URANUS

URANUS

BEN BOVA

TOR

A TOM DOHERTY ASSOCIATES BOOK

New York

URANUS

Copyright © 2020 by Ben Bova

A Tor Book
Published by Tom Doherty Associates
120 Broadway
New York, NY 10271

www.tor-forge.com

Tor® is a registered trademark of Macmillan Publishing Group, LLC.

The Library of Congress Cataloging-in-Publication Data is available upon request.

ISBN 978-1-250-29654-2 (hardcover)
ISBN 978-1-250-29655-9 (ebook)

Our books may be purchased in bulk for promotional, educational, or business use. Please contact your local bookseller or the Macmillan Corporate and Premium Sales Department at 1-800-221-7945, extension 5442, or by email at MacmillanSpecialMarkets@macmillan.com.

First Edition: 2020

Printed in the United States of America

0 9 8 7 6 5 4 3 2 1

TO SPIDER ROBINSON:
friend, fellow writer, troubadour

Know myself? If I knew myself I'd run away!

Johann Wolfgang von Goethe

book one

THE WHORE

Orbital Station *Haven*

There were thirty of them, eleven women and nineteen men, their ages ranging from late teens to approaching senility, standing wide-eyed, gaping at the trees and shrubs and—beyond the Glassteel dome above them—the blue-gray clouds of the planet Uranus.

Pointing toward the bland-looking planet, their group leader said sternly, "That world's name is pronounced 'YOU-ra-nus.'" His craggy face dead serious, he went on, "I don't wanna hear any wiseguys call it 'Your-ANUS.' Unnerstand me?"

The thirty newbies nodded and mumbled assent.

His ham-sized fists planted on his hips, Quincy O'Donnell nodded back at his new charges. "All right, then," he said, the flat twang of his native Boston still unmistakable in his creaky tenor voice, "let's get on with it. The minister is waitin' to greet you."

They were standing in the garden, a wide swath of Earthly greenery planted and lovingly tended by the inhabitants of *Haven*, the spindly ring-shaped space station swinging in orbit around the huge planet Uranus. In the distance, they could see several towers rising high above their level. And overhead there was more real estate: green empty acres, small clusters of towns that looked sparkling new, untouched as yet.

A whole new world, built inside the ring of metal and plastic that encircled them.

Not one of the dozen newcomers moved a centimeter. They were all gaping at the habitat spreading as far as the eye could see, even above their heads. They stared wide-eyed, frozen in wonderment.

It's hitting them, O'Donnell said to himself. For the first time, the reality of it is making itself felt. You're a long way from Earth, he told them silently. And there's no goin' back. This is your new home. Permanently.

"All right now, that's enough of sightseein'. Let's get moving."

They stirred, reluctantly. But they moved in response to his command. Good. They'll learn to obey orders, they will. Or suffer for their sins.

O'Donnell turned and led the newbies along the winding brick path that led through the profuse foliage to the waiting auditorium. Thirty more poor souls, he said to himself. Thirty more lost waifs searchin' for paradise. Well, maybe they'll find it here. If not here, I don't know where on God's green Earth they'll find a place to rest their poor bones.

Then he reminded himself that they weren't on God's green Earth, not anymore. They were damned near three billion kilometers from Earth, out at the ass end of the solar system, swinging endlessly around the planet Uranus.

O'Donnell clenched his teeth tightly. There you go again, Quincy old boy, swearin' like you haven't been taught better. Remember to include that sin in your next confession.

"C'mon," he shouted. "The minister is waitin' for yez."

data bank

uranus is the third largest of the solar system's eight planets, orbiting beyond beringed saturn, out in the cold and lonely darkness of the sun's most distant children.

More than four times larger than Earth, Uranus orbits nearly three billion kilometers from the Sun. Uranus's year is slightly more than eighty-four Earth years. It spins around its axis every seventeen hours and four minutes.

While the planet's mass is 14.5 times more than Earth's, its density is merely 1.3 times greater than that of water. Its atmosphere—at least the uppermost part of it—is composed mainly of hydrogen and helium, the two lightest elements, with significant amounts of methane and ammonia. The temperature of its cloud tops is truly frigid: more than 197 degrees below zero Celsius.

Uranus is *weird*. The other planets of the solar system have axial tilts ranging from Jupiter's 3.1 degrees to 26.7 degrees for Saturn. Earth's axis is tipped 23.4 degrees, a tilt that produces its seasons.

Uranus, though, is tilted 97.9 degrees from vertical. Its north pole points toward the Sun for part of its year, while half a Uranian year later (some forty-two Earth years) its south pole points Sunward. And unlike all the other planets, Uranus spins from east to west, *retrograde*, in astronomical parlance.

Uranus has rings circling over its equator. Thin, dark rings of meteoric bits of rock and metal, barely visible except on those rare occasions when they happen to catch a glint of sunlight.

Curious scientists from Earth sent dozens of unmanned probes into orbit around Uranus, and deep into the placid blue-gray clouds that cover it from pole to pole. They were only partially successful in unveiling the planet's secrets. *Something* collided with Uranus early in the solar system's history, the scientists reasoned, banging its axial tilt so far from vertical. *Something* apparently sterilized the planet-wide ocean that lies beneath Uranus's methane and ammonia clouds. Unlike the oceans of Jupiter and Saturn, and even the more-distant Neptune, the ocean of Uranus is dead: no living creature has been found there, not even single-celled protoplasms.

Interest in Uranus faltered in the face of such discouraging discoveries. A sterile planet, dead, lifeless. Scientific probes were sent elsewhere. Uranus was a dead end, literally.

Until the self-styled Reverend Kyle Umber conceived his plan of building a haven for Earth's poor, disenfranchised, forgotten men and women, in orbit around the planet Uranus.

KYLE UMBER

++
++

Quincy O'Donnell led his thirty foundlings along the bricked path that led toward the auditorium. That's how he thought of his charges: foundlings, orphans, the "wretched refuse" of their native Earth, poor, ignorant, hopeless.

But Reverend Umber will give them hope, give them learning, give them a reason to live and to praise God. O'Donnell had seen it happen to earlier arrivals at this mission station set in deep space.

Thanks to optical recognition technology the auditorium doors swung open automatically as O'Donnell led his little troop toward them. The thirty followed O'Donnell inside, goggling at the lofty ceiling, the broad expanse of pews, row after row of benches and—up atop the stage—a row of high-backed wooden chairs that looked stiff, stern, uncomfortable.

All empty. The vast, high-ceilinged auditorium was empty except for their little group. Unadorned. No pictures on the blank walls. No statues or images of any sort on the empty stage before them. Their footsteps echoed off the metal walls. They were awed into silence.

O'Donnell sat them in the front row of seats, grinning inwardly at their wide-eyed stares. The auditorium was bare, undecorated, windowless, yet it still astounded each one of them into silence.

For several moments, they sat before the raised stage, glancing around uneasily, unsure of what they were about to face.

Then the Reverend Kyle Umber came walking silently, smilingly, out of the right wing of the stage. He seemed to glow against the shadows behind him. Dressed in a simple suit of pure white, Umber looked down at the new arrivals with a smile that lit up his entire face.

It was an ordinary sort of face, roundish, with healthy pink cheeks and a full crop of reddish-brown hair swept back from his forehead and falling to his shoulders. Umber was short, thickset, with heavyish arms and legs beneath his immaculate white jacket and trousers.

He walked to the edge of the stage and—as several of the newcomers rose to their feet in automatic reflex—he hopped off the edge of the stage and landed like a well-trained acrobat on the balls of his feet exactly in front of the newbies.

A wide smile on his ruddy face, Kyle Umber spread his arms and said, "Welcome to *Haven*. Welcome to your new home."

The people who had gotten up hesitated a moment, then crumpled back into their seats, almost shamefaced. Quincy O'Donnell—who had seen the minister's hijinks before—remained standing in the aisle, arms folded across his broad chest, resisting the urge to applaud.

Umber said, in a soft, intimate voice, "I hope you'll forgive my dramatics. I get a kick out of making that little jump. To me, it sort of illustrates the much bigger jump each of you has made—the jump from teeming, overcrowded, decaying Earth to the new paradise we are working to create here at *Haven*."

A few of the new arrivals chuckled appreciatively.

"I suppose you're wondering why I established this refuge, this sanctuary nearly three billion kilometers away from Earth.

The reason is simple: I wanted to create a haven far from Earth and its troubles, a refuge where men and women like yourselves could find peace, and love, and a meaningful life.

"*Haven* is that place. It is a new world, a world that you will help to build, literally, with your own hands and hearts and skills. A refuge where you can live in dignity and harmony, far from the evils and temptations of Earth. Here in *Haven* you will build a new world. On Earth you were considered the worst samples of humankind. Here in *Haven* you will become the best examples of human capabilities. Together, you and I, we will create the best out of the worst.

"*Haven* is the place where the human race will be reborn, clean, new, strong and free. And *you* will be reborn as well— clean, new, strong and free."

Absolute silence through the vast, echoing auditorium. The newcomers were totally fixated on the Reverend Kyle Umber.

"If you are ignorant, we will teach you. If you have skills or knowledge, we will put them to use in building this new world. Put your past behind you! A new life is opening for you, God is giving you a new chance to live the life He wants you to live."

"Amen!" shouted one of the women.

Smiling, Umber nodded and said, "Amen indeed. We have a stupendous task before us. We will build a new world here, literally. We will—together, you, me and all of us—we will extend and enlarge *Haven* so that we can accept as many of Earth's forgotten millions as possible.

"We will build new habitats, new man-made worlds that will house and protect and educate all who come here seeking shelter and wisdom and safety. We will endure hardships and dangers. We will conquer fear and hate. We will create a true human paradise here in the darkness, so far from the lifegiving Sun. We will triumph over ignorance and poverty and hatred.

"Together, you and I and the others, together we will prevail. We will triumph."

The thirty newcomers rose to their feet as a single entity and cheered lustily. The sound of their enthusiasm echoed throughout the vast, nearly empty auditorium.

Kyle Umber bowed his head in silent acknowledgement of their approval. He stood silent and unmoving until the newbies sat back in their chairs.

Raising his head to look at them again, his smile benign, his eyes aglow, Umber went on, "This is a monumental task we have set for ourselves. It will not be accomplished easily or quickly. But we will prevail!"

Again the thirty jumped to their feet, clapping their hands lustily. Quincy O'Donnell, still standing in the aisle at the end of the row, smiled inwardly. He had seen this performance before. The minister always stirred the newbies with his vision.

As the newcomers settled back into their seats again, Umber half turned back toward the stage and said, "Now I want you to meet the person who has made all this possible: Evan Waxman."

EVAN WAXMAN

From the same right wing of the stage stepped a tall, lean, elegant man, stylish despite the casual pearl-gray slacks and untucked light yellow shirt he wore. Smiling at the newcomers, he went to the corner of the stage and came down the steps there in an easy, loose-limbed gait.

"This is Evan Waxman." Umber introduced him. "Our benefactor and great good friend."

Waxman was a full head taller than Umber, his chiseled features handsome, confident. His hair was dark and cut short; his skin pale, ashen. He waved one hand carelessly at the newbies and smiled at them with dazzling teeth.

"Hello everybody," he said in a clear deep voice. "Good to meet you."

Umber reached up to pat Waxman's shoulder. "Mr. Waxman is really the founder of our feast. He has spent a good part of his family's fortune to construct *Haven* out here in the wilderness. The debt we owe him can never be repaid—in money."

Waxman bowed his head humbly, then spoke up. "What I have donated to Reverend Umber's cause is only money. I was glad to do it. Reverend Umber has shown me that there are much more important things than mere wealth, things like loyalty, and generosity, and a vision for the future."

"And a few billion international dollars to donate," Umber added, with a happy smile.

"That's merely money," Waxman repeated, "money that I am glad to give, money that is being turned into this sanctuary, this retreat where you and he and I—together—can create a refuge where we can build new lives for ourselves, where we can learn to live in peace and harmony."

One of the newcomers—thin, frail, dark of skin and eye—raised a questioning hand.

Waxman nodded to him.

The newbie slowly got to his feet, glanced shyly around at his companions, then asked, "Is *Haven* strictly a Christian endeavor, or is it truly open to people of all faiths?"

Waxman turned toward Umber, whose smiling face grew quite serious.

"We believe that God is served by all faiths. People from every corner of the Earth try to worship God in the ways that make sense to them. Here in *Haven* we have no specific denomination of worship. All are free to worship God in his or her own way."

And he called out, "Roman Catholic decor, please."

Suddenly the auditorium was transformed. The stage became an altar with a three-story-high crucifix hanging behind it. Windows topped by pointed arches appeared along the side walls, each showing a magnificent stained-glass image of a Biblical scene.

The newbies gasped in awe.

Umber called, "Lutheran decor, please."

Instantly the dramatic pictures and images disappeared, replaced by quietly dignified simplicity.

Smiling broadly, Umber called, "Thank you. End presentation."

The auditorium returned to its original bare simplicity.

"We have decor schemes for more than forty different religious affiliations, including Moslem, Hindu, even Baha'i."

"What about agnostics?" asked the questioner. "Or outright atheists?"

Umber's smile widened, gentle, understanding. "Whatever your faith—or lack of it—you will be welcome in *Haven*. After all, the God who created the universe knows what is in your heart. His vision is all-encompassing."

"I'd like to add something to that," Waxman said, his brows knitting slightly. "I am an agnostic. The religion that my parents followed—the religion I was indoctrinated with as a child—that religion taught that faith is a gift, given freely by God." With a shrug of his shoulders, Waxman went on, "Well, I never received that gift. I wish I had, but somehow it's eluded me. Yet here I am, working shoulder to shoulder with Reverend Umber to help build *Haven*."

"You say 'to help build *Haven*,'" one of the other men called, from his seat. "How large do you intend to make this habitat?"

Umber spread his arms. "As large as we can. And we intend to build more habitats, to house more immigrants. *Haven II* is already under construction next to us. We intend to take all those who seek shelter and solace and peace into our community. There will never be an end to this endeavor; we will keep growing as long as we need to."

"Where's the money going to come from?"

"From generous patrons such as Mr. Waxman, here," Umber replied. "And from others like him. God will provide, never fear."

raven marchesi

sitting on the aisle seat of the auditorium's front row—next to quincy o'donnell standing out in the aisle—raven marchesi watched and listened intently to Kyle Umber and Evan Waxman.

They're good salesmen, she thought. Smooth and slick. Promising heaven and peace and joy. But what's it going to cost us?

Raven always worried about the costs of life, from the time she'd been six years old in the decaying slums of Naples, within sight of the smoldering old Mt. Vesuvius, looming over her.

Her home—such as it was—had been buried in Vesuvius's latest eruption. No one came to her neighborhood to warn the people to get out. Most of them were buried when the skies rained white-hot ashes and choking gas.

But Raven had noticed the exodus of private cars and hired buses from the high-rent condominiums on the edge of her run-down district; she followed barefoot the evacuation trail of her wealthier neighbors. She had no parents to guide her; her only warning of the coming eruption was the evacuation by the rich.

Her earliest memories were of the seedy, roach-crawling, rat-infested orphanage where she'd grown up. She'd been ten years old when she had her first period—and her first sexual experience. She quickly learned that sex was a sort of equalizer: as poor and ragged as she was, sex was the one path to money and safety open to her.

As she grew into a slim, sleek, dark-haired beauty, she learned about sex. She learned how to turn the sweaty passions of men—and women—into money and a scant measure of security.

She was nearing twenty when one of the occasional police sweeps scooped her off the streets and landed her in a dark and dismal jail. Her cell was crowded with other women: some defiant, some bitter and hopeless, some offering themselves to the prison guards. She almost laughed at the irony of it. I'm back among the rats and the filth, she told herself. Back where I started.

To her surprise, the next morning she was taken by a pair of guards from her overcrowded cell to a tiny office several levels above the cellblock. The cramped little room had a single slit of a window, set too high in the wall for Raven to see the street. Nothing out there but a jumble of slanted rooftops. Bright warm sunshine made the sky glow.

A dumpy, overweight woman in a starched white blouse and dull gray skirt came in and sat behind the table that took up almost all the room's floor space. The table was bare except for a hand-sized notebook computer. A stiff wooden chair stood empty in front of the table. On the stone wall behind the table a large round clock silently showed the time flowing by: almost 10:00 A.M.

"Sit," said the woman, in a voice like a cobra's hiss.

Raven sat. Her stomach rumbled slightly; she'd had nothing to eat except a candy bar the night before.

The woman flicked her computer open and, without looking up, asked in Tuscan dialect, "Your name?"

Noting that the woman's fingers bore no rings, Raven replied, "Raven Marchesi, signorina."

The woman looked up at Raven, her brow cocked. In English

she said, "Let's leave my marital status out of this, Miss Marchesi."

Raven nodded and replied in barely accented English, "Very well."

Continuing in English, the interviewer asked, "Your occupation?"

Raven shrugged. "Sex therapist."

The woman said to her computer, "Whore."

"No!" Raven protested. "I—"

"A sex therapist?" The woman scoffed. "Where did you get your degree?"

"I've been trying to save enough money for the classes, but—"

"Shut up! You're a whore and we both know it."

Raven glowered at her but said nothing.

The woman went through a series of questions, almost automatically. Just as mechanically, Raven gave answers—some of them the truth, the rest fables from her imagination.

At last the woman closed her notebook and studied Raven's face for long, silent moments. The clock's second hand swung silently.

"The police can hold you here for twenty-four hours, then they are required to turn you loose. Is that what you want?"

"Of course."

With a bitter smile, the woman said, "You won't get much sleep during those twenty-four hours."

Raven shrugged her slim shoulders. "It won't be the first time."

"I can offer you something better."

"Sex with you?" Raven sneered.

The woman seemed shocked, repelled. "Sex? With you? Good lord, no!"

"You might like it," Raven said.

Looking halfway between disgusted and ashamed, the woman said sternly, "I am empowered to invite you to join a journey to a space habitat named *Haven*, orbiting the planet Uranus. It will be a one-way journey; you will spend the rest of your life there. Not as a prisoner or a convict. *Haven* is a self-sufficient community for the poor and disadvantaged. You can start a new life there. A better life."

The woman spoke for more than twenty minutes, nonstop, promoting the advantages of the *Haven* habitat. After ten of those minutes, Raven was ready to sign up and start a new life.

She made up her mind when the woman told Raven that during the flight out to the distant planet, she would undergo medical procedures that would cleanse her of any narcotics or disease organisms her body housed.

"You'll arrive at Uranus clean and healthy," the woman promised, "ready to begin a better life. A new beginning for you."

A new beginning, Raven said to herself. A new, clean life. It might even be true.

a new home

Now, seven weeks later and billions of kilometers from Naples, Raven sat in Haven's auditorium and studied Kyle Umber and Evan Waxman as they explained about the world they had created here at the cold, dark end of the solar system.

The *Reverend* Kyle Umber, she said to herself. He doesn't look like a priest. Doesn't act much like one, either. She had known her share of priests back in Naples. Some were furtive, haunted. Others were haughty, self-important, even sadistic. Umber looked like a pleasant-enough man, smiling, friendly. But Raven thought she detected a hard shell beneath his amiable exterior.

The man is *dedicated*, she decided. Driven to build this new paradise far from the filth and indecencies of old Earth. Behind his smiling eyes was a dedication, a mission, an inflexible drive to make his vision into reality.

Not him, she decided.

She turned her chestnut-brown eyes to Evan Waxman. Tall, graceful, rich. Good smile, the kind of smile that comes from never having to worry about where your next meal might come from, or where you can spend the night. *Successful*, she realized. Clever enough to be born to incredibly wealthy parents.

And now he's spending most of that wealth on Umber's

Haven. On the dream of a place where the poor can begin to lead new lives. Where they can leave their miserable existences behind them and start out fresh.

Like what the priests told us about God and heaven and a perfect life. Does Evan Waxman really believe that? Truly? She guessed not. But she decided that her best path to safety on this new world was to be enfolded in the wings of this very wealthy Evan Waxman.

But how to get to him? How to make him notice me? Raven realized she was dressed in the dreary uniform they had given her aboard the spacecraft that had carried her and the others from Earth. Mousy-gray, shapeless baggy trousers and an equally loose-fitting long-sleeved blouse.

He'd never notice me in this sack, she thought. How to attract him? How?

Standing in front of the row of new arrivals, Kyle Umber clasped his hands together and said, "All right, that's enough from Evan and me. Now Mr. O'Donnell will show you to your quarters. You'll have the rest of the day to yourselves, and tomorrow you'll begin your new lives as citizens of *Haven*. May God be with you."

With that, Umber turned and headed for the stairs that led up to the stage.

Waxman, beside him, asked in a voice loud enough for all the newcomers to hear, "Aren't you going to jump up onto the stage?"

Umber laughed and shook his head. "Thou shalt not tempt the Lord our God," he said as he took to the stairs.

Quincy O'Donnell led the thirty new arrivals out of the auditorium and down a long, straight passageway. No decorations on the walls. No pictures or windows. Nothing but bare metal

and closed, unmarked doors. Raven could see that the passageway was not actually straight: it curved, in the distance, rising
up and out of sight. But as she walked along with the others, it
seemed perfectly flat. Strange, she thought.

Raven maneuvered past a rail-thin woman and a pair of
reasonably healthy-looking young men to come up next to
O'Donnell.

He towered over her, big and beefy, the expression on his
florid face absolutely neutral, as if he were actually walking in
his sleep.

"Will it be much farther?" Raven asked him, in a small voice.

O'Donnell's face came alive instantly. Looking down at her,
he asked, "Why? Is anything wrong?"

Raven temporized, "I've got a cramp in my leg."

"A cramp?"

"I'm not accustomed to walking so far," she said.

"Oh . . . well, we're almost there. See?" He pointed. "There
are nameplates on the doors here. Your quarters'll be just a little
bit further on."

Raven nodded and conspicuously bit her lip.

"Are you in a lot of pain? Maybe—"

"No," she said softly. "I can manage." And she made herself
limp ever so slightly.

O'Donnell looked confused, upset, almost guilty. "Only a
few more meters now," he said.

"That's good," said Raven. Inwardly she smiled at the big
oaf's concern. Easy pickings, she said to herself.

Sure enough, the doors on either side of the passageway
started to show the names of the thirty newcomers. One by
one they entered their quarters. Raven caught glimpses of the
compartments inside: they didn't seem very spacious, but they
weren't cramped, either. Nice enough, she thought. Above

everything else, they seemed *clean*! No rats, no spiderwebs, no water seeping down the walls.

At last they came to her place. The nameplate on the door read MARCHESI, R.

O'Donnell clicked the lock and slid the door open for her. Then, with a sweeping gesture, he ushered Raven into her new home.

She took two steps inside, then stopped.

"Is it all right?" O'Donnell asked, from out in the passageway.

Raven saw a sofa, a pair of sling chairs, a coffee table. To the right was a kitchen, with sink, refrigerator, shelves stocked with various cartons and bottles. To her left was an open door and, beyond it, a bed neatly made with sheets and a blanket and plump pillows with real pillowcases over them!

"Is it all right?" O'Donnell asked again.

"It's wonderful!" Raven cried.

Then she turned, stepped outside again, threw her arms around his neck and kissed O'Donnell on the lips. "It's wonderful," she repeated.

O'Donnell's face flamed tomato red.

"Well . . . it's all yours," he managed to mutter as he disentangled himself from her arms.

Raven stepped back into the living room. *Her* living room. Her very own. Dimly she heard the door slide shut behind her. Suddenly alone in her new home—*her own home, all to herself*—she raced into the bedroom and jumped full-length upon the bed.

It was soft and warm and safe. Raven had never been so happy in her life.

a new life

Raven woke to the sound of an insistent buzzing. She opened her gummy eyes, blinked several times, then sat up on the bed. It was real. The room, the bed, the warm coverlet tangled around her bare legs.

"It's not a dream," she said aloud.

Looking around, she saw that her bedroom walls were a soft yellow, the ceiling blank white.

My bedroom, she said to herself. My own bedroom, all to myself. And out past that door is a living room and a kitchen.

The buzzing rose a notch. Turning, Raven saw that it came from a phone console on the night table next to her bed.

"Phone answer," she called out.

A woman's face appeared on the phone's small screen.

"Good morning, Miss Marchesi. You are scheduled for an orientation interview at oh-nine-hundred hours. The time is now oh-seven-thirty."

"Where is my interview going to be?" Raven asked.

The woman's brunette features froze for a moment, long enough for Raven to realize that this wasn't an actual live person, but a computer image.

"Your interview will take place in your quarters at oh-nine-hundred hours. One hour and twenty-nine minutes from now."

"Thank you," said Raven.

The phone screen went blank.

Raven got up, showered, wrapped a towel around herself, then rummaged through the kitchen and made herself a bowl of cereal and a cup of strong black coffee. By 8:48 A.M. she was dressed in another of the dreary, baggy outfits that she'd found hanging in her closet.

My closet, she told herself. My very own closet in my very own bedroom in my very own apartment. She felt like dancing.

But she sat, demure and ladylike, on the living room sofa. They're probably watching you, she told herself. You'd better behave like a proper lady.

Precisely at 0900 hours the front door buzzer hummed. Raven got up from the sofa, went to the door, and stopped, puzzled. She could not see any buttons or latches or controls for opening the door. Nothing but a small screen beside the door that showed a middle-aged woman, slim and good-looking, with well-coiffed short blond hair, standing out in the passageway.

Suddenly desperate, Raven called out, "How do I open the door?"

The woman outside broke into a bright smile. "Just say 'Open please.' The mechanism is tuned to your voice."

Raven glared at the door and muttered, "Open please."

The door slid open.

"Hello," said the blond woman as she extended her hand. "I'm Cathy Fremont. I'm your orientation leader."

Raven clasped her hand and gestured her into the living room. The door slid shut behind them.

"I'm sorry to be so stupid," said Raven as she led Cathy Fremont to the sofa.

"This is all new to you, isn't it?" Fremont replied as she sat down.

"Yes, it is."

"You speak English very well, Raven. Is it all right for me to call you by your first name?"

"Yes, of course," said Raven, sitting herself on the sling chair nearest the sofa. "I speak Italian, English, Spanish, German, a little Greek and a smattering of a few other languages."

Fremont made an obviously forced smile. "How clever of you."

Raven cocked her head slightly. "In my profession you learn languages quickly."

"Your *former* profession," said Fremont.

"Yes, of course. My former profession. I'm starting a new life here, aren't I?"

"Indeed so."

It was a long day. Without leaving Raven's apartment, Fremont used the living room's wall screen to show her the layout of station *Haven*, everything from the cafeterias and formal dining rooms to the clinic and the recreational facilities. Raven took it all in, asking questions, nodding at the answers.

As noon approached, Raven went to the kitchen and found the makings for sandwiches. Cathy Fremont nibbled away happily without stopping the orientation for more than a moment or two.

Inwardly, Raven was asking herself, How can I get close to Evan Waxman? How can I make him notice me?

As the digital readout at the bottom of the wall screen reached 4:00 P.M. Fremont said, "I think that's enough for one day. Tomorrow you will take a battery of aptitude tests, so we can determine what kind of work you're best suited for."

Dropping her eyes respectfully, Raven said, "I'm afraid I don't have much experience at anything useful."

Fremont smiled reassuringly. "Oh, don't be too sure of that. We've found great stores of talent among our new arrivals, talents that most of them didn't realize that they had."

Raven smiled back at her, but she thought, Is fellatio one of the talents you're looking for?

FiNdiNg tALENt

FOR the next three months, Raven attended school. Back in Naples she had been forced to go to school whenever the authorities picked her off the streets.

"For your own good," they would tell her. "To improve yourself."

But the dreary classes in the stifling, oppressive rooms taught her nothing except an unbearable yearning to get out, get free, get back on the streets where she could use her brains and her body to live on her own. Even a beating was better than sitting through the droning lectures and pretending to read the stupid books they forced on her.

Here on *Haven*, though, school was very different. She studied in her apartment, engrossed in virtual reality programs that immersed her in the subjects she explored. History became real to her: she lived in ancient Rome, in modern Euro-America. She saw how mathematics worked and stored the new knowledge in her brain. She learned how her own body worked, and marveled at the wonderful intricacy of her cellular machinery.

Without realizing it, at first, Raven began to learn.

She learned how the habitat *Haven* was governed, how the poor, ignorant newcomers were transformed into productive, intelligent citizens who actually helped to govern the habitat's growing population.

I could become a councilwoman, Raven realized one afternoon. I could be one of the people who gives orders, who makes decisions, who directs how the others live.

Evan Waxman would have to notice me then, she told herself.

She made friends among the other newcomers, and even among the people who had been there longer, who were now part of the government of *Haven*. One of those friends was Quincy O'Donnell, the big, beefy watchman who had guided Raven's group when they'd first arrived at *Haven*.

One afternoon, as she was taking lunch in the main cafeteria after a morning of exhausting examinations by the education department's central computer, Quincy O'Donnell came up to her table carrying a tray loaded to its edges with a salad, a sandwich, a hefty slab of pie, a big cup of juice and a dainty jewel of chocolate topped by a pink sliver of candy.

"D'you mind if I sit with you?" he asked, his voice quavering slightly.

Raven gave him a minimal smile and said, "No, I don't mind at all. Sit right down."

O'Donnell placed his tray carefully on the small table across from her and settled his bulk in the spindly-legged chair.

Then he picked up the tiny chocolate piece delicately, in two fingers, and placed it on Raven's tray.

"For you," he said, the expression on his heavy-featured face somewhere between expectant and apprehensive.

"Why, thank you," said Raven, surprised.

O'Donnell broke into a sloppy grin, then grabbed his sandwich and tore a huge bite out of it.

Raven smiled demurely at him. By the time they had finished their lunches they were chatting like old friends.

They got up from their chairs, O'Donnell towering over her.

"I . . . uh," he stammered, "I thought . . . well, maybe we could have dinner together sometime."

Keeping her smile fixed in place, Raven replied, "That would be nice."

O'Donnell nodded happily and mumbled, "I'll call you."

"Fine," said Raven. Then she watched the big man lumber away, as if fleeing some ogre.

He'll be easy to keep on a leash, she told herself as she watched his retreating back. Like a big puppy. Just don't let him get too close.

When she got back to her apartment, Raven's wall screen showed a notification to appear at Cathy Fremont's office at 0900 hours the next morning.

She sank down onto the sofa in her living room, staring at the message on the screen, biting her lip in consternation. What have I done wrong? she asked herself, alarmed. She wondered, Maybe I shouldn't have agreed to have dinner with Quincy. Maybe . . .

With a shake of her head, she decided it was pointless to try to guess why she'd been summoned. Just go to Fremont's office and face the music, she told herself.

But her dreams that night were of old Naples, dark and filled with danger.

The next morning, Raven marched herself to Fremont's office, rehearsing in her mind what she would reply to any accusation her orientation leader would level at her. I didn't do it. I didn't know it was against the rules. I won't do it again.

But she didn't know what "it" was.

Cathy Fremont rose from her desk chair as Raven stepped into her office.

"Good morning," Fremont said cheerfully.

Raven muttered a "good morning" and slipped into the chair before Fremont's desk.

Hiking a thumb toward the viewscreen on her office wall, Fremont smiled and said, "You've done very well with your studies. Your grades are among the highest we've ever seen."

Taken aback, Raven replied merely, "They are?"

"Yes, they are," Fremont answered happily. "There's a first-rate mind inside your skull, Raven."

Raven blinked with surprise.

Fremont stared at Raven for a long, unsettling moment. Here it comes, Raven thought. She softens me up with good news, and now comes the sledgehammer.

But Fremont's smile widened slightly as she leaned back in her desk chair and said, "I think you might be able to help us with a situation that's about to arise. That is, if you want to."

"Help you?"

"You've probably never heard of Tómas Gomez, have you?"

Raven shook her head.

"I thought not. He's an astronomer, from Chile, in South America."

"An astronomer," Raven echoed.

"He's coming here to *Haven* because he wants to study Uranus. We need someone to show him around, get him settled, familiarize him with our habitat."

Suddenly it clicked in Raven's mind. I haven't done anything wrong! She doesn't want to punish me. She's asking me to help her!

"You want me to be his guide?"

"Yes. Only for his first few days. Help him get his feet on the ground, so to speak. Help him get his equipment set up."

Raven said, "I don't know anything about astronomy."

"That's no problem. What we need is someone to make Gomez feel comfortable here in *Haven*. Get him settled in. I believe he plans to stay here for at least a year, perhaps longer."

"I can do that," Raven said.

Before she could think about how she might make the man comfortable, Fremont's smile evaporated.

Raising a warning finger, Fremont said, "We know about your life back in Naples, Raven. That's all behind you now. We are not asking you to treat Gomez as a sexual customer. In fact, I think he would be shocked and horrified if you even hinted at such behavior."

"Of course," Raven said softly. But she was thinking, We'll see.

TÓMAS GOMEZ

TWO days later, Raven met Tómas Gomez at the reception area just outside Haven's main docking port.

The place was busy, as usual. Raven saw troops of newbies being led by officers like Quincy O'Donnell, gaggles of young men and women goggling at the broad expanse of the arrival center and the busy chatter of the newcomers and their hardworking guides.

She recognized Tómas Gomez from the photos she'd seen in his file. He was walking slowly among the crowd, his head pivoting as if he were searching for someone to meet him.

He was just about Raven's own height, stocky, his hair dark and straight, his face the light brown of uncured tobacco leaf. Ordinary face, broad cheeks, his eyes just slightly slanted, not oriental but mestizo. Native American heritage, Raven realized, using some of the history lessons she had recently absorbed.

"Señor Gomez?" she asked as he stepped across the lines painted across the reception area's floor.

He stopped and stared at her. Raven had spent most of her evenings studying a computer course in dressmaking, and had altered her baggy, saggy uniforms into tighter, sleeker outfits.

"I am Tómas Gomez," he replied, in English.

Switching to English herself, Raven extended her hand as

she said, "Hello. I am Raven Marchesi. I'll be your guide for your first few days here in *Haven*."

Gomez's face lit up with a broad smile. "I'm very pleased to meet you, Ms. Marchesi."

"Raven," she said.

"Raven," he repeated, still smiling.

Raven led Gomez down into *Haven*'s living area, and through the intersecting passageways to the compartment that had been assigned as his living quarters. It was much like her own: living room, kitchen, bedroom, bath.

"This will be your home while you're living here," she said cheerfully.

His eyes flicked to the travel bags sitting by the door to the bedroom. "My equipment?" he asked. "Where is my equipment?"

Raven tugged the phone from her hip pocket as she asked, "Do you have an identification number for it?"

Gomez nodded and spelled out a nine-digit string of alphanumerics.

Raven's phone showed that the equipment was being taken to one of the habitat's docking ports.

"I must go see it," he said.

With a smile that she hoped showed self-assurance, Raven said, "We can see it from here."

"Really?"

"Of course."

It took three tries, but at last Raven got the living room's wall screen to show six bulky crates being unloaded in a docking area by a team of robots and their human overseer.

Gomez slowly sank onto the sofa and stared at the screen as if it showed his whole life being delivered.

"That's your equipment?" she asked softly.

Gomez nodded, his eyes glued to the screen.

Raven sat down beside him, fully an arm's length away. "What's in the packages?" she asked.

Without taking his eyes from the screen, Gomez replied, "Spectrographs, sampling equipment, a boring machine, computer systems to operate them all."

Little by little, Raven got Gomez to explain what the equipment was supposed to do.

"Vessels that go into Uranus's ocean are cut off from contact with us, here in space," he told her. "The ocean absorbs ordinary electronic transmissions. Even laser beams are distorted beyond comprehensibility."

Raven nodded in what she hoped were the right places. Dimly, she understood that ships sent into the planet-wide ocean down on the planet were on their own, any signals they sent out were cut off by the seawater.

"Then how do you control them?" she asked.

Gomez shook his head, still without looking at her. "We can't control them. They are preprogrammed. All we can do is hope that the programming works."

"You mean you don't know if it works or not?"

At last his head turned toward her. "No. Not yet."

Raven stared at him.

"Something happened to Uranus," Gomez said, his voice stronger than before. "Something knocked the whole planet sidewise and sterilized its ocean. I hope to learn what that something was."

She saw an intensity burning in his coal-black eyes, a fury.

"By sending a submarine into the ocean," she said.

"To the bottom of that ocean," Gomez corrected, his face set in rigid determination. "I'm going to dredge up samples from the seabed and bring them back here for analysis. I'm going to find out what happened to the planet billions of years ago."

Raven simply stared at him. She couldn't think of anything to say.

And suddenly Gomez's iron-hard expression melted into an embarrassed smile. "I'm sorry," he told her. "I tend to get carried away with my own importance."

"No," Raven countered. "I think it's exciting . . . wonderful. What happened to this planet? It's a marvelous mystery."

"And I'm a marvelous egotist to think that I can solve it."

"Somebody will, sooner or later," Raven said. "Why not you?"

"That's the big question, isn't it?"

Before Raven could think of a reply, Gomez's phone buzzed.

"Answer, please," he called out.

The scene of the docking port vanished and Evan Waxman's handsome face appeared on the screen.

"Dr. Gomez," said Waxman. "Welcome to *Haven*."

"Thank you, Mr. Waxman."

"I wonder if you could drop in at my office tomorrow morning?"

"Of course," said Gomez. "What time would be convenient for you?"

"Oh, nine, nine thirty."

"I'll be there at nine," Gomez said.

"Fine. See you then."

And Raven's pulse quickened. I'll go with you, she said silently to Gomez. I'm going to meet Evan Waxman!

meeting

Raven was up at six. She showered, then dressed carefully, noting that the dull and shapeless uniform that was standard dress for newcomers now looked trimmer, more form-fitting. Not sexy, perhaps, but at least it hinted that there was a desirable woman beneath the gray fabric.

She called Gomez and arranged to meet him at his apartment at 0730 hours. Then she led him to the closest cafeteria for breakfast. Once they finished eating, she used her phone's scanner to guide them and led Gomez to Waxman's office. Gomez rapped on its door at precisely 0858 hours.

The door slid open and they stepped into an anteroom, where a female assistant—lean, almost gaunt, with hollow cheeks and pale blue eyes, her light brown hair cut in short, wild spikes—rose silently from her desk to greet them with a cold stare.

Gesturing to the door beside her, she smiled slightly and said, "Go right in, Dr. Gomez. Mr. Waxman is expecting you."

Raven followed the astronomer into Waxman's private office.

It was considerably smaller than she had expected. Waxman was standing behind a trim little curved desk, smiling at Gomez. He didn't seem surprised or upset that Raven was with him. In fact, his smile widened at the sight of her.

"Dr. Gomez," said Waxman, coming around the desk, arms extended in greeting. "I'm very pleased to meet you."

Then he turned slightly toward Raven. "And you must be Ms. Marchesi."

Raven smiled back at him, but said nothing.

"Sit down, make yourselves comfortable." Waxman pointed to the plushly upholstered chairs in front of his desk.

As Raven sat down, she glanced around the office. No bookshelves, no furniture at all except for a hip-tall cabinet lining the wall to the right of Waxman's desk. The walls were crowded with images, though: photographs of streets, houses, park squares in a city that was built on hills by a big lake of some sort.

"Salt Lake City," Waxman explained, noting Raven's interest. "I was born there. So was Reverend Umber."

"You were childhood friends?" Raven asked.

Waxman smiled thinly. "Not exactly. As a matter of fact, we met in the city jail."

"Jail?" Gomez blurted.

"It's a long story," Waxman said, waving one hand as if to shoo it away. "Today I'd like to learn about what you intend to accomplish here, Dr. Gomez, and how we may help you to succeed."

For the next hour and then some, Gomez expounded on the unsolved mysteries of Uranus's lopsided configuration and its seemingly barren worldwide ocean.

Waxman nodded here and there, frowned with puzzlement, clasped his hands together on his desk. Raven tried to follow Gomez's narration, but the words seemed to flow over her like a tidal wave. Soon she felt that she was drowning. But she made herself nod, too, whenever Waxman did.

At last the astronomer wound down. "I know this is a lot to aim for, but I have only this one chance to study the planet. The

Astronomical Association back on Earth decided to fund this
one expedition. Period. Either I find what has made Uranus so
unique or I return home empty-handed."

Straightening in his high-backed desk chair, Waxman gave
the astronomer a piercing gaze. "We will, of course, assist you in
every way we can. Manpower, computer time, communications
back to Earth—whatever you want, simply ask me."

Gomez dipped his chin in acknowledgement. "Thank you so
much, Mr. Waxman, I—"

"Evan; please call me Evan."

"Evan," Gomez said. "And I am Tómas."

Waxman smiled pleasantly as he turned his head toward
Raven. "And you, Ms. Marchesi? May I call you Raven?"

Raven smiled back brightly. "Certainly . . . Evan."

Without an official acknowledgement, without anyone telling
her or even asking her, Raven became Gomez's de facto assistant. She oversaw the unloading of his equipment in the docking area, and when his submersible arrived, several days after he
had, she watched the crew that Waxman had assigned carefully
installing the instruments into the spherical-shaped submarine.

She dined with Gomez almost every night, but except for
that first meeting, she heard nothing from Evan Waxman. He
didn't notice me, Raven told herself disconsolately. I sat there
across the desk from him and smiled my best but he paid me no
notice.

How can I attract his attention? she asked herself.

And got no answer.

Her work with Gomez, though, absorbed more and more of her
time. While the astronomer busied himself in checking the sub-

mersible's instrumentation and plotting its course through the Uranian ocean, Raven took on all the "household" details of his existence.

Not once in all those days—and evenings—did Gomez give the slightest indication that he was sexually attracted to her. He might as well be my brother, she complained to herself. Or a priest.

It was at that moment that it struck her. He *is* a priest, of sorts, she realized. He's married to his profession. His god is the universe, and he's dedicated himself to uncovering its secrets. He has no time for romance or even sex.

Could I break through his shell? she wondered. And if I did, would it make Evan Waxman notice me?

bOdY aNd SOUL

+++
+++

To her surprise, Raven was summoned, not to Waxman's office, but to the presence of the Reverend
Kyle Umber.

She was preparing dinner for herself and Gomez one evening when she received an instruction on the wall screen of her
living room to appear at the minister's office the next morning.
At precisely the specified time—1100 hours—Raven stood before the double doors that fronted Umber's suite of offices. The
doors slid open silently.

She stepped just inside the doorway. No one was there. This
outer office space was filled with eight consoles, each displaying
circular data screens blinking faster than the human eye could
follow. No sounds. Raven could hear no hum or buzz. No noise
at all. The screens flashed and flickered madly with no person in
the room to monitor them.

Before she could think of anything to say or even blink her
eyes, a flatly emotionless robotic voice said from a speaker in the
ceiling:

"Welcome, Ms. Marchesi. Please proceed along the middle
aisle to the door on the far wall."

Feeling a little uncertain, Raven walked past the busily flashing computer consoles toward the door, which slid open as she
approached it.

She stepped through, into a garden.

It had a high, dome-like ceiling, barely visible through the branches of the trees and shrubs that lined the walkway curving through the foliage. Flowers bloomed everywhere and the air was scented with their fragrance.

"That's right," a human voice spoke out of nowhere, "just walk along the path."

The seamless golden path curved left, then right, then ended at a magnificent broad desk of teak and inlaid precious metals. Behind the desk stood the Reverend Kyle Umber, smiling beneficently.

"Welcome, Ms. Marchesi," Umber said, spreading his arms in salutation. He was dressed in a spotless white suit that seemed almost to glow. Raven half expected a halo to be hovering above his thick shoulder-length reddish-brown hair.

She realized that Umber's desk was subtly raised above floor level. Even though she was standing, she had to look slightly up at him. She approached the desk and saw that there was a single stiff-looking chair placed in front of it.

"Please sit," said Umber, gesturing to the chair. "Make yourself comfortable."

The chair didn't look comfortable, but Raven sat slowly down on it. To her surprise, the chair seemed to shift, almost to flow, until it conformed to her body shape.

Umber sank into his own high-backed black plush chair. Leaning forward and resting his forearms on the desktop, he asked solicitously, "May I address you as Raven?"

Raven nodded wordlessly.

"Good. And you may call me Reverend Umber."

Raven almost smiled. The power game, she said to herself. The Reverend Umber isn't above playing the game. Well, I can play it too.

"I was very honored to receive your call," she said, in what she hoped was a properly humble tone.

"We've been watching your work with Dr. Gomez," said Umber, "and I must say that I, for one, am quite happily impressed with it."

Raven looked up into Umber's round, pink-cheeked face with its auburn hair sweeping down to his shoulders, and smiled.

She said, "I'm trying to help Dr. Gomez all I can."

"That's good. Very good. I'm sure God will reward your efforts."

"I hope so."

"We have noticed, however, that you have not attended any religious services of any kind since arriving here in *Haven*."

Raven put on an expression of contrition. "I have no religion," she said, softly, sadly.

Umber nodded sorrowfully. "In your former life, I suppose the word of God didn't reach you."

"Hardly."

"But here in *Haven* you have begun to change your life. Don't you think you might try to meet God halfway?"

"I don't know how," she replied, in a near whisper.

"I could help you."

Despite herself, Raven's eyes widened with surprise. *He's coming on to me! This man of God wants to lay me!*

"I . . . I don't know if I'm worthy of your help, sir."

"Not my help," said Umber gently. "God's help."

Raven bowed her head as she asked, "What must I do?"

"Attend services at the main chapel tomorrow at six A.M."

"Chapel services?"

"Get to know God and what He expects of you. His yoke is light, His way is the path to salvation."

Raven was too surprised to reply. *Does he actually mean what he's saying? Is he really trying to save my soul? He's not after my body?*

mind and spirit

using her apartment's computer, Raven found that the habitat's main chapel was actually the big auditorium she and the other new arrivals had been taken to on her first day in *Haven*.

The following morning, she arrived at the auditorium a good ten minutes before six, wearing one of the dreary gray outfits that hung in her closet. She slipped quietly through the heavy wooden double doors. . . .

And stepped into another world. The auditorium had been transformed into a chapel. It was only half filled with worshipers, but the vast chamber soared above their bowed heads like a magnificent vision of heaven. Stained glass windows lined both sides of the nave, displaying beautiful scenes of saintly men and women in strikingly bold colors. At the front of the chapel, behind the many-colored marble altar, stood a mammoth image of the crucified Christ, staring out from His cross, a beatific smile on His bearded face despite the bloody nails through His hands and feet and the cruel crown of thorns pressed down upon His head.

She remembered the brief glimpse of this setting from her first day at *Haven*, but somehow, with the chapel half filled with kneeling worshipers, it all seemed more powerful, more stirring.

Raven thought the Christ image was staring directly at her, as if there were no one else in the church. It took an effort of will for her to tear her eyes away from its hypnotic gaze.

Standing on trembling legs at the rear of the church, Raven saw a splendidly robed priest rise to his feet at one side of the altar and raise his hands in blessing.

A voice from nowhere filled the cathedral, pronouncing, *"Dominus vobiscum."* The congregation replied in unison, *"Et cum spiritu tuo."*

"Ite, missa est," said the priest, his arms raised in blessing.

As one, the people replied, *"Deo gratias."*

Then the people—men and women, a few children—rose from their pews and walked slowly along the central aisle, heads bent reverently, past Raven, who was still standing by the massive rear doors. No one spoke a word. To Raven it seemed as if they had all been struck dumb.

She stood there until the last of the worshipers filed past and left the church, leaving it empty, silent.

Suddenly a crisply authoritative voice boomed, "Scrub the Catholic setting. Cue up the Quaker façade."

The beautiful cathedral disappeared like a lamp suddenly clicked off. The church went totally dark for a moment, then a new vision lit up before Raven's astonished eyes. Somehow the church was now much smaller and utterly unadorned. No stained glass windows, no elaborate crucifixion scene, no marble altar. The walls were bare, simple black and white.

A handful of plainly dressed people began filtering into the church. Raven shook her head, as if to clear it, and stumbled back into the walkway outside, which was filling up with pedestrians striding along, talking, laughing, living lives that Raven could understand.

* * *

By the time Raven got back to her quarters, she had made up her mind that she would not return to the chapel, or cathedral, or auditorium, or whatever it was. Not for me, she told herself. If Reverend Umber ever asks me about it, I'll tell him I tried but it didn't work for me.

She wondered if that was the right way to go. But she knew that joining a congregation of worshipers, bowing and kneeling and repeating phrases that were thousands of years old—that was not for her. If she did it, she would be playacting. She felt no sense of belonging among those people. None whatever.

The message light was blinking at the bottom of her living room screen. A message from Tómas, she saw. She called out, "Play message, please."

Gomez's broad-cheeked mestizo face appeared on the screen, looking distraught. "Raven, I need your help. I'm ready for the final checkout of the submersible, but I can't find the checklist that inventories the sub's consumables. I've looked everywhere but I can't find it! Do you know where it is?"

Raven almost laughed. It's probably in your back pocket, she said silently to the image on her screen, filed away on your personal notebook.

Instead, she made herself look almost as serious as he did, then called out, "Reply to message."

Gomez's image shrank to a corner of the screen as Raven said aloud, "I'll come over and help you look for it, Tómas. I'll be there in five minutes."

She sent the message, shut down the screen, then got up and went to her front door, heading for Gomez and problems that she understood.

ШАXMAN'S FILE

The spherical submersible craft sat in a cradle of plastisteel beams in the middle of the docking area. A trio of robots paced slowly around its globular shape, examining every seam and joint along its length. Tómas Gomez stood up on the raised balcony high above, intently watching the automatons, his personal notebook clutched in both hands.

Raven climbed the spiral metal staircase and stood beside Gomez, keeping her face blank, noncommittal, hiding the amusement she felt. Wordlessly, she took the notebook from Gomez's hands.

Sure enough, the checklist that he'd been unable to find was tucked among the data filed in his notebook, along with a lifetime's collection of notes, blueprints, photographs and other miscellanea.

As she watched Gomez's intent face staring down at the robots and the submersible, Raven thought, He really would be lost without me. He's like a very bright little boy, brilliant but absentminded. I wonder who looked after him on Earth?

Raven knew from peeking into Gomez's personnel file that he was unmarried, unattached. He seemed to have time only for his work, his research, his passion to unlock the secrets that Uranus hid at the bottom of its planet-girdling ocean.

She turned her head slightly to gaze down at the submersible. It was a perfectly rotund shape of dark metal, designed to withstand the immense pressures at the bottom of Uranus's sea.

My rival, Raven thought. He doesn't have time for anything or anyone else. I'm playing second fiddle to a machine.

Almost, she laughed. Almost. But she was thinking, once that contraption goes into the ocean, once it's cut off from communication with him, once he's alone up here without his precious toy—that's the time when he'll have no one to talk to, no one to console him, no shoulder to cry on. That's when I'll get him.

Yet a voice in her head asked, Why bother? You don't need him. He can't raise your status in this imitation heaven. Waxman's the one with power. Waxman and Umber. But Umber's not available and Waxman is.

That evening, after a solitary dinner in her own kitchen, Raven looked up the station's computer file on Evan Waxman.

Born to great wealth. Married twice, twice divorced. Met Kyle Umber when the reverend was serving a brief prison term for leading a protest against a state law that allowed people to hunt and kill the few brown bears still living in the national forests. Spent almost all his family's considerable fortune to construct this space station in orbit around Uranus, the station that Umber christened *Haven*. Devoted his life to working with Umber, helping him turn *Haven* into a refuge for Earth's downtrodden poor.

Raven shook her head in disappointment. Nothing there, she concluded. Nothing that lets me see inside the man. Nothing but a shining, glorified biography that was probably written by a public relations organization.

Her phone buzzed, startling Raven out of her musings.

"Answer, please."

Evan Waxman's handsome features appeared on her living room wall screen.

"Good evening," he said, with a smile.

"Mr. Waxman," said Raven, surprised.

"Evan."

"Evan."

"I see that you're examining my biography."

Raven felt a pulse of alarm. "I . . . I was curious about you."

Waxman's smile widened slightly. "Why don't you come over to my quarters and I'll tell you the story of my life."

"Your quarters?"

"I've opened a bottle of very good Amontillado, and I really don't like to drink alone."

Raven's thoughts swirled through her mind as she heard herself answer, "I'm not really dressed to go visiting, I'm afraid."

"You look fine to me. Nothing to be afraid of."

"I don't know . . ."

"Please."

She recognized the expression on his face. She had seen it many times before, on many faces.

"Well, if you think it's okay . . ."

Waxman broke into a handsome grin. "I won't tell Reverend Umber if you won't."

Raven smiled back at him. "All right. I'll be there in a few minutes."

As she strode up to Waxman's door, it slid open automatically for her. Stepping inside, she saw the man standing in the center of his living room, wearing a deep burgundy jacket over black trousers, a long-stemmed wineglass in one hand.

Waxman's apartment seemed little different from her own. Slightly bigger, but the furnishings were very similar. The walls were hung with paintings, though: scenes of cities from the distant past, ancient Rome, Athens, other cities that Raven did not recognize.

Gesturing toward the images, Waxman said—almost sadly—"The glories of yesterday. Many of them have been drowned in the greenhouse floods."

"How sad," Raven murmured.

Brightening noticeably, Waxman said, "I promised you some wine."

He turned toward the coffee table that rested in front of a sofa that was remarkably like the one in Raven's own quarters. A slim bottle of wine stood in an ice bucket on the coffee table and a glass exactly like the one Waxman was holding rested beside it.

"Amontillado," Waxman said. "I first discovered it in a story by Edgar Allan Poe. Been fascinated by it every since."

Raven shook her head. "I never heard of it."

He bent down, put down his own wine glass, and picked up the bottle and the empty glass. "I hope you like it," he said as he poured.

Raven took a cautious sip. The wine tasted slightly bitter, almost tart.

"It's good," she lied.

Waxman nodded and gestured to the sofa. "Let's get to know each other better," he said.

WAXMAN'S STORY

Raven sat on the couch. Waxman sat next to her, close enough for her to smell the cologne he was wearing.

"I've read your personnel file," he said, with a whimsical smile. "Is all that true?"

Raven made herself smile back at him. "Most of it."

"It must have been a very difficult life. You must be glad to be here now."

"I'm very happy to be here. For the first time in my life, I feel safe."

Waxman took a long pull from his wine glass. Then he smiled and asked, "Even now?"

Raven blinked at him. "Are you suggesting that I shouldn't feel safe now?"

His smile shrank noticeably. "The male ego is a very fragile thing, you know."

Keeping her expression serious, Raven replied, "Sometimes the male ego turns violent."

"You poor thing."

"No, I'm not a poor thing. I'm a survivor. I've lived through hell, back on Earth. Now I'm striving for heaven."

Waxman leaned back on the sofa and turned his eyes toward

the ceiling, which sparkled with twinkling stars. "You've been talking with Umber, I see."

"Once."

"And do you intend to become one of his converts? One of his saved creatures?"

For several moments Raven did not answer. Her mind was spinning different responses to Waxman's question. Finally she said, "I intend to become a free and independent woman, able to stand on my own feet and go my own way, without depending on anyone else."

"That," said Waxman, "is well nigh impossible. Everyone needs others to depend on. One person alone can't make it in human society."

"I intend to try."

"Then why did you come here tonight?"

Raven hesitated again. At last she shrugged and answered, "Old habits die hard."

"Ah."

"I shouldn't have come. I shouldn't have given you the impression that I was . . . available."

Waxman sighed. "And I shouldn't have given you the impression that I'm a predator."

Raven stared at him. "You're not?"

He grinned at her. "Not entirely."

"I suppose this is where you tell me the story of your life."

"You haven't looked it up?"

"Your biography looks like a public relations job."

He nodded. "And so it is."

"What's the real story?"

"Too dull to repeat. Until I met Kyle."

"Reverend Umber."

"Yes. He changed my life. Quite literally. Before I met him

I was just a rich kid, like so many others. Just drifting through life. No ambitions, no goals."

"And Reverend Umber changed that?"

"He did indeed," said Waxman. "At first I thought he was crazy. Build a habitat orbiting the planet Uranus? Create a haven for Earth's poor, downtrodden? For the forgotten masses, the people left to vegetate on the outskirts of our glorious inter-planetary society? It sounded like pie in the sky. Fantasy. A pipe dream."

"And yet you're here."

"I am indeed. I'm here among your huddled masses, yearn-ing to breathe free. I'm here helping that madman build a better world."

"That's kind of wonderful."

"It is that," Waxman said, with some fervor.

Raven thought it over for a few silent seconds. Then she asked, "So where do you go from here?"

He made a noise somewhere between a chuckle and a grunt. "Where do we go? Onward and outward. Enlarge *Haven*. Bring more of your downtrodden brethren here. Build additional habi-tats. Start a new nation—free, clean and safe for all."

Raven shook her head. "There are some terrible people among Earth's poor. Horrible people."

"I know," Waxman said, sighing. "I've been warning Umber about them. But he sees only the good in them."

"You've got to protect him against them."

"I try. We use computers to scan their records. We test them before we allow them to come to *Haven*."

Raven remembered how she had maneuvered through the tests. She wondered how many others had done the same. How many murderers and thieves and hopeless scoundrels was Rever-end Umber allowing into *Haven*?

"Umber thinks God will turn all the refugees into saints," Waxman said.

"That won't happen, will it?"

"Hardly."

"How can we protect him from the predators?"

Waxman's brows rose in surprise. "We?"

"I want the reverend's plan to succeed," Raven said. "I want *Haven* to be everything Reverend Umber hopes for it."

"So do I."

"How do we do that?" she asked.

Leaning closer to her, Waxman said, "Well, to begin with, you might consider working with me instead of that astronomer."

Raven pretended surprise. "Oh, I couldn't leave Dr. Gomez! He's like a little boy. He'd be lost without someone to look after him."

"Really?"

"Really."

Waxman studied her face for several silent moments. Raven tried to look sincere and a bit uneasy.

At last Waxman said, "Well, if that's the way you feel . . ."

Raven got to her feet. Waxman looked up at her, then stood up too.

"I . . . I'm sorry," Raven stammered. "I'd love to work with you, I really would. But I couldn't leave Dr. Gomez, really, I couldn't."

"I see," said Waxman, flatly, tonelessly.

She started toward the door. "I appreciate your offer. I really do."

Almost wistfully, Waxman said, "I really need an assistant. Someone bright and . . . well, capable."

Lowering her eyes, Raven said, "Not now. Not yet."

"I understand," said Waxman.

He walked her to the apartment's front door. As it slid open, Raven said, "Thanks for understanding, Evan."

He smiled ruefully.

"You're a real gentleman."

"Then why do I feel like a real idiot?"

Raven stood on tiptoes, gave him a peck on the lips, then swiftly stepped out into the passageway. As she strode hurriedly away from Waxman she smiled to herself.

Leave him hungry for more, she told herself. He'll be back.

into the ocean

Gomez had turned his living quarters into a command center. The living room was crammed with buzzing, humming, blinking pieces of equipment. The only place Raven could find to sit down was the sofa, next to Gomez himself.

The astronomer looked as tense as a live wire stretched almost to the breaking point. The wall screen across the living room showed the submersible, floating in space outside the *Haven* habitat. The screen's audio system was counting down the seconds to the sub's launch.

Gomez's eyes flicked from one piece of droning, chattering equipment to another. Every light showed green as the audio's countdown continued smoothly, but the astronomer looked as anxious as a man facing a firing squad.

Raven put out her hand and rested it on Gomez's thigh. He took no notice of it. His head swiveled back and forth, peering at the various consoles as if he were keeping them functioning by his own willpower alone.

"T minus ten seconds," the audio voice intoned.

Gomez's already taut posture stiffened even more. Raven thought that if ever he devoted this much concentration to lovemaking he'd be a marvelous partner.

"... four ... three ... two ... one ... ignition," said the monitor's emotionless voice.

For an instant nothing seemed to happen. Then the globular submersible disappeared. It flashed out of sight faster than Raven could blink.

Gomez pointed a trembling finger at one of the consoles. "It's on its way," he croaked, his voice hoarse with tension.

The wall screen showed a telescope's view of the submersible dwindling against the background of Uranus's blue-gray clouds.

Raven sat wordlessly beside Gomez as the astronomer turned his head slowly to stare at each and every one of the consoles littering his living room. She didn't know what to say, what to do.

The telescope still showed the submersible hurtling closer to Uranus's unbroken expanse of clouds. Off in the upper right corner of the screen swirled the dark circle of a mammoth storm, the size of Asia.

"We won't be able to see it once it enters the clouds," Gomez muttered. It was the longest sentence he'd spoken to Raven in more than an hour.

"We won't see it enter the sea?" she asked.

"No. But we'll know when that happens. All the telemetry will cut off."

"It will go silent."

"Yes." With a wry smile, Gomez added, "Then I'll know how my father felt when I left our home and went to the university."

"But you could write to him, talk to him by telephone," said Raven.

"I could have."

Raven reached for his hand. "It will be all right, Tómas. Everything's going to be fine."

He nodded, but answered bleakly, "There's only a few thousand things that could go wrong."

"It will all go right."

"I wish."

"You'll see." Raven pushed herself up from the couch and headed toward Gomez's kitchen. "I'm starved," she called over her shoulder. "Aren't you hungry?"

Gomez shook his head silently.

The red phone signal began flashing at the bottom of the view screen. "Incoming call from Mr. Waxman," said the screen's voice.

"Take his message," Gomez commanded.

Waxman's handsome face filled the screen. "I'm sure you're watching the sub's entry into Uranus's clouds, Tómas. But once your baby dives into the ocean and is cut off from communicating, why don't you join us in the main lounge? Most of your crew is here, ready to celebrate. Quite a few others, as well. We'd all like to see you and congratulate you on a successful launch."

The screen went blank, except for a REPLY? prompt.

Before Gomez could say anything, Raven called from the kitchen, "We'd be happy to join you. Thanks."

Gomez stared at her with real hostility burning in his eyes. "I'm not going to any party!"

"Yes, you are," said Raven firmly. Then she repeated to the screen, "We'd be happy to join you, Evan. Thank you." She hesitated a moment, then commanded, "Transmit message."

MESSAGE TRANSMITTED, appeared on the screen.

Rising to his feet, Gomez complained, "I'm not in the mood for a party."

"You could use some relaxation," said Raven. "Once the submersible is in the ocean you won't be able to communicate with it. Why not unwind a little bit? We won't have to stay very long. Just let people admire you, Tómas. Be a little bit human."

Gomez shook his head and mumbled something too low for Raven to make out. But once the submersible splashed into the ocean and its link with him was cut off he trudged reluctantly alongside Raven to the main lounge.

Raven could hear the thumping music while they were still twenty meters from the lounge's door. They're having a party, she realized. Letting off steam. Celebrating a successful launch.

Gomez looked somewhere between frightened and angry.

"What if something goes wrong?" he asked, in a near whisper. "What if the sub malfunctions or sinks?"

"But it hasn't," Raven countered, tugging at his arm. "It's all gone fine so far, and you're the man everyone wants to see and congratulate."

"Maybe. But—"

"Come on, Tómas! Put on a smile!"

He tried to smile. Raven thought it looked ghastly. But they were approaching the doors of the lounge, and the music from inside blared loud enough to make her wince. Raven realized she hadn't danced since she'd arrived at *Haven*, months ago. I deserve a little fun, she told herself.

The doors slid open automatically and the noise was enough to knock a person flat. Raven flinched momentarily, then, without even looking at Gomez, she stepped into the raucous, swirling party. Gomez hesitated at the doorway, as if frightened to enter the lounge.

"There he is!" someone shouted.

The music stopped abruptly, and some thirty or more men and women converged on them.

They pushed past Raven and surrounded Gomez, the men shouting congratulations and pounding his back, the women staring at him. Raven stepped away, thinking, This is Tómas's party. His moment in the spotlight. His time to shine. I hope he enjoys it.

Gomez seemed bewildered at first, but within a few moments he was grinning at the men and women clustered about him. One of the women, lithe and leggy, several centimeters taller than Gomez himself, folded herself into his arms and—as the music resumed its thumping beat—began twirling with him across the floor. Raven saw that the woman was dancing, with Gomez shuffling along clumsily. But he was smiling.

The congratulatory group quickly broke into couples that swirled across the dance floor.

"May I have this dance?"

Raven turned. There was Evan Waxman, tall, elegantly dressed in a form-fitting jacket of royal blue, smiling at her. She placed her hand in his and let him lead her out onto the dance floor.

Over the blare of the music Waxman fairly shouted into Raven's ear, "Looks like your lad is enjoying himself."

Raven nodded. "I think this might be the first time he's ever been the center of attention."

"Ah," said Waxman, "everyone should be the center of attention every now and then."

"Yes, I suppose so."

Waxman chuckled. "It's a good thing that every resident of *Haven* has been medically examined and cleared of sexual diseases."

Raven blinked with surprise, then muttered, "I suppose so."

"That includes me, of course."

She made herself smile up at him. "Me too," said Raven.

the morning after

Raven awoke from a deep, languorous sleep. Evan Waxman lay beside her, snoring gently, a satisfied smile on his lips.

Tómas! Raven thought, her eyes snapping wide open. She remembered seeing him dancing happily with one woman after another. Then she'd lost track of him.

I've got to get back to my place and track him down. Softly, slowly, she slipped out of bed and headed for the bathroom. Evan had been a surprisingly gentle lover, she recalled. He knew how to help a woman enjoy sexual intercourse.

By the time she left the bathroom, fully dressed once again, Waxman was sitting up in the bed with the sheet covering his groin and legs.

"Leaving?" he asked, with a thin smile.

"I've got to locate Tómas," Raven said. "He's—"

"He's in good hands," said Waxman. "He trundled out of the lounge last night with a woman on each arm."

Despite herself, Raven broke into laughter.

Still sitting on the bed, Waxman said, "Thank you."

Dipping her chin slightly, she replied, "Thank *you*."

"I wish you'd come and work with me, Raven. I need you."

"In bed?"

He grinned ruefully. "Yes, of course." Before Raven could reply, Waxman added, "But more than that. Much more. I need an assistant, Raven. An assistant with a first-class mind."

"Me?" Raven felt truly surprised.

"You," Waxman answered.

"I'm just a refugee, Evan. I don't have any education, no experience—"

"You learn quickly. Gomez would be lost without you."

"Yes, I suppose he would."

"I need you, too. I truly do."

Feeling torn, Raven said, "But Tómas . . ."

"He's got nothing to do now that his sub is in the ocean. He doesn't need you now."

"But once his submersible comes up again, he'll have his hands full of data to interpret."

"I've got this entire fucking habitat to look after!" Waxman snapped, his voice rising. "Umber can sit up there on his private Cloud Nine, but I've got to make certain this habitat functions properly."

"I know."

"Then help me! I need your help."

Raven studied his face. He seemed sincere enough, but she thought she knew what he was really saying.

"Evan, I can spend my nights with you."

"And I can spend my nights with any one of a hundred women living in this habitat. It's you that I want—and not just in bed. I want you to help me run this funny farm. I need you!"

Raven went over and sat on the edge of the bed. "I wish that was true."

"It is!" Raising his right hand, he swore, "So help me God!"

"But I don't know anything about running a habitat. I don't have any education."

Waxman's earnest expression eased into a smile. "I can teach you. Me, and the computers. Then there's hypno-learning. You can get an education while you sleep!"

"While I sleep?"

He nodded.

"But what about Tómas?"

"I'll get one of my staff people to help him. As you said, there's nothing for him to do until his sub pops up from the ocean."

"True," Raven said uncertainly.

"By then he'll have forgotten about you," Waxman said firmly.

Raven shook her head. "I don't know. . . ."

Waxman let a small sigh escape his lips. Then he said, "All right, let's try it this way: You take on the position of my assistant while Gomez's submersible is in the ocean, out of contact. When his sub shows up again we can re-evaluate where we stand. Fair enough?"

For long moments Raven sat on the edge of the bed, her mind spinning. Waxman stared at her, studying her, waiting for her decision.

"All right," she said at last, more than a little uncertainly. "Let's try it that way."

Waxman broke into a wide grin. He put out his hand toward her. "Agreed!"

Raven let her hand be engulfed by his. "Agreed," she said, in a near whisper.

She expected him to pull her next to him for another bout of lovemaking. Instead he released her hand and, smiling, told her, "Now go and find Gomez and break the news to him."

Surprised, Raven got up from the bed and headed for the door.

Waxman called after her, "I'll expect you at my office tomorrow at oh-nine-hundred hours."

She turned her head back toward him and nodded. "Oh-nine-hundred."

By the time Raven got to the apartment's front door and stepped into the passageway outside, she felt puzzled, confused. *He really wants me to become his assistant? He isn't just trying to screw me?*

Then she smiled and started striding along the passageway, toward her own quarters, telling herself, *But that doesn't mean I can't screw him.*

LOVE

Raven phoned Gomez as soon as she returned to her quarters. No answer. She asked the habitat's personnel monitor to locate him, but the monitor reported he was nowhere to be found.

He went off with a pair of women, Raven remembered from the night before. *Haven*'s security cameras scanned every square centimeter of public space aboard the habitat: passageways, parks, restaurants, shops, maintenance facilities, laboratories, storage areas, the hospital, offices. But private living quarters remained private. No security cameras watched them.

Where could Tómas be? Raven wondered.

She asked the security system to scan again. He's got to be somewhere, Raven told herself.

And there he was, trudging along one of the passageways down among the habitat's docking facilities. What's he doing there? Raven wondered. His submersible isn't there anymore, it's gone into Uranus's ocean.

"Tómas," she called. "Can you hear me? It's me, Raven."

He looked up at the sound of her voice. "Raven. Where are you?"

"In my quarters. Come and join me. I'll make some breakfast."

* * *

Raven expected Gomez to be joyful, happy about his night with the two women he'd walked off with. Instead, as he sat at the kitchen's tiny foldout table, he seemed morose, dejected ... guilty?

She placed a plate of eggs and faux bacon before him and asked, "Did you enjoy your party?"

He looked startled.

Raven carried her own plate from the microwave oven to the miniature table and sat down opposite Gomez. "You certainly were the center of everyone's attention."

Gomez nodded glumly.

"Come on, eat your breakfast before it gets cold."

He poked at the eggs.

"What's the matter, Tómas?" Raven asked, smiling at him. "Didn't you have a good time?"

He stared down at his plate.

"Two women," Raven prompted. "You must be pretty tired."

He looked up at her. "I wish it had been you."

Raven's mouth dropped open. "Me?"

"I love you, Raven."

She stared at him, thinking, He's spent the night with two women and he tells me he's in love with me? Something inside her wanted to laugh at his hangdog expression, but something stronger kept her from doing that.

She heard herself ask, "You love me?"

"I do."

Raven thought, You'd better put a stop to this, right here and now.

She said, "That's very sweet of you, Tómas, but you can't really mean it."

"I do mean it. I love you." The expression on his face was full of misery.

Raven shook her head. "Maybe you think you do, but—"

"I know what I feel. I love you!"

"Tómas, do you know what I was before I came here to *Haven?*"

"I don't care."

"I was a whore! I fucked men for money. Women too. I was a whore!"

"But you're not anymore."

"I'm not? What do you think I was doing while you were making out with your two friends?"

"I don't care."

"Well I do," Raven said, her voice burning with the anger inside her. "I'm still a whore and I'm not interested in a moon-struck scientist who's feeling guilty about having an enjoyable time last night."

He stared at her, his deep brown eyes unblinking, steady and firm.

"Tómas, this is impossible!"

Gomez pushed his chair back from the table and slowly rose to his feet. Standing, he said softly, "I know you can't love me. I know I'm nothing in your eyes. But I thought that if I told you how I felt . . . how I love you . . . it might make a difference."

Raven remained seated. She looked up at him and said, "You'll forget about me." Before he could protest she went on, "It's better that you do. I'm very flattered that you think so highly of me, but I'm not the woman you think I am. It will be better if we don't see each other again."

Gomez bit his lip and nodded. Silently he turned and walked out to the front door and left Raven's apartment.

For long moments she stared at the door once it closed behind him. Then she sank her head in her arms and began to cry uncontrollably.

Education

Once she regained control of her emotions, Raven went into her living room, phoned Waxman and—without hesitation—asked him to find someone else to assist Gomez.

His expression on her wall screen was somewhere between surprised and amused.

"You don't want to work with him anymore?" Waxman asked.

Sitting alone on her sofa, Raven replied, "I think it's better if I don't. I think I should devote all my attention to learning what I need to know about being your assistant."

"Wonderful!" said Waxman. "You can start this evening, at my place. Dinner for two."

Raven smiled thinly. "Evan, you told me to report for work at oh-nine-hundred. I'm serious about learning to be your assistant. I mean it."

He flourished a hand in the air. "Certainly! And I'm happy that you feel this way. I'll see you in my office at oh-nine-hundred hours, then."

"Good." Glancing at the clock on the kitchen counter, Raven saw that she had more than twenty minutes to get to Waxman's office.

"And you can forget about tonight. I'll find someone else to dine with."

Raven started to reply, but held her tongue. Of course he'll find someone else, she told herself. He must have a whole harem of women waiting for him to crook his finger at one of them. I'm just another conquest for him.

"Fine," she said flatly.

She made herself smile more brightly at his image on the screen. Waxman smiled back. Raven was surprised that he didn't lick his lips.

It was a strange romance, Raven thought. Every few nights Waxman invited her to his apartment and Raven went willingly, knowing what he expected. They spent those nights in bed together, exploring the many ways a man and a woman can give pleasure to each other. But once the habitat's lighting system turned on its daylight mode, Raven became a student. She studied the complexities of *Haven*'s physical layout, the organization of its government and population, the balances of power and authority, who made decisions and who carried out those decisions.

For the first time in her life, Raven began to see how a community as massive and complex as *Haven* was actually put together, how it ran, how everything functioned.

Waxman was a gentle, accommodating lover. Insistent, but not too demanding. She smiled at his relaxed attitude. So sure of himself. He seemed truly concerned about her education, prodding her to learn and teaching her how to *use* what she learned in the day-to-day affairs of the habitat.

The nights he spent with her were very different, though. He made Raven feel as if she were the only woman in the universe that he cared for. But then he would go days, even weeks, before calling her to his bed again.

She did her best to satisfy him, knowing that she had plenty of competition for his affections. Meanwhile, she learned—even in her sleep.

Waxman gave her a pair of tiny buds that she could worm into her ears. Once her breathing and heart rates showed she was deeply asleep, the buds stimulated her brain directly and she awoke much more knowledgeable than she'd been when she'd fallen asleep.

During those weeks, every now and then she'd notice Quincy O'Donnell's hulking figure, usually at a distance, his eyes on her. It made her feel slightly uncomfortable, but whenever the big man got close enough to speak to her he invariably mumbled a "Hello" and then shambled off, as if embarrassed.

She saw Gomez too, usually in one of the habitat's cafeterias at lunch time. He too seemed stiff and uncomfortable at first, but after a few weeks his attitude loosened enough so that he would sit at the same table with her. Gomez would ask her how she was. Raven always replied positively but noncommittally.

"I'm fine, Tómas. And you?"

He shrugged. "The sub's still down at the bottom of the ocean, poking around the seabed." Than he added, "I hope."

Leaning over her lunch tray, Raven asked, "When is it supposed to come back?"

"In two weeks. If it's still functioning properly."

"You won't know until then?"

Gomez shook his head slowly.

"It must be maddening," Raven said.

"Oh, it's been sending up message drones on schedule," Gomez replied, his hangdog expression unchanging. "Everything seems to be going along as designed."

"That's good."

"But it hasn't found anything. The seabed is just a collection of stones and sands. Nothing interesting. Nothing at all."

"What are you hoping for?" Raven asked.

"Something!" Gomez blurted. "Anything! A sign of life. A seashell, a strand of biologically active chemicals. But there's nothing down there. That ocean is as lifeless as a dead chunk of rock. It looks like my investigation isn't turning up a goddamned thing."

Raven didn't know what to say, how to make him feel better.

"And that means my career goes down the toilet," he added. "I'm dead meat."

"No," Raven snapped. "That can't be true. I can't believe that."

"Believe it," he said, his face a picture of misery, defeat. "The university went way out on a limb to fund my project, and I'm not going to have anything to show for it. Not a goddamned sonofabitchin' thing."

"But isn't that a worthwhile finding?" Raven asked. "It's a result that nobody knew before."

"That the planet is sterile?" He hm'phed. "Big fuckin' deal."

"It's a surprise, isn't it? I mean, the other gas giants—Jupiter, Saturn, Neptune—they all have biospheres, don't they?"

Gomez nodded. "But Uranus doesn't."

"How come? What makes Uranus different?"

He hunched his shoulders. "Whatever makes Uranus different must have happened very early in the solar system's history, when there were lots of planetesimals whizzing through the system. One of them smacked into Uranus, knocked it over sideways, sterilized it."

"So you're proving that that's what happened, aren't you?"

"I guess," he admitted slowly. "It all happened so far back in the system's history—billions of years ago—that we can't really be sure of who did what to who."

"To whom," Raven corrected.

"Whatever."

She saw that he was really down, staring inescapable defeat in the face.

Putting on a smile, Raven said, "Well, maybe you'll find something that your submarine dredged up from the sea floor once you get it back here."

"Or maybe I should just put an electric probe in my mouth and scramble my brain permanently."

"Don't talk like that!" Raven snapped. "This isn't the end of the world."

"It's the end of my world," said Gomez.

He pushed his chair back, got to his feet, and slowly walked toward the cafeteria's exit doors. Raven stared at his retreating back. Then she noticed that he hadn't touched his breakfast. His tray lay there on the table, just as it had been when he'd first put it down.

book two

THE MANAGER

rust

Raven spent her days studying and learning how Haven was administered—and occasional nights in Waxman's bed.

On one particular morning, he met her in his outer office as she came in from the passageway outside.

"Raven," he said, with a beaming smile, "you, of course, know my executive assistant, Alicia Polanyi. Alicia, I want you to be the first to know that Raven Marchesi, here, is now my new administrative assistant."

Raven felt surprised, even delighted. Until she saw the expression on Alicia Polanyi's sallow face.

Polanyi measured Raven with her eyes, which were glacial-blue, the color of an Arctic iceberg. Her light brown hair was cut spiky-short, her face cadaverous with sunken cheeks and nothing more than a thin, faintly pink line for lips, her body lean to the point of emaciation. She was wearing a single-piece uniform that hung on her bony frame, two sizes too large.

No competition, Raven thought as she extended her hand toward Polanyi's cadaverous fingers.

"Congratulations," Polanyi said, her voice flat and dark.

"Raven's going to be working with me here in the office from now on," Waxman announced. "She'll need a space for herself, with a desk, console, all the trimmings."

"I'll take care of it right away," said Polanyi, her icy blue eyes never moving from Raven's face.

Waxman smiled brightly, then said to Raven, "Come on into my office. We have work to do."

Raven turned and followed Waxman into the inner office. But she could feel Polanyi's eyes burning into her back.

It took less than a day for a team of robots and a single male supervisor to create an office all her own for Raven. It was several doors down the passageway from Waxman's suite, and she had to go past Polanyi's cold-eyed stare to get to Evan's office, but she got accustomed to that.

Although there was no written record of it, casual conversations with other staff members over the lunch tables in the cafeteria told Raven that Waxman and Polanyi had once been lovers.

"She was a knockout in those days, less than a year ago," said one of Raven's newfound office mates. "But that was before she started toking Rust."

Raven knew better than to ask obviously pointed questions. She just let the office gossip gradually fill her in. Rust was apparently a hallucinogenic, a powerful narcotic.

"It lifts you up to the stars," one of the office crew told her— the guy who had supervised the robots that had built her office. "But then it drops you down into a pile of shit."

Raven understood what they were saying: stay away from Rust.

But a few days later, she found a line in an invoice buried among the other office records. Just a single line. It was a bill for the sale of ten kilos of Rust. Close to a million international dollars! Raven got up from her desk and headed for Waxman's office.

As she strode down the corridor, she remembered that Tómas's submersible was due to break out of the ocean tomorrow and return to the habitat. She hadn't seen Tómas in several days. Was he hiding from her?

But she put her thoughts of Gomez aside as she stepped into Waxman's outer office and locked eyes with Alicia Polanyi, who nodded silently to Raven and touched the keypad that opened the door to Waxman's private office. All without a word spoken by either of them.

That's what Rust does to you, Raven told herself as she swept past Polanyi's desk. Alicia is the wreckage of what had once been Evan's mistress. Don't let that happen to you!

Waxman was seated at his desk. The wall screen to his right showed a view of Uranus, blue-gray and bland as usual, except for a cyclonic swirl of dark clouds near the planet's north pole.

Without preamble Raven asked, "What is Rust?"

Waxman's face froze. For a heartbeat he just stared at Raven, unmoving, his mouth slightly open, his eyes unblinking. Then he asked, "Rust?"

"There's a charge for Rust on invoice 26-953," Raven said.

Waxman shook his head. "That's not possible."

Pointing to the desktop screen, Raven said, "Take a look."

Waxman hesitated a brief moment, then took a breath and called up the invoice. He scanned every item. "I don't see any mention of Rust."

Raven stepped around his desk and stared at the screen.

"I saw the entry," she insisted.

Leaning back in his desk chair, Waxman said coolly, "It's not there now."

"It's been erased."

For an eternally long moment Waxman stared into Raven's eyes. She stared back, unflinching.

At last he said, "It wasn't supposed to be there. One of the accounting robots made an error."

"We're buying narcotics?"

Waxman eased into a sly smile. "No. We're selling the stuff."

"Rust?" Raven asked, in a voice half an octave higher than a moment earlier. "We're selling Rust?"

"To whoever wants to buy it," said Waxman. "How do you think we keep this habitat running?"

Raven stepped over to one of the chairs in front of Waxman's desk and sank into it.

"We're selling narcotics?"

"Down in the Chemlab Building we manufacture the drug called Rust. It's our major export item."

"But it's illegal."

"Not here. Not aboard *Haven*. There's no law against it here."

"But on Earth . . . on the other worlds, the Asteroid Belt . . ."

Waxman tilted his head slightly. "They have their laws, we have ours."

It took several moments for Raven to process what Waxman was telling her. Then she asked, "What does Reverend Umber have to say about this?"

"Nothing. Not a thing. He closes his eyes and doesn't get in our way. He acts as if he doesn't know anything about it."

"But he does know?"

With a shrug, Waxman replied, "Of course he knows. But I can tell you this: he doesn't *want* to know."

An almost delirious laugh bubbled out of Raven's throat. "This entire habitat—this haven of refuge—it's built on money from narcotics."

Waxman shrugged again. "Politics makes strange bedfellows, Raven."

"This isn't politics," she retorted. "It's drugs! It ruins people. Kills them!"

"They kill themselves," Waxman said sternly. "We don't force anyone to use the stuff. They pay good money for the privilege."

Nodding toward Waxman's office door, Raven said, "Like Alicia."

"Like Alicia," Waxman agreed. "She's working hard to get off her habit. She might even be successful, sooner or later."

"Sooner or later," Raven echoed.

Waxman leveled a stern gaze at her. "That's up to her. People bear the responsibility for their actions, you know."

"I know that narcotics can sizzle your brain, turn you into a zombie, kill you."

"That's not our fault. We simply sell the stuff. We don't force anyone to use it."

A picture of some of the people she knew in Naples filled Raven's mind. No, she thought, you don't force anyone to use the drugs. You just make them available. You just lay them out in front of them, like offering candy to a baby. You pocket their money and leave them to tear themselves apart.

But she said nothing. She knew that Waxman would not tolerate any objections from her, any questions, any doubts.

Instead, she asked, "You pay for this whole habitat with the money you make from Rust?"

With a shake of his head, Waxman smilingly replied, "Oh no, not at all. Most of the habitat's money comes from good-hearted people who honestly want to help the poor. They donate money and tell themselves they're doing good."

"And they stay in their mansions and live their lives and think everything's okay."

Waxman sighed. "That's about the size of it. We help the good, honest, high-minded citizens of the worlds to feel they're doing the right thing."

"While you make millions from selling Rust. Or is it billions?"

"Not quite billions," Waxman answered with a thin smile, "but it's getting close."

"I see."

"Now that you know," Waxman told her, "naturally I'd like you to keep quiet about it. No sense advertising it all through the habitat. Not that it's illegal here, remember. It's perfectly legal."

But slimy, Raven thought. Dirty. Filthy.

Unaware of what she was thinking, Waxman went on, "We try to keep a low profile here in the habitat. We've used Rust to help pacify some of our rowdier residents, of course. There's always a few who slip through the screening process—as you did."

Raven saw that he was staring at her, his face set in a mask of authority. Automatically, she made herself smile back at him. "Why Evan, I thought you liked me."

"I do," he said, breaking into a sunny smile. "I like you very much, Raven."

Like you once liked Alicia, she thought.

His expression hardening again, Waxman said, "But I want this Rust business kept as quiet as possible. Loose lips sink ships . . . and sailors."

the Prodigal returns

Raven went to the main auditorium to watch the recovery of Gomez's submarine. Tómas had invited her to his quarters, but she couldn't make herself accept his invitation. That would be too close, she told herself. It might give him ideas. Better to stay separated.

Waxman had declared an official holiday, so the auditorium was already crowded, and more people were coming in to watch the sub's return, standing and staring at the big screens that hung on every wall. So far, they showed nothing but Uranus's blue-gray clouds.

Raven was surprised—almost shocked—when she saw Tómas shouldering his way through the crowd that had gathered in the auditorium. Heading toward her.

"Tómas!" she called to him. "What are you doing here?"

His face looked tense, worried. "Same as you," he shouted over the hubbub of the crowd. "I've come to see if my sub had survived its mission."

"But not in your quarters?"

"I couldn't stand being alone," he said, stepping beside her.

And you wanted to be with me, Raven said to herself. Well, there's nothing I can do about it. He's here. She realized that she was glad that Gomez had come to be with her. And that her reaction was anything but wise.

The speakers set into the auditorium's ceiling announced, "Breakout from the ocean in thirty seconds."

"If she breaks out," Gomez muttered. "If she's intact. If nothing happened to her while she was down on the sea bottom."

A different voice sang through the speakers, "Breakout attained at oh-nine-seventeen hours GMT."

The crowd roared out a lusty cheer. Raven threw her arms around Gomez's neck. "She's okay! She made it!"

Gomez's grin could have lit up a major city. They both stared at the wall screens, which still showed nothing but Uranus's endless expanse of clouds.

"It'll take almost an hour to climb through the atmosphere and break out of the clouds," said Gomez tensely.

They waited. Nearly quivering with anxiety as they stood in the middle of the crowd, they stared at the pole-to-pole expanse of blue-gray clouds, together with all the others, half-listening to the scraps of conversation from the people around them.

". . . atmospheric turbulence . . ."

". . . wind shear in the clouds . . ."

Raven was surprised to hear so much talk about the conditions in Uranus's atmosphere. These people didn't sound like poor, ignorant dregs of civilization. They had learned something, many of them, since they'd arrived at *Haven*. She realized that she wasn't the only one who had been educating herself.

Then a tiny dark speck appeared against the blue-gray clouds.

"There she is!" someone shouted.

"No, that's just—"

But even as the people stared at the screens, the cameras in orbit around the planet zoomed in on the unmistakable image of the spherical submersible rising above Uranus's clouds and heading for the habitat.

"She's made it!"

"She's coming home!"

The crowd roared. People swarmed around Gomez, grabbing for his hand, pounding him on the back. Women kissed him. Men grinned and laughed as if they were responsible for the submersible's return. Raven stood aside and let Tómas bask in his moment of glory.

But after a few moments the big grin on his face faded. He nodded good-naturedly at the crowd and said, "Now we must examine the samples from the seabed that the sub has carried to us. Now we have to find out whether or not the planet is truly sterile."

That didn't diminish the crowd's enthusiasm one iota. Raven watched them as they smiled and nodded and pawed at the astronomer. One woman stepped up to Tómas, brazenly wrapped her arms around his neck and kissed him squarely on the lips. Gomez sputtered and gulped for air, half delighted, half embarrassed.

Standing off at the edge of the crowd, Raven realized that Tómas was right: his real work was just beginning.

Eventually the crowd broke up into knots of men and women talking, discussing, gesticulating while they slowly walked out of the auditorium. Raven watched Gomez as the crowd gradually melted away from him. Your fifteen minutes of fame have ended, she said to him silently.

Gomez seemed to understand. He turned and headed for the nearest exit, without even a nod toward Raven. Heading back to work, heading for his real love, his urge to uncover the mysteries of Uranus.

Despite herself, she sighed. But when she turned and started for an exit she saw Quincy O'Donnell standing a few steps away from her, big, hulking, the expression on his face halfway between expectant and cringing.

Raven made herself smile at him. "Hello, Quincy."

"Hello, Raven," he said, his eyes glancing this way and that. "How are you?"

As Raven headed slowly toward the nearest exit, she replied, "I'm fine. And you?"

Walking beside her, Quincy asked, "Are you busy tonight? Can I take you to dinner?"

Raven hesitated. She saw the big oaf's anxiety in his deep blue eyes. Why not? she asked herself. Keep him on the leash.

"That would be nice," she said, as she extended her hand toward his.

Raven spent the day in her quarters, studying. Precisely at 7:00 P.M. she heard a tap on her door. The viewscreen next to the door showed O'Donnell out in the passageway, wearing a sharply creased pair of new-looking trousers and a powder-blue hip-length shirt, nervously biting his lip.

He's dressed up for me, she thought.

She cleared the wall screen she'd been working with, got to her feet and commanded the door to open. O'Donnell stood there uncertainly, like an oversized child wondering what was expected of him.

"Come in, Quincy," said Raven. As he entered, Raven turned toward her bedroom and said over her shoulder, "I'll only be a minute."

O'Donnell led Raven to the habitat's fanciest restaurant. She wore a form-hugging outfit she had created from one of the shapeless uniforms in her closet; it complemented his outfit nicely.

As they sat off in a corner of the restaurant, at a table for two, Raven asked, "What are you up to these days?"

A wide grin broke across his rugged, ruddy face. "I've been promoted, I have. I'll be supervising one o' the teams of robots buildin' the new wheel."

"Really? That's wonderful. Congratulations."

And for the rest of their dinner, O'Donnell described his work on the extension of *Haven*'s habitat. The new wheel they were constructing would double the station's capacity.

"It'll be a duplicate of this structure, right down to the last weld," he said happily.

As the robotic waiter delivered their desserts, Raven said, "I didn't know you were an engineer."

Still beaming happily, O'Donnell responded, "I wasn't, not until last Friday. I been studyin' in my sleep, y'know, learnin' structural engineering—at least, enough to qualify for a supervisor's slot. I'm risin' up in the world, I am!"

Raven realized she wasn't the only one using hypno-learning to advance herself.

She said, "Quincy, that's wonderful."

"On this job, we'll be workin' outside, you know. Out in space. It won't bother the robots, of course, but I'll have to wear a space suit, just like the astronauts!"

"That'll be exciting," Raven enthused.

"One o' these days I'll be a full-fledged engineer, with a diploma and everything."

"That will be grand," Raven said, feeling honestly delighted for him.

"It will," he said happily. "It will."

He walked her back to her quarters. Raven stopped at her door, stood on her tiptoes to give him a peck on the lips, and said, "Thanks for a lovely dinner, Quincy."

He beamed happily.

"And congratulations again on your new position."

He nodded, fidgeting uncertainly before her closed door.

"Good night, Quincy."

For a moment he was silent, staring down at her. Then, "Good night, Raven."

He turned and started down the passageway. Raven stared after his shambling, hulking form for a moment, then swiftly opened her apartment's door, stepped inside, and slid it shut again.

She leaned against the closed door, thinking, The higher he gets in the engineering field, the harder it will be to control him. Remember that.

the drug trade

morning after morning, Raven went to Evan Waxman's office, past the piercing cold blue eyes of Alicia Polanyi, and learned more about the intricacies of managing habitat *Haven*.

More than four thousand people lived in *Haven*, almost all of them refugees from the slums and villages of Earth. They were the forgotten ones, the voiceless ones, bypassed in the surging rush for wealth, for pleasure, for opportunity that their more fortunate brethren pursued. Most of these poor, downtrodden men and women were trying to better themselves, striving for education, for a new place in this new world.

"We don't seem to have many children here," Raven said to Waxman, as she stood in front of his desk.

Leaning back in his desk chair, Waxman said carelessly, "No, we don't. By design."

"By design?" Raven echoed, surprised. "But I would think that families—especially families with small children—they're the ones who need our help the most."

Waxman replied casually, "You'd think that, wouldn't you?"

"Don't you?" she asked.

He shook his head. "It's too late for them. We don't want to become a charity ward for young families. For women without husbands and a half-dozen brats clinging to their skirts."

"But they're the ones who need the most help!"

"Maybe they do, but they'd soak up most of our resources. And for what? So that they can go out and make more children? We're not running a family clinic here. We want single, unattached men and women who can learn and grow, who can manage themselves positively and help this habitat to prosper."

"By selling Rust." The words were out of Raven's mouth before she could stop them.

Waxman stared up at her for a long, silent moment. Then, "That bothers you, doesn't it?"

She stared back at him as she sank into one of the chairs in front of his desk. At last she admitted, "Yes, it does."

"You didn't do drugs while you were on the street in Naples?"

"Of course I did," Raven replied. "You couldn't survive without something to take the edge off."

"Small stuff, I imagine."

"That was all I could afford, Evan. Marijuana, coke now and then . . . I even tried Ecstasy once in a while."

"But not Rust."

"I didn't know Rust existed until I got here."

Waxman smiled mirthlessly. "And here I thought you were smart enough to steer clear of it."

Thinking of Alicia, in the outer office, Raven said, "I would have, if I had known its long-term effects."

He shook his head. "No, you wouldn't. Oh, you might have tried to stay away from it, but sooner or later you'd try some. Just as an experiment, you'd have told yourself. But you'd have tried it."

Raven let her eyes drop. "You're probably right. There were times when I would have tried anything, just to get through another night, just to survive."

Waxman's stony expression softened. "I'm glad you didn't, Raven. I'm glad you came here to *Haven*, instead." In a low voice she replied, "So am I."

That evening, after dinner alone in her quarters, as Raven pored over a text on political organizations, her door announced, "Reverend Umber is at the door."

Surprised, she looked up and, sure enough, the door's tiny viewscreen showed Umber standing outside in the passageway, decked out entirely in white, as usual.

"Door open!" she called, as she got up from the sofa.

The door slid open, and Reverend Umber stepped in, looking uncertain, perplexed.

"I'm not intruding, am I?" he asked, as the door slid shut behind him.

"Not at all," said Raven as she cleared the wall screen she'd been reading from. "Come right in."

Umber stepped hesitantly toward the sling chair next to the sofa and gingerly lowered himself into it.

"Can I get you something?" Raven asked. "Coffee? Tea?"

"Plain water, please."

Raven went to the kitchen and drew a glass of water from the sink's faucet.

"I'm sorry to barge in on you like this," Umber began.

"It's okay. I was just studying."

She handed him the glass and sat down on the edge of the sofa.

"Studying. That's good. Very good."

Raven peered at his round, pink face. He was smiling at her, yet somehow she felt that he was troubled.

She started to apologize. "I know I haven't been attending church services—"

Umber waved a hand. "That's entirely up to you. We each find God in our own way."

Raven nodded her thanks. A silence fell between them.

After several seconds, Raven asked, "What do you want to talk to me about?"

Umber flushed noticeably and ran a hand through his long, auburn hair. Then he uttered a single word:

"Rust."

Surprised, Raven blinked. "Rust?"

"It's a narcotic. I'm sure that Evan has told you about it."

"Yes, he has. He *warned* me about it, actually."

Umber nodded and clasped his hands together. "I'm uncomfortable that we're selling Rust to anyone who has the wherewithal to purchase it. He's turning *Haven* into a drug dealership!"

"He's not selling it to any of our residents," Raven said.

"True enough. They can't afford it. But people who can afford it buy it from him. Kilo after kilo. Drug dealers. Millionaires. Society people. Entertainment stars."

"Evan says it's perfectly legal."

With a shrug of his shoulders, Umber replied, "Oh, I'm sure it is. Evan is very clever that way."

"But it bothers you."

For a long wordless moment Umber stared at her. She realized that his eyes were light gray, almost silver.

"Yes, it bothers me. I believe that Evan is doing the devil's work."

"Have you spoken to him about it?"

"Many times. He nods and smiles and pays me no attention."

"But you're the head of this community," Raven said. "Why can't you—"

Umber stopped her with an upraised hand. "I may be the nominal head of this community, my dear, but Evan Waxman is actually running *Haven*."

"How can that be? I thought—"

Shaking his head sadly, Umber said, "It's the Golden Rule, my dear. He who has the gold makes the rules."

"I know he handles the administration for you."

"For himself. Oh, Evan's been very kind and extremely generous. But he runs this habitat to suit his purposes, masquerading as my faithful backer and administrator."

It took Raven several moments to digest what Umber was telling her. At last she asked, "What can you do about this?"

"That's why I've come to see you," said Umber.

PLAN OF ACTION

Raven stared at the minister. Somehow Umber's round, florid face seemed inexpressibly sad. His silvery eyes, though, were focused squarely on her.

"Me?" she squeaked. "What can I do?"

Umber shrugged his round shoulders. "I wish I knew! But we've got to do something. It's wrong to be selling Rust. It's the devil's work!"

Raven nodded her agreement, but asked again, "How can you stop it? How can you get Evan to stop it?"

"I tried to at yesterday's Council meeting. I got voted down, sixteen to two, including my own vote."

"So the Council is with him."

"I realize now that Evan himself picked most of the Council members. I trusted him. I let him handle the governance of *Haven* and he's turned the habitat into a narcotics trafficking center."

Again Raven asked, "How can you stop him?"

"I don't know! I was hoping you might have some idea."

"But I'm a newcomer here. A nobody. Evan's picked me to be his assistant, but that doesn't mean anything. He could drop me anytime he wants to."

"You're sleeping with him," said Umber. It wasn't an accusation, not even an objection. Merely a statement of fact.

"Yes, I am," said Raven. Then she added, "Now and then."

"You're closer to him than anyone in this habitat."

"But that doesn't mean . . ." Raven ran out of words. She didn't want to carry her thought to its logical conclusion.

Umber's eyes went wide as he realized what Raven was thinking. "No!" he shouted. "No violence! I won't be a party to violence!"

For an instant Raven's mind filled with the scenes of violence she had witnessed: many of them aimed at her.

"No violence," she agreed, in a near whisper. Then she asked, "But then . . . what?"

The outraged flush in Umber's cheeks faded. More quietly he answered, "I wish I knew."

A fine couple of collaborators, Raven thought. Neither one of us has the slightest idea of what to do.

She admitted, "I don't think I could talk Evan out of selling Rust. He thinks he's doing it for the good of the habitat—at least, in part."

Umber shook his head. "It's always easy to convince yourself you're doing what is needed, what is helpful, what is right—when in fact you're doing the devil's work."

Raven said, "If only we could get the people who're buying the junk to stop. Take away the market for it."

"I don't see how we could do that."

"You're a respected man of God," Raven told him. "Maybe you could contact the organization that links all the settlements we've made through the solar system . . ."

"The Interplanetary Council?"

"Yes. Ask them to convene a meeting to find a way to stop the sale of Rust."

Umber shook his head. "But *Haven* doesn't belong to the IC. We've never applied to join."

Raven smiled at him. "Then we should."

implementation

"I can't contact the Interplanetary council," umber objected. "Evan has my phones tapped, I'm sure. He wouldn't let me put through a call to Earth."

Raven understood where he was heading. "You think I could? As your representative?"

With a shake of his head, Umber replied, "I would think Evan monitors all our communications with Earth and the other settlements throughout the solar system."

"You mean he wouldn't allow you to talk to anyone who might . . ."

"Who might be connected to the Interplanetary Council," Umber finished for her.

The two of them sat in her living room, silently staring at each other. In her mind, Raven pictured how the habitat's phone links to Earth and the other human settlements throughout the solar system worked.

You've studied this, she told herself. You've read about the system linking *Haven* to Earth and the rest of the solar system.

Communications satellites, she remembered. We put through a call to Earth. The call goes from the habitat to one of the commsats in orbit around Uranus. From that satellite to another one in orbit around Earth, and then down to the phone you're trying to reach.

She murmured, "If I could make a direct contact to one of the commsats outside this habitat . . ."

Umber's face brightened. "Without using a phone here in *Haven*."

"No one in *Haven* would know about it," she continued. "We could reach the IC without Evan finding out."

"Yes," said Umber. But then his expression clouded over once again. "But how could you do that?"

A smile lifted Raven's lips. "I think I know a way."

"Go outside?" Quincy O'Donnell's beefy face frowned down at Raven.

They were having lunch together at one of *Haven*'s crowded, noisy restaurants. The more noise the better, Raven thought. Makes it harder to snoop on what we're talking about.

"Outside, like you do," she said to him. "I'd love to see the work you're doing."

He shook his head slowly, ponderously, from side to side. "That's not allowed, Raven. Safety regulations."

"But it would only be this one time," she coaxed. "And just for a quick visit. Couldn't you bend the rules a little? For me?"

O'Donnell was still shaking his head. But he said, "I could lose my job. If anything happened . . ." His voice trailed off.

Raven decided to play her trump card. "I'd be ever so grateful to you, Quincy. Really grateful."

His head shaking stopped. From across their narrow table he stared down at her. In a tone that was almost pleading, he insisted, "The regulations are for your own safety, Raven."

"But you'd be there to protect me."

"Yes . . . but . . ."

"Afterward we could have dinner together. In my quarters."

He swallowed visibly. "Dinner."

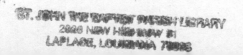

"Just the two of us."

"The two of us."

"I'd really be grateful, Quincy."

She could see the wheels turning behind his deep blue eyes. "Well," he muttered, "you are the assistant to Mr. Waxman, after all."

"That's right," she agreed. "I could write up a work assignment or something, so your responsibility would be covered."

"That you could," O'Donnell agreed.

For the first time in her life, Raven felt like a conspirator. Hell, she told herself, I *am* a conspirator. Quincy O'Donnell looked uneasy when, two days later, he took her down to the station where the suits for extravehicular activity were stored. They walked slowly, carefully, past the rows of empty suits hanging in storage, seeking one small enough to fit Raven properly.

O'Donnell insisted on having her walk through all the safety procedures with a pair of technicians who trained people for work outside the habitat's sheltering walls. Then she went through a standard test in one of the habitat's docking centers, working in the suit carefully, slowly, inside an exercise chamber pumped down to vacuum.

She had to do her training exercises on her own time, during lunch hours or after full days of working with Waxman. She didn't want Evan to know what she was up to, of course. He seemed to have no inkling. Waxman worked with Raven as usual, and spent his nights rotating through his harem.

Good, thought Raven. Keep yourself busy, Evan. Still, she did her best to keep him happy on the nights when he crooked his finger at her.

EVA

+++
+++

Raven stood nervously by the airlock hatch, decked in a nanofabric space suit and glassteel helmet. Quincy O'Donnell loomed next to her, dwarfing her diminutive figure. Like her, O'Donnell was enclosed in a semitransparent nanofabric EVA outfit. Somehow it made him look even bigger and lumpier than normal.

It was well past the dinner hour. The exit chamber was otherwise empty except for a pair of technicians, one male and one female, sitting at the control consoles on the balcony that ran high above the metal-walled chamber.

"Ready for extravehicular activity?" sounded in Raven's helmet earphones.

She heard O'Donnell reply, "Ready."

The hatch before them swung open ponderously. Beyond it was the airlock chamber, bathed in lurid red light, looking dark and dangerous.

O'Donnell's voice croaked, "Raven, switch to freak two."

She lifted her left arm and pressed the button for frequency two. Now she and Quincy could speak to one another without anyone else hearing them.

"Are you sure you're ready for this?" Quincy's voice sounded worried in her helmet earphones.

With a courage she did not truly feel, Raven nodded inside her helmet and answered, "I'm ready."

"All right then." He gestured toward the open airlock chamber. "Ladies first."

Her insides fluttering, Raven stepped carefully over the hatch's coaming and into the airlock's interior. O'Donnell clumped in behind her and the heavy hatch swung slowly closed.

The airlock was surprisingly large, big enough to handle a half-dozen people in space suits or even sizable pieces of equipment.

"Alone at last," O'Donnell quipped. Raven smiled at him, then realized he couldn't see it through her helmet's visor in the chamber's dim lighting.

"Ready for depressurization?" she heard the female monitoring technician ask.

"Ready," said O'Donnell.

A clattering sound penetrated the insulation of Raven's helmet. She saw a trio of lights on the chamber wall next to the outer hatch: green, amber and red. The green light winked out and the amber turned on. The clattering noise seemed to dwindle, grow fainter.

After several moments, Raven couldn't hear the sound at all, although she still felt its vibration through the thick soles of the boots she was wearing.

Her mouth felt dry. She remembered from her training sessions that there was a water nipple just beneath her helmet's visor, but she couldn't locate it without her hands to search for it.

At last the vibration dwindled into silence.

"Here we go," Quincy said.

The amber light went dark and the red one turned on. Vacuum, Raven thought. We're in vacuum now.

Even as she thought that, the outer hatch began to swing open. And beyond it was the universe.

Raven's mouth dropped open. She gaped at countless swarms

of stars hanging unblinking against the utter blackness of space. On the rocket journey from Earth, she and the other passengers had been seated in a windowless compartment. There were video screens on the seatbacks in front of each passenger, of course, but they didn't give a hint of the sheer magnitude of the vast universe outside.

Now Raven saw it all, stars and nebulae hanging there as far as she could see, blazing magnificently. Off to one side curved the bare-boned skeleton of what would one day be *Haven II*. But it was the splendor of the stars that mesmerized her. They weren't twinkling. They hung out there staring at her, as if they were judging her, deciding if she were fit to be in their company.

O'Donnell broke the spell. He reached for the clip at the end of her safety tether and pulled it out from its housing. No noise. Not a sound. Just the slightest tremor of a silent vibration.

"I'll attach this to the cleat outside the hatch," she heard O'Donnell saying. "Wouldn't want you to go floatin' off to infinity now."

Raven nodded wordlessly, still staring in awe at the stars.

O'Donnell went to the edge of the hatch, attached Raven's safety line and then his own to the cleat on the station's skin out there, then turned back toward Raven.

With a stiff little bow, he said, "The universe awaits, my dear."

Raven stepped carefully to the rim of the hatch and then, after taking a deep breath, she pushed through into emptiness.

She knew that she wouldn't be truly in zero gravity as long as she was connected to the rotating space station. Still, as she floated away from the habitat's structure she felt her stomach fluttering and her throat constricting.

Then she heard O'Donnell's voice: "Oh Lord, I love the beauty of Thy house, and the place where Thy glory dwelleth."

Turning in mid-emptiness, Raven asked, "What was that, Quincy?"

She could hear the embarrassment in his voice. "Oh, it's nothin'. Just . . . ah, just a little somethin' I say whenever I go outside. It's from the Twenty-fifth Psalm."

"It's beautiful," said Raven.

He floated up behind her and grasped both her shoulders. "There's nothin' like it. The universe. God's creation."

"It certainly is magnificent," Raven agreed, staring at the wonder and glory of the stars.

He turned her to face the unfinished skeleton of what would become *Haven II*.

"That's where I work," he said, with real pride in his voice. "Me and a handful of robots."

For almost a half hour Raven hung there nearly weightless while O'Donnell pointed out the intricacies of the structure that was being built. The bare metal assembly formed a complete circle, exactly the same size as *Haven* itself, but it was only a skeleton, empty, incomplete. Halfway across its diameter Raven caught the flashes of welding tools as a team of robots worked steadily, tirelessly.

Pointing, O'Donnell told her, "That's goin' to be the main reception area for newbies, same as we have here on the original *Haven*. And there"—his gloved hand shifted—"will be the command and control center. Lots of electronic gadgetry will go in there. And we'll connect the new module to the original down there, at their hubs."

Raven nodded and smiled in the right places, knowing that Quincy couldn't see it through the tinting of her helmet visor but feeling that he needed some reward for this unauthorized visit.

At last she said, "Oh! While we're out here, can I make a call to Earth?"

"From here?" O'Donnell asked. "Why not from inside?"

"It's more private outside here, isn't it?"

Sounding puzzled, O'Donnell answered, "I suppose so."

"It's for Reverend Umber," she stretched the truth. "I've been so busy with you lately, I haven't had the time to do this for him."

O'Donnell's tone sounded wary, skeptical, but he said, "I suppose it'll be okay."

Raven touched her helmet to his and gave him an awkward nuzzle. "Thanks, Quincy!"

He sputtered and floated slightly away from her.

Raven had memorized the number of the Interplanetary Council's executive director, Harvey Millard. She switched to her suit's private line, then spoke the string of numbers into her helmet microphone.

"I'm calling on behalf of the Reverend Kyle Umber, the head of the *Haven* habitat in orbit around the planet Uranus. Reverend Umber would like to request that the Interplanetary Council consider allowing habitat *Haven* to join the Council. He awaits your reply."

There, she thought. It's done. The message is on its way. She knew it would take some two and a half hours for her message to reach Earth, and the same amount of time for Earth's reply to get back to the habitat.

She remembered something a Vietnamese businessman had told her, one night long ago as he was slowly removing her clothing: Even the longest journey begins with a single step.

I've taken the first step, Raven said to herself.

communications failure

++

After their little extravehicular sojourn, Raven and O'Donnell returned to the habitat and wormed out of their nanofabric space suits, then made their way to her quarters. She put together sandwiches for the two of them while O'Donnell busied himself pouring wine from the kitchen's scant supply of bottles.

At last they moved to Raven's bedroom. O'Donnell seemed flustered at first, eager yet somehow at the same time hesitant— not reluctant, but unsure of himself.

"Raven," he breathed as she unbuttoned his shirt, "you don't have to do this, you know."

She looked up into his flushed face. "You don't want to?" she asked, all innocence and disappointment.

"I want to!" he exclaimed. "But . . . well . . . maybe we shouldn't . . ." His face was an image of conflict.

Raven stood on tiptoes and kissed him lightly on the lips. "Well, why don't we just get into bed together and see what happens."

"Okay . . . I guess . . ."

Raven watched him watching her as she stripped. Then she pulled down the covers and slipped into bed, with him still there, gawking.

She patted the sheet next to her. "Come on, Quincy."

Red-faced with inner conflict, O'Donnell peeled down to his

skivvies and walked around to the other side of the bed. Even with his undershorts still on, she could see that he was erect.

He's a virgin! Raven realized. He's never done this before.

O'Donnell climbed into bed beside her. The mattress sagged noticeably.

"I don't . . . ," he began.

Raven shushed him softly as she put a hand on his chest and then slowly slid it down to his groin. He made a sound halfway between a sigh and a moan.

"It's all right, Quincy," she whispered to him. "Everything's going to be fine."

When she awoke the next morning O'Donnell was gone. His side of the bed was a jumble of twisted sweaty sheets; even his pillow was shorn of its casing. Raven sat up in bed, then got to her feet, pulled a robe out of the closet and padded into the kitchen as she cinched it around her waist.

Quincy was nowhere in sight. But he'd left a sheet of tablet paper on the kitchen table.

I LOVE YOU, was scrawled in block letters across the paper.

Raven sank onto the kitchen chair and fought back tears.

She was a few minutes late arriving at her office. It had somehow taken Raven longer than usual to shower, dress, and gobble a breakfast bun.

Her desktop screen bore a command. SEE ME AS SOON AS YOU GET IN. EVAN.

Alicia Polanyi was not at her desk as Raven entered Waxman's outer office. Good, she said to herself. Polanyi's silent, accusatory stares distressed Raven.

Waxman was at his desk, speaking through his computer screen to one of the engineers. He waved her to the padded chair in front of the desk without missing a syllable of his ongoing discussion.

Raven sat and tuned out Waxman's voice. *Quincy's going to be a problem*, she told herself. *One night in bed and he thinks he's in love. Probably wants to marry me.* She almost smiled at the thought. *But she realized, I'm going to have to handle him carefully. Let him down gently.*

Waxman ended his phone discussion, cleared his desktop screen, turned and smiled at Raven.

"And how are you this fine morning?" he asked, his smile showing teeth.

"I'm fine," Raven said. "And you?"

Waxman pursed his lips, then answered, "I've got a bit of a problem, Raven."

"Oh?"

"That call you put through to the IC."

Raven felt her entire body stiffen.

Calmly, still smiling, Waxman went on, "I don't allow calls to the Interplanetary Council for a reason, Raven. I control all communications with Earth. I and I alone."

"Oh. I didn't know."

"Whether you did or not is immaterial."

Raven stared at him. The man was still smiling, yet his expression made her shudder.

"Your call came to me. It never was sent to Earth."

"I see."

"No, you don't see," said Waxman. "But you will. You and your oaf of a boyfriend."

"Quincy's not my boyfriend!"

"Perhaps not," Waxman said, his smile turning dangerous. "But he's going to be."

PUNiShMENt

++
++++++++++++++++++++++++++++++++++++

Trying to keep her breathing under control, Raven asked, "What do you mean?"

Waxman leaned back in his desk chair, his eyes never leaving Raven's face.

"You tried to go around me, Raven. You tried to make contact between Umber and the Interplanetary Council."

"I . . ."

"Don't bother denying it." Waxman leaned forward in his chair, placed both his forearms on his desktop. "I can't trust you, Raven. But I can punish you. You and the lummox who helped you."

Raven heard herself protest, "Don't blame Quincy! He didn't know what I was doing. He had no idea."

"He's got to learn to be more careful. And you have to learn to be more grateful to me."

"I am, Evan. I'm very grateful. For everything you've done—"

"You've betrayed me, Raven. After all I've done for you." Waxman shook his head sadly. "I can't let that betrayal go unpunished. You've got to learn to be obedient."

"Wh . . . what do you mean?"

"You're going back to your old life, Raven. Once a whore always a whore. But this time you'll be working for me."

Raven blinked at him. "I don't understand . . ."

"How could you?" Waxman's smile turned malicious, nasty.

He pulled open a desk drawer and took out a thin vial containing a reddish dust.

"You were curious about Rust, weren't you?" He held the vial between two fingers and shook it slightly. "Well, this is what the stuff looks like. You notice the vial is half empty? The other half is floating in the air of this office. You've been breathing it since you walked in here."

Raven's eyes went wide. That's why Alicia wasn't at her desk! she thought. But Evan's sitting there, breathing in the Rust, and he's—

Reading the expression on her face, Waxman said, "I'm wearing nose filters, Raven. But you're not."

Raven's immediate thought was to get out of this office, this trap that Evan had set for her. She tried to push herself out of the chair, but her legs wouldn't support her. Then she saw that Waxman's desk was dissolving, its side softening, liquefying, dripping onto the carpeting like the wax of a melting candle.

With a malicious smile Waxman said, "I can see that the Rust is taking effect. Good."

Raven watched as Waxman's desk faded away. Still seated in his chair, he too began to melt and stretch out into a long multi-colored ribbon.

"Enjoy your trip, Raven." Waxman's voice boomed in her ears as she felt herself dissolving, liquefying, sliding into another dimension.

She couldn't move, couldn't even blink her eyes. She stared as the world around her coalesced into a kaleidoscope of vivid, pulsing colors.

Raven was floating, rocking gently on a sea of surging colors. She felt hands on her body, stripping her, groping her, pawing her, and all she could think was *More! More!* Time was stretching like taffy. She lost all awareness of who she was, what she was, all lost in the overwhelming sensations of being stroked, touched, caressed.

The first lash of the whip made her scream, but the only words she heard were "More! More!"

Floating on a sea of frenzy, she writhed and twisted, but strong, powerful hands held her as Waxman's voice boomed like the trumpet of a god, "You're a whore, Raven. That's all you've ever been and all you'll ever be."

And she was screaming, sobbing, "Yes! Please! Please!"

Her body pulsed and writhed with agony that was exhilarating, overpowering, stretching her consciousness and her bodily sensations beyond endurance.

Everything went dark. She thought she must be sleeping, but this was much deeper. She could feel nothing, hear nothing, see nothing. Only darkness and a throbbing pain deep inside her.

She awoke, alone and naked in a bare little room. A cell. A prison. She propped herself on one elbow. Nothing to see except cold gray walls.

She heard a sound. The soft fall of a naked foot. All around her a cluster of men came into focus, naked, erect, intent. And Alicia Polanyi stood among them, also naked and smiling mirthlessly down at Raven.

"Welcome to my world, Raven," Polanyi said, with a cheerless smile.

The men crowded around her, seized her arms and legs and lifted her off the cold bare floor. One of them stepped between her outstretched legs, grinning wickedly. "I'm first," he said, grinning down at her naked, struggling body. "But I won't be the last." The other men laughed and gripped Raven tighter.

An animal roar shattered the gray-walled cell. The locked

door crashed to the floor. The men grasping Raven dropped her painfully onto the cement floor as a huge apparition took form in their midst.

"Quincy," Raven whimpered.

Another man's form coalesced between Raven and O'Donnell. "It's not your turn yet," said Evan Waxman. Unlike the others, Waxman was wearing a multicolored floor-length robe that shimmered with his every motion.

O'Donnell stared at him. "You promised me," he growled.

Waxman smiled knowingly. "Not just yet, Quincy. We're not finished having our fun with her."

For an eternally long moment, O'Donnell stood before Waxman, blinking uncertainly, his hands balled into fists, his hairy chest heaving. Then he glanced down at Raven, lying helpless and naked on the cold bare floor.

"You're finished!" O'Donnell bellowed. And he swung a backhand swat at Waxman that sent him staggering to the floor.

The other men scattered and disappeared. O'Donnell stepped down and lifted Raven gently in his arms, then turned and started for the open doorway. Beyond the door was light, so bright it hurt Raven's eyes.

Raven heard a sharp *zing* and felt O'Donnell shudder, but the giant of a man lumbered through the door and staggered out into the brightness.

The light hurt Raven's eyes. She squeezed them shut as Quincy carried her in a staggering trot along the habitat's long, curving passageway. She could hear him puffing, panting, feel his hairy chest heaving while his big meaty hands held her naked body close to his.

Raven didn't know if anyone else was in the passageway. She kept her eyes shut tight against the painful overhead lights. She heard no voices, no footsteps, sensed the presence of no one except Quincy's massive body lumbering along the passageway.

She felt his chest rising and falling as he puffed along, felt the warmth of his body, the sheen of his sweat.

Where are you taking me? she asked silently, too exhausted and drained to speak aloud.

At last she sensed him slowing down. She cracked her eyelids open enough to see the double-doored entrance of the habitat's hospital. Quincy banged a bare foot against one of the doors and it swung open.

Raven closed her eyes again but she heard voices, male and female:

"Who the hell—"

"What do you think you're doing?"

"What's wrong?"

She gave up her fragile grip on consciousness and let herself slide into oblivion.

confrontation

quincy o'donnell watched the medics take raven's
naked form from his arms and wheel past him, into
the hospital's main corridor.

Suddenly he realized with a shock that he was standing in the hospital lobby totally naked. The medical personnel and waiting patients were staring at him. He didn't know what to do, where to go.

One of the nurses—a short, dark-skinned Asian—came to him, bearing a full-length hospital gown.

"It's disposable," she said in a near whisper to Quincy as she stood on tiptoes to spread it over his broad shoulders. "Just flush it down a waste chute when you're finished with it."

Red-faced with embarrassment, Quincy muttered his thanks as he struggled into the gown. It barely reached his mid-thighs and he worried that it would rip down the back, but he felt un-utterably grateful for it.

He marched himself, barefoot, back through the passage-ways toward his quarters. People passed by him, staring, some grinning, but one look at the grim expression on his face kept them from saying anything.

He reached his apartment finally and sat heavily on his un-made bed. Waxman, he thought. He did this to Raven. Prom-ised me she and I would be together, and when I got there she was naked and shivering while Waxman and all those other men looked down and pawed at her.

He saw again Waxman's sadistic, gloating face in his mind's eye. His fists clenching automatically, Quincy told himself, "I'll have to see him."

He lay back on his unmade bed and tried to sleep. But the visions of Raven in that cold room, naked, helpless, while Waxman gloated over her, filled his mind whenever he tried to close his eyes.

Quincy was surprised when he awoke. Turning on the bed, he saw that it was a few minutes past 6:00 A.M. Very deliberately, he got to his feet, showered, shaved, dressed in a work uniform, threw the hospital gown down the disposal chute, and headed for Waxman's office. He passed two different cafeterias on his way there, but didn't have the faintest urge to eat anything.

Waxman's office was locked when he reached it. Quincy decided to wait out in the passageway. He stood there like a Praetorian guard until Alicia Polanyi showed up, blinked with surprise, then let him into the outer office.

"You want to see Mr. Waxman?" she asked, curiosity knitting her lean face. "Do you have an appointment?"

"No," said Quincy as he settled himself in one of the chairs along the office's wall. "I'll wait for him."

"Shouldn't you be out with your construction team?"

"They're robots. They're already programmed. I need to see Mr. Waxman."

At that moment the door to the passageway outside slid open and Waxman stepped in. He stiffened with surprise as Quincy rose from his chair like a looming thundercloud.

"O'Donnell," Waxman said stiffly. "I should have expected this." Without even a glance at Alicia, Waxman strode to the door to his private office, which slid open automatically as he told Quincy, "Come on in."

Quincy followed Waxman through the doorway and firmly shut the door as Waxman slid into his desk chair.

"So what do you want?" Waxman asked, looking up at Quincy. "Disappointed that you didn't get your chance with her? That can be—"

Quincy planted his massive fists on Waxman's desk and leaned over until he was nose-to-nose with the man.

"You leave her alone," he rumbled.

"Raven? She's a whore, for god's sake. You can't—"

Grasping the front of Waxman's shirt and lifting him up from his chair, Quincy repeated, "Leave her alone."

Waxman grasped Quincy's fist in both his hands, but couldn't budge them from his shirt front.

"You try to touch her again," Quincy told him, "and I'll kill you. I'll break your face and crush your ribs and dance on your dead bones. Understand me?"

Waxman sputtered, swallowed hard, and finally managed to squeak, "I understand you."

Quincy released him. Waxman collapsed back into his sumptuous dark chair.

"Good," said Quincy. Then he turned and left the office.

A moment later Alicia Polanyi appeared at the doorway, distressed. "Are you all right?"

Waxman was breathing heavily, his eyes on the doorway that Quincy had gone through.

After a few moments, he nodded shakily. "Yes. All right. No damage done." He sat up more erectly, drummed his fingers on his desktop, then said, "Get the chief of the robotics department on the phone for me."

"Yes, sir." Polanyi went back to the outer office, sliding the door shut behind her.

Threaten me, will he? Waxman seethed inwardly. The big Irish idiot. We'll see who lives and who dies.

awakening

++
++

Far, far in the distance she heard voices. Women, for the most part, talking about—her, Raven felt sure, but she couldn't quite make out the words they were using. Too soft, too hushed, too guarded.

She sank back into the oblivion of unconsciousness, all sensation gone, all memories nothing more than a faint, distant picture of Vesuvius hulking against the blue Neapolitan sky. After a while the volcano shifted, transformed into the hulking form of Quincy O'Donnell, grim and silent.

Time lost all meaning. Raven floated on nothingness as Quincy's bulky form dissipated, dissolved into blank nothingness.

"Can you hear me?"

The voice sounded familiar, somehow.

"Raven, please open your eyes. It's time for you to wake up."

Alicia? Raven wondered.

It took an effort of will as she tried to force her eyelids open.

Alicia Polanyi was bending over her, her cold blue eyes staring at Raven, her cadaverous face grave, utterly serious.

"Wake up, Raven," she said softly, almost begging. "Please wake up."

Raven blinked twice, three times.

"I'm awake," she croaked. Her throat felt sandy dry, scratchy.

Alicia's gaunt face broke into a thin smile. "Thank God," she whispered. "Thank God."

Raven realized she was lying in a hospital bed. The ceiling, the walls were soft white. The room was narrow, cramped; she thought she could almost touch both walls without moving from the bed by stretching out her arms. Machines somewhere were chugging and beeping. She felt weak, fragile.

"I was . . ."

Alicia placed a finger gently on Raven's lips. "Don't try to talk. Rest. Sleep. You're all right now."

But Raven tried to push herself up to a sitting position. And failed. She had no strength. She lay back on the hospital pillow and stared at Alicia.

"What happened?" she mumbled. "How did I get here?"

Alicia's thin lips almost smiled again. "Quincy O'Donnell brought you here. With a tranquilizer dart embedded in his back, he carried you in his arms from Evan's little playroom to the hospital."

"Playroom?" Raven asked.

"You're all right now," Alicia said. "The Rust has been flushed out of your system. The medics got to you in time, thanks to your big boyfriend."

"Quincy's not . . ." Raven couldn't finish the sentence. She knew whichever way she said it would be wrong.

"You sleep now," Alicia Polanyi said gently, getting to her feet. "The medical staff will take care of you."

A sudden alarm made Raven's body tense. "Evan! He did this to me."

With a nod, Alicia agreed, "Just as he did to me, more than a year ago. But I didn't have a giant of a man to save me."

"Quincy."

"He pulled you out of Evan's little playroom and brought you here. He saved your life."

"Quincy," Raven repeated, more softly as sleep closed her eyes.

When she awoke again the Reverend Kyle Umber was standing beside her bed, in his customary chaste white suit, staring down at her with sorrowful eyes.

"Good morning," he said softly.

For the first time, Raven noticed there was a view screen on the wall of her room. It showed an image of Uranus: blue-gray, serene, bland.

Surprised, Raven mumbled, "Reverend Umber."

"How do you feel?" Umber asked.

Raven realized that she felt strong, sound. As she pulled herself up to a sitting position she saw that she was wearing a disposable hospital gown, as pure white as Umber's suit. The bed rose behind her, almost noiselessly.

"I'm all right . . . I think."

"You had a close call. The percentage of Rust in your blood was very high."

"Evan did that to me," she snapped.

Umber shook his head. "When I heard that you were here in the hospital I immediately asked Evan what he knew about it. He told me he'd been in an all-night meeting with the maintenance staff. There's been an accident on the construction of *Haven II*—"

"He was gang-banging me!" Raven cried.

Umber shook his head sadly. "Seven members of the maintenance division affirmed that they were in conference with Evan all that night."

"They're lying!"

With a helpless shrug, Umber said, "How can we prove that? It's your word against theirs."

The word of a whore against the manager of this entire habitat, Raven thought.

"He's evil," Raven whispered. "Evan's a monster."

Reverend Umber nodded sadly. "He's drunk with power. I've tried to change him, bring him to God's grace, but . . ." He shook his head. "I've had no success with him. Not yet."

"I'll kill him," she hissed.

Umber's face went white with alarm. "No!" he barked. "Evil is not the answer."

"It wouldn't be evil," Raven insisted. "It would be justice. God's justice."

For a long silent moment Umber looked down upon Raven sadly. "Don't try to assume the powers of God. That way lies death and damnation."

Raven started to reply, but held her tongue. The reverend doesn't understand. He doesn't know how truly evil Evan is. In her mind she saw again Waxman's cold smile as the men pawed and penetrated her.

At last she said, "I know you're right, Reverend. But it's hard to forgive."

"Christ forgave those who crucified him. From the Cross, bleeding and dying, he forgave them all."

Raven nodded, but inwardly she thought, I'm not Jesus Christ. I'm not God.

* * *

After a few more attempts to comfort her, Umber left her room, head bowed unhappily. A nurse came in with a luncheon tray. And an announcement. "Good news, Ms. Marchesi. You passed all the diagnostic tests. You'll be free to leave this afternoon, after your physician sees you and signs off on your case."

And go where? Raven asked herself.

She was finishing the last morsel of soyburger on her tray when Evan Waxman stepped through the doorway of her narrow room.

Smiling brightly at her, Waxman said, "They tell me you'll be able to return to work tomorrow."

Raven glared at him.

Stepping to the side of her bed, Waxman lowered his voice and continued, "Don't be sullen. You tried to go around me and paid the penalty for that. Let's allow bygones to be bygones."

"Bygones?" Raven shouted. "You call what you did to me 'bygones'?"

Waxman shook his head sadly. "Raven, my dear, nothing happened to you. You weren't raped. You weren't even molested."

"The hell I wasn't!"

His smile only slightly thinner, Waxman explained, "That's the beauty of Rust, my dear. That's why it's in such demand. It affects the mind, not the body. It builds elaborate fantasies inside your brain."

Raven glared at him, unbelieving.

Waxman sat himself on the edge of her bed. "Think, Raven. You've been thoroughly examined by this hospital's very meticulous machinery. And probed by the medical staff. They haven't found you injured in any way; no scars, not even any bruises. Perfectly sound of limb and body."

"I was gang-rapcd," Raven snarled. "While you watched. And smiled. And laughed."

"All in your imagination, my dear. All in your mind. The Rust produced a fantasy for you."

"For *you*, Evan."

His smile thinning somewhat, Waxman admitted, "Well, yes, I produced the scenario for your dramatics. But it all happened in your mind, not your body."

"I don't believe you."

Spreading his hands innocently, Waxman said, "Raven, I wouldn't hurt you. Not really. I'm rather fond of you, actually."

"You're a monster."

"Perhaps," he admitted carelessly. "But the only scars you're carrying as a result of our little endeavor are in your mind, not your body."

"I don't believe you."

"It's true. I promise you. The hospital staff, the diagnostic systems that examined you from top to toe, they all show that you are physically unharmed."

"Physically," Raven echoed.

Getting to his feet once more, Waxman said, "The brain, Raven. That's the most important sexual organ of all. And thanks to Rust, we can manipulate it virtually any way we like."

Glowering at him, Raven muttered, "You're a monster, Evan."

"Perhaps," he replied. "But if you want to survive here, you'll do as I tell you."

Raven said nothing, although she was telling herself, Silence means assent. Let him think that. Do what he wants. For now.

Waxman went as far as the door before turning and telling Raven, "Oh, yes, that lumbering oaf O'Donnell. He was killed two days ago. An accident on the job he was supervising outside on *Haven II*'s construction. Damned fool misprogrammed one of the robots he was managing and it tore his head off, helmet and all."

aLLiaNce

++
++++++++++++++++++++++++++++++

Raven sat on the bed, stunned. Quincy is dead? The question reverberated in her mind. Dead? Killed? Because he helped me. It's my fault. I killed him.

She bent over and cried until no more tears were left.

Eventually, a pair of doctors came into her room—one male and one female—and gave her a peremptory examination. Vision, reflexes, a quick check of her innards with a handheld scanner.

"You're good to go," the male doctor said cheerily, as he scrawled his signature on the processor in his hand.

"Everything looks fine," added the woman smiling beside him.

You didn't look into my mind, Raven said silently. You didn't see the sickness in there.

"You can get dressed and leave," the man said, "whenever you're ready."

"Before five P.M.," the woman added.

They left Raven sitting on the bed, wondering where her clothes might be. Then she remembered that when Quincy brought her to this hospital she had no clothes on.

The thought of Quincy welled up inside her again. But Raven forced it down, away. He's dead and there's no bringing him back. From somewhere deep in her memory she remembered a schoolteacher telling her, "Life belongs to the living. Don't bury yourself in useless mourning."

No mourning, Raven told herself. But vengeance, justice, payback—those are worth living for.

The door to her narrow stall opened and Alicia Polanyi stepped in, a capacious handbag on one arm.

"Are you all right?" Alicia asked.

Raven nodded. "So they tell me."

Hefting the handbag, Alicia said, "I brought you some clothes. Evan gave me the combination to your apartment's front door."

"Very generous of him."

Alicia's lips twitched in what might have been the beginning of a smile. "He can be generous—when he's getting what he wants."

"He wants me back at the office tomorrow," Raven said, without moving from the bed.

Alicia nodded. "I know."

"I can't go back there! I can't look at his face without wanting to kill him."

"You've got to. If you don't, he'll see to it that no one will employ you. You'll be dumped into the unemployable pool. You'll end up selling yourself again."

Raven said, "I've been there before."

"You don't want to go back there," Alicia said, her sallow face lit with inner fire.

"I want to kill him."

"Evan?"

"Evan."

Alicia stared at her for a long, silent moment. At last she whispered, "So do I."

Raven blinked at her as she digested Alicia's words. Then she felt herself smiling.

"Then let's do it. You and I. Together."

"Don't be crazy."

"I mean it," Raven insisted. "It won't be murder. It would be execution. He killed Quincy."

Alicia nodded again. "Yes, he did, didn't he?"

"Justice," Raven murmured.

With a shake of her head, Alicia said, "I couldn't do it."

"Why not?"

"He's too strong. Too powerful. If we tried it and failed . . . think what he'd do to us."

"What's he doing to us now?" Raven countered. "Do you want to spend the rest of your life with him pulling your strings?"

A long silence. Then Alicia whispered, "No. I don't."

"Then let's kill him."

Alicia's eyes went wide. "Do you think we could?"

"We could try."

"But if we fail . . ."

"We'd be no worse off than we are now. We're his slaves, Alicia! He points his finger at us and we perform anything he wants."

"But with Rust it's all . . . imaginary."

"Murdering Quincy wasn't imaginary."

"True."

"And what he made me do." Raven shuddered at the memory. "It might have been all in my mind, but he watched it somehow. He *enjoyed* watching it."

Alicia's skeletal face went solemn. "He's enjoyed watching me, too. Many times."

Raven swung her legs off the bed and stood up. "He's killing us a centimeter at a time. We've got to stop him, once and for all."

"Do you really think we could do it?"

"Maybe. I don't know. But we've got to try. I'm not going to let him kill me, torture me to death."

"Me neither!"

The two women clasped each other in a sisterly embrace.

As Raven swiftly pulled on the clothes that Alicia had brought, a sudden thought seared her consciousness.

"Our conversation is being recorded!" she realized. "It's part of the hospital's data system."

Alicia nodded, tight-lipped. "We've got to erase it."

"Can you do that?"

"If we act quickly enough. I'll go back to my office and erase the record. Then, at the end of the workday, I'll meet you in your quarters."

Raven nodded. "I'll wait for you there."

PLANNING

Raven returned to her apartment and waited impatiently for Alicia to show up, pacing back and forth through the living room, her mind churning.

Was Alicia able to erase the hospital's recording of our conversation? Is she really going to work with me or was she lying about it? Is she working for Evan?

That thought sent an electric current through her. Is she so attached to Evan that she'd betray me? Or worse, maybe Evan controls her so completely that she's spilling her guts to him right now! Raven stopped her pacing and stared at herself in the mirror hanging over the sofa. I'd be better off dead, if that's the case.

The doorbell buzzed. Raven turned and stared at the screen by the door. Alicia Polanyi. Alone. By herself. No one with her.

"Door open!" she called out.

Alicia stepped into her living room, but not before casting a quick glance back over her shoulder.

Raven realized, "He can see that you've come to my quarters."

Alicia forced a smile. "Raven, there are tons of records from all the cameras installed throughout the habitat. He'd have to spend all his time sifting through them if he intended to keep watch on you."

Taking in a deep, calming breath, Raven said, "I suppose so." But then she thought about it. "Couldn't he set up an automated search system to watch my door?"

"He could," Alicia answered. "But he'd ask me to do it for him. Evan is smart, but he hardly ever does his own dirty work."

Raven smiled cooly. "That's what assistants are for, I guess."

As she gestured Alicia to the sofa, the phone announced, "Incoming call."

Both women froze. The phone continued, "From Dr. Tómas Gomez."

Raven breathed again. "Phone answer," she said, as Alicia sat tensely on one end of the sofa.

Gomez's broad-cheeked tan face filled the wall screen on the other side of the room. He looked alarmed, his dark eyes wide, his hair disheveled.

"Raven!" he called, as if he were floundering in a heaving ocean. "I need your help! Right away! This idiot that Waxman assigned to assist me is no good at all. I need you!"

Raven blinked at him. "Tómas, I'll be happy to help you, but I'll have to get Mr. Waxman's permission first."

"Do it! Please!"

"First thing in the morning," she replied. "I promise."

"I'm going to call him now," Gomez said.

"He won't answer you, not after office hours. Not unless it's an emergency."

"This *is* an emergency! It's urgent! All my work will be useless unless I can get someone to help me."

"I'll do what I can, Tómas."

"Please!"

"I'll speak to Mr. Waxman first thing tomorrow morning."

"Please," Gomez repeated.

Raven thought she should ask Tómas to have dinner with

her, calm him down, soothe him. Then she glanced at Alicia and decided that it would only cause complications.

"I'll call you as soon as I've spoken with Mr. Waxman," she said.

"Promise?"

"I promise."

"Thank you!" Gomez said, as if she had just stepped in front of a bullet aimed at his heart. "Thank you!"

Once the screen went dark, Alicia asked, "Is he always so churned up?"

"His work means everything to him," Raven replied.

"So he assumes it should mean everything to you, as well."

Raven realized the truth of it. "I suppose he does."

"Scientists." Alicia made it sound like a curse. And suddenly Raven recognized that she was right. It *is* a curse, she told herself. Scientists like Tómas are truly cursed; they've cursed themselves with a curiosity that must be satisfied, if they're ever to find peace.

Sitting herself down on the sofa next to Alicia, Raven asked, "So what are we going to do about Evan?"

Two hours later they still sat—at the tiny kitchen table—facing each other, the question totally unanswered.

PLAYING WITH FIRE

Raven slowly pulled herself to her feet and started taking the dinner dishes to the kitchen sink. Alicia got up too, as if she weighed ten tons, and cleared the narrow kitchen table of the rest of their dishes.

"This isn't going to be easy," she said as she stood beside Raven at the sink.

"We'll figure it out," Raven said. "There's got to be a way."

"We're playing with fire."

Raven almost smiled. "The lessons in anthropology that I'm studying in my sleep showed me that early humans who played with fire changed the course of history."

Alicia nodded, but said, "Did your lessons show you how many of them got burned?"

They both returned to their jobs the next morning: Alicia to Waxman's outer office and Raven to her cubbyhole down the hall. Once Alicia told her that Waxman had shown up, Raven strode to his office, stepped past Alicia at her desk, and rapped on the partially open door to Waxman's private office. She stepped in before the man could respond.

"Raven!" he said, looking up from his desk. "What a delightful surprise."

Ignoring his remark, Raven said, "Tómas Gomez called me last night. He was frantic—"

"I know," Waxman said, his expression souring. "He left a message for me that was more than half an hour long."

"He needs my help. He's like a little boy who can't find his toys."

"Aptly put," said Waxman. "How long do you think you'd be away from this office?"

She temporized, "A few days. Maybe a week or so."

Waxman stared at her for a long, wordless moment. "And we were just starting to get along together so well."

Standing there before his desk, Raven replied, "That's finished, Evan. I won't be taking Rust again."

He smiled thinly. "That's not for you to decide."

"Yes it is. I ordered nose filters just like yours. They'll be delivered to my quarters this afternoon." Raven didn't reveal that it was Alicia Polanyi who scoured through the habitat's catalogues, found the filters, and ordered them. Plus a pair for herself.

Waxman's narrow smile disappeared. "Did you now?"

"I did."

Waving one hand carelessly in the air, Waxman said, "All right, go ahead and drudge for Gomez. I hope you enjoy the work."

"Thank you, Evan," said Raven. And she turned and left his office.

As she passed Alicia's desk, she made the slightest of nods. Alicia smiled slightly.

Waxman's voice came through the open doorway of his office, "You just make damned certain you've cleaned up all the tasks you've been working on here before you go start babysitting that astronomer."

Without breaking her stride, Raven answered over her shoulder, "Of course, Mr. Waxman."

Once Raven got back to her own cramped little office, she called Gomez.

Before she could say a word, he asked breathlessly, "Is it all right? Did he give you permission—"

"Yes, Tómas," Raven interrupted, smiling. "I'll start working with you tomorrow morning."

"Tomorrow?" Crestfallen. "But I need you today! Now!"

With the slightest shake of her head, Raven replied, "I've got to clean up the work I've been doing here, Tómas. It'll take me the rest of the day and well into the evening."

"That long."

"That long," she confirmed. "But I'll be at your laboratory first thing tomorrow morning. Without fail."

He nodded ruefully. Without his expression changing in the slightest Gomez asked, "Can you have dinner with me tonight?"

Raven made herself smile. "I'm afraid not. Too much work to get through. I'll probably just have a snack here in my office."

"Oh. All right. Okay." His face looked miserable. "I'll see you first thing tomorrow."

"Without fail," Raven replied, trying to make it sound as cheerful and bright as possible.

Her desktop screen went blank.

Evan Waxman leaned back in his plush desk chair and drummed the fingers of both his hands against the thighs of his perfectly fitted trousers.

She thinks she's getting away from me, he said to himself, his face clouding over. She thinks she can walk out on me.

There are plenty of other fish in the sea, a voice in his head reminded him. Yes, Waxman admitted, but once you let one get away the others will notice it. It will give them ideas.

Raven's got to be brought under control, he concluded. I can't let her walk away from me. She's not leaving until I'm finished with her.

He sat up straight in his chair and called for Alicia.

She appeared almost instantly at his office door.

Eying her gaunt figure, Waxman said, "I want you to set up a surveillance watch on Raven Marchesi while she's working with Gomez. I want to see everything she and that astronomer are doing together."

Alicia Polanyi nodded obediently. "Right away, Mr. Waxman," she said.

countermeasures

slightly bleary-eyed from having slept only a few hours, Raven got out of bed, showered, dressed, and grabbed a sweet bun for breakfast. She was still chewing its last remains as she left her apartment and headed for Tómas Gomez's quarters, halfway across *Haven*'s main wheel.

She tapped at his apartment's door once and it slid open immediately. Gomez was asleep at his desk, head resting on his arms amid a clutter of papers and fingernail-sized video chips.

Like her own quarters, Gomez's place was not spacious. But he had turned it into his personal laboratory. The living room was filled with diagnostic devices, machines that could display and analyze the recordings that the submersible had made down at the bottom of Uranus's globe-girdling ocean. Viewscreens covered the walls, all of them blank, silent.

Looking at Gomez's slumbering form, Raven realized that he must have worked all night. Just as I did, she thought. Worked until he collapsed.

Suddenly Gomez snapped awake. His head popped up and his bloodshot eyes went wide as he focused on Raven.

"You're here! Thank God!"

Raven smiled down at him and said, "I'm ready for work, Tómas."

"Thank God," he repeated.

Gomez was not nearly as disorganized as Raven had feared. It was just the sheer amount of data that his submersible had accumulated and sent to the surface during its mission into Uranus's sea bottom that had overwhelmed him.

Raven pulled up one of the chairs in front of his desk and started sorting out all the papers and chips. Using the skills she had learned at Waxman's command, she began to bring some order out of the seeming chaos. By lunchtime Gomez was actually grinning happily.

Smiling back at him, Raven suggested, "Why don't you go take a shower and get into some clean clothes, Tómas? Then we can have lunch together."

The astronomer looked stricken. "I must smell pretty bad, huh?"

"I've smelled worse," Raven said. "But you do need a shower and a change of clothes."

He scrambled out of his desk chair. "Yes, you're right. I'll get to it right away."

And he scurried to the bedroom like an embarrassed teenager. Raven saw that his bed was covered with still more chips and printouts. She smiled at his back as he dashed through the door, then she turned to her work again.

The data she worked with meant nothing to her. Only numbers and alphabetical designations. But she sorted them patiently as her mind drifted to Evan Waxman and his expectations, his demands.

Evan won't willingly let me out of his control, she knew. How can I make him believe I'm still under his domination without actually giving in to him?

She realized she'd already taken the first step. The nose filters will protect me from breathing in Rust, she knew. Evan won't like it but there's nothing he can do about it, not without violence.

Raven had known violence in her earlier life. She'd been beaten and savaged by some of the meanest, toughest thugs of Naples's dark underworld. She'd survived, but only at the cost of convincing one hood after another that she was willing to do anything for his pleasure.

Evan's not like that, she understood. He's smarter. And meaner. Rust is his perfect weapon. It doesn't harm its victims—except in their minds.

Rust creates fantasies. It makes its victims live out those fantasies in their imaginations. No physical damage. But she remembered the pain of the whips, her helpless agony when the men were having their fun with her.

And somehow Evan participates in those fantasies. He takes part in them. He enjoys them. He invades my mind and plays with me. While I do whatever he wants me to do.

There's got to be a way out of this, she told herself. There's got to be an escape route, a countermeasure that I can use to protect myself.

The only countermeasure she could think of was refusal. Refusal to take the Rust. Refusal to play Evan's game, refusal to allow him to play with her.

But that path led to danger, she knew. He could overpower me easily enough. The imaginary "friends" that he used to work me over could be replaced by real, actual men. And then where would she be?

She was still struggling with that question when Tómas came back into the cluttered living room, glowingly clean, beaming from ear to ear.

decisions

Evan Waxman sat at his desk, also thinking about his relationship with Raven.

She's only one woman, he told himself. Why worry about her? There are plenty of others. But he kept thinking of how exciting, how wonderfully abandoned she was under the influence of Rust. She'd do anything, and ask for more.

So what? he asked. So was Alicia, back when we started. And a dozen others. Don't get your life snarled around one woman. There are plenty of others, and more coming in on every shipload that arrives here.

Almost, he convinced himself. Almost.

But then he thought, If I let Raven walk away from me, what message does that send to Alicia and all the others? I'm in charge here, goddammit! They do what I want them to do, or else. If I let Raven walk away, then others will try to follow.

I can't allow that, Waxman told himself. I've got to bring her back under my control. Totally. She doesn't leave me until I'm finished with her. And it's got to be done so that all the other little slashes see it and know it and understand that I tell them what to do and they do it.

I'm not going to allow Raven or any other of these available twats to get away from me. There's only one way out for them.

Like that big oaf O'Donnell. The only freedom they'll ever find is death.

Nodding to himself, he called to his intercom, "Alicia."

She slid his office door open immediately.

Waxman smiled at her. That's the kind of response I want, he told himself. I call and she comes.

"Yes, Mr. Waxman?" Alicia asked from the doorway.

Gesturing to the chairs in front of his desk, he said, "Come in. Sit down."

Alicia did as she was told.

Waxman studied her gaunt face for a silent moment.

Then, "How friendly are you with Raven Marchesi?"

Alicia's eyes flashed wide for a moment. Alarm? Waxman asked himself. The question had startled her.

Swiftly composing herself, Alicia answered, "I had dinner with her once, in her quarters."

"You two get along well?"

"Well enough."

Waxman went silent for several heartbeats. Then he slid open one of his desk drawers and pulled out the half-empty plastic vial of Rust.

"You know what this is, of course," he said.

Alicia stiffened slightly. "Rust."

Dangling the tiny vial between two fingers, Waxman asked, "Do you think you could get into Raven's quarters and sprinkle this inside her refrigerator? Without her knowing it, of course."

Alicia Polanyi stared at the vial hanging from Waxman's fingers, her lips pressed together into a thin bloodless line. He smiled at her. How long has it been since our last session with this stuff? Waxman asked her silently. Months. And it still has its pull. She's staring at it like a starving man gazing at a full-course dinner.

"It took several weeks for the medical team to clean that junk out of my system," Alicia said.

"I know," Waxman responded. "But I'm told you've requisitioned nose filters for yourself, so there's no danger of your inhaling any of it."

Alicia couldn't take her eyes off the tiny plastic tube half filled with the reddish narcotic. But something was going on behind those ice-blue eyes, Waxman saw. Something was churning in her mind.

"Well?" he prodded.

"I . . . I'd rather not have anything to do with it, if you don't mind."

"But I do mind, Alicia. I mind very much. I want you to do me this favor. You'll be perfectly safe, I promise you."

She finally shifted her gaze to Waxman's slyly smiling face.

"And what do I get in return?"

Waxman leaned back in his sculpted chair. "Ah. The old quid pro quo."

Alicia said nothing.

Almost laughing, Waxman said, "Well. I won't offer you another Rust trip. That would be too cruel, after all your hard work to get over your addiction."

She nodded silently.

"What would you like? What can I offer you?"

"I . . . I'll have to think about that."

Spreading his arms wide, Waxman said, "Name your price. Anything in this habitat that you want."

"I'll think about it," Alicia repeated. "This is a surprise."

His smile disappearing, Waxman said, "Well, think quickly. I want your answer before the end of the day."

"Yes, sir," Alicia said. And she got up from the chair and

hurried to the outer office, leaving Waxman staring at the door sliding shut between them.

Alicia sat at her desk, her thoughts spinning. *Anything in this habitat that you want*, he said. Anything. She knew what she really wanted. She wanted to be away from Evan Waxman and his cruelly smiling face, his lustful hands, his filthy pleasures. She wanted to be back on Earth, free, rich enough to live as she wished, where she wished.

But Evan would never allow that. She might have rid herself of the need for Rust, but he would never allow her to leave the habitat and get entirely away from him.

What to do? Who could she run to? She dared not contact Raven. Evan would find out and punish her. Maybe kill her, just as he'd had Quincy O'Donnell murdered.

She did not want to serve Evan Waxman anymore, not for another day, not for another hour, another minute. But how to get away from him? How?

It was late in the afternoon before she made up her mind.

Checking her desktop video, she saw that Waxman was deep in conversation with one of the habitat's councilmen. They were talking about the construction of *Haven II*. Quincy O'Donnell's death had put a crimp in the construction schedule, from what they were saying, but that would be smoothed out soon enough.

Alicia tapped out the number for Tómas Gomez's quarters, and there was Raven, seated beside the astronomer, scrolling through a long, incomprehensible list of alphanumeric symbols.

I can't call her, Alicia said to herself. Evan might find out. But maybe . . .

She thought over the idea that had cropped up in her mind nearly an hour earlier. At last she decided that it could work.

There was some risk involved, of course, but sitting here doing nothing was riskier.

Checking back on Evan, she saw that his conversation with the councilman was finished. Time to act, she told herself.

Alicia Polanyi got to her feet, stepped to the door to Waxman's private office, and rapped on it firmly.

ACTIONS

++
++

without preamble, Alicia said to waxman, "I want to
set up a boutique."

Waxman's brows climbed toward his scalp. "A boutique?"

"A shop for women. A place where they could buy stylish
clothes, jewelry, shoes . . . that sort of thing."

His eyes narrowing slightly, Waxman said, "We already have
shops for women."

Stepping farther into his office, Alicia said, "Yes, I know. But
they're more like military depots than shops where a woman
can choose from the latest fashions."

"That's Umber's doing. He wants our people to dress pretty
much alike. And besides, that keeps the price of clothing low.
Nobody can out-do her neighbors. No competition between the
women. Or the men, for that matter."

"But women like to dress up," Alicia countered. "Why should
we all go around wearing the same uniforms?"

"From what I've seen," Waxman answered, "lots of women
make their own alterations on their clothes."

Alicia nodded vigorously. "Yes. Of course they do. No
woman really wants to go around in the same uniform as everybody else."

"A women's clothing shop," Waxman mused.

"It could make a profit for the habitat," Alicia coaxed. "Only a small one, at first, but . . ."

For a long, silent moment Waxman stared at her as he thought, She wants to get away from me. She wants to set herself up as someone to pay attention to.

With a shake of his head, he told Alicia, "This is something that's beyond my authority. You'll have to get Reverend Umber's permission."

Clamping down on the thrill of excitement she felt, Alicia asked, "May I speak to him about it?"

Waxman clearly was not pleased with the idea, but he reluctantly agreed, "I suppose so."

"Oh, thank you, Evan! I'm so grateful!"

Waxman nodded, thinking, We'll see just how grateful you are the next time I invite you to my quarters.

Now comes the hard part, Alicia told herself.

It was late in the afternoon. She carried the plastic tube half-filled with Rust in the pocket of her slacks as she headed for Raven's quarters.

Evan can track me through the cameras set up along all the passageways, she knew. But once I'm inside Raven's place there won't be any surveillance devices watching me. She knew this from the long months she had spent as Waxman's assistant. Private quarters were kept private, at Reverend Umber's insistence.

"We'll have no Peeping Toms in *Haven*," the reverend had commanded.

Other men and women strode along the passageway as Alicia approached Raven's quarters. Aside from a nod or a smile, they paid scant attention to her. She had memorized the combination to Raven's front door. No pulling out a slip of paper when she was ready to tap out the entry code. It's got to look as if I'm

going into my own place—which was several dozen meters farther down the corridor.

No one seemed to pay any attention to her as she quickly
fingered the lock's combination. The door slid open smoothly
and Alicia hurriedly slipped inside, then slid the door shut again.

She went into the kitchen and glanced at the little refrigerator sitting beside one of the storage shelves. She pulled the tube
of Rust from her pocket and, after scanning the kitchen's ceiling
for a sign of a surveillance camera, threw the vial and its contents into the disposal chute.

The chute's door snapped shut, but not before Alicia saw the
flash of light that meant the vial and its contents had been va-
porized, utterly destroyed, broken into their constituent atoms
by the disposal's laser system.

Then she pulled a small pad from her other pocket and
scrawled on it: *Meet me in the main cafeteria as soon as you can.*

She signed the note with a single sweeping *A*, then pressed
it onto the kitchen table. Again she looked up and scanned the
ceiling. No sign of surveillance cameras. Still, she felt nervous.

Alicia wanted to phone Raven, but feared their conversation
would be tapped by Waxman. Instead, she made her way to the
main cafeteria, found a table for two off in a corner far from the
serving counters, and waited for Raven to show up.

book three

THE ASTRONOMER

Living room Laboratory

+++
+++

Tómas Gomez sat in the makeshift laboratory that had once been his living room. The room was jammed with instrumentation—sensors, computers, diagnostic monitors—humming and beeping and flashing flickering images on their viewscreens.

He sat at the room's tiny desk, staring glumly at the symbols scrolling down his desktop screen.

Nothing, he moaned inwardly. The submarine had scooped up more than a hundred samples of the seabed's rocks and sands, which were now carefully laid out across the floor of the docking area where the submersible itself was resting, halfway across the habitat's circular structure from Gomez's apartment. Automated cameras and diagnostic analyzers slid slowly along an elevated trackway, carefully examining each specimen and automatically televising the imagery to Gomez's desktop computer screen.

Nothing but rocks and sand.

Gomez looked up from his screen, across the narrow desk at the chair where Raven had been sitting. After a ten-hour-long day with him, she had left for dinner. She had asked Gomez if he wanted to come with her to the main cafeteria, but he had declined, glued to his self-imposed vigil.

Chemical analyses of the ocean bottom's sands showed nothing but sand. Ordinary sand that had been sitting on the floor of the sea for billions of years. The same for the samples of rocks that the submarine had dredged up. Natural, commonplace rocks, nothing unusual about them, nothing that suggested anything surprising.

Nothing, Gomez told himself. Nothing but natural materials, no hint of anything that hadn't been there since the planets were formed, nearly four billion years earlier.

He felt a surge of anger welling up inside him, a dark tide of violence.

To come all this way, to battle past the committees, the officials sitting behind their desks with their nods and smiles while they decided the course of my life, to fight my way out here to fucking Uranus and send the submarine to the bottom of the fucking ocean and find—*nothing*! Not a goddamned mother-humping shred of evidence, not a shit-faced pissing hint of anything beyond the natural crap that's down there—it was more than he could bear.

His whole life hung in the balance. Finding nothing meant that he had spent the past three years of his life in vain, and the university committee had spent more than three billion international dollars—for what? A few scoops of rocks and sand.

I'm ruined, he knew. I'll be known everywhere I go as the idiot who spent a fortune proving that there's nothing on Uranus worth studying. Nothing that a gaggle of grad students can't categorize and write a paper about that nobody will bother to read.

Slowly, Gomez pushed himself to his feet. Deep in his guts he felt a burning, raging urge to smash the machines that surrounded him, to destroy the technology that had failed him, to destroy himself and his pointless, worthless life.

How can I face them? he seethed inwardly. How can I go back to Earth with nothing to show them? Better to die here and get it over with.

He took a deep, shuddering breath. And sat down again. Staring at his desktop screen, he let his stubby fingers tap out the command to keep reviewing the results of the submarine's excursion, to continue searching for something, anything, that might give a hope of discovering a new revelation.

He lost track of time. The images on his screen blurred into a slowly scrolling list of failure, of defeat, of the end of all his hopes and dreams.

In his mind's eye, he saw himself returning to Earth, reporting his failure, being assigned to some backwater study that would drown him in meaningless details. Add another decimal point to somebody else's analysis, clean up the work that this group of researchers has published, teach classes to bright and eager newcomers who've never heard of your work, sink deeper and deeper into obscurity.

Then a voice from deep within him said, Well, you had your chance and you took it. You tried, but the thing you were searching for just wasn't there. It's not your fault. It just isn't there.

It's not my fault, Tómas agreed. But I'll carry this albatross around my neck for the rest of my life.

He realized that his desktop's screen was blinking.

ANOMALY.

The letters flashed across the list of alphanumerics that filled the screen.

ANOMALY.

A glitch somewhere, Gomez told himself. He spoke to the voice-activated computer program. "Examine anomaly."

The screen immediately showed a small piece of twisted metal, one of the hundreds of samples the submarine had returned from Uranus's seabed.

Gomez blinked at the image. Nothing unusual about it, he thought. The data bar at the bottom of the screen showed that the sample was slightly less than eight centimeters long.

A scrap of metal, Gomez thought. We've brought up hundreds of similar bits. Natural enough: metal chunks scattered among the sand and rocks.

"Chemical analysis?" he asked the computer.

Letters took shape over the image. Gomez read aloud:

"Iron, ninety-five percent.

"Carbon, two point five percent.

"Manganese . . .

"Nickel . . ."

His jaw dropped open.

"Steel," he whispered, as if afraid that if he spoke the word any louder the analysis would disappear from his screen.

He swallowed nervously, then asked the computer in a trembling voice, "Conclusion of analysis?"

The computer's synthesized voice answered, "The imaged sample is composed of steel."

Steel.

Gomez felt his heart thumping beneath his ribs. Steel! STEEL!

Steel does not exist in nature. It is created in ovens, in blast furnaces. Created by intelligent beings!

Gomez stared at the letters of the analysis, and the image of the twisted piece of metal in the screen's background.

He leaped up from his chair and shouted, "Steel! It's steel!"

standing there at his desk, slightly bent over, staring at the computer screen, his whole body shaking, his heart racing, gomez repeated to himself in
a heartfelt whisper, "Steel! Steel created by intelligent inhabitants of the planet Uranus."

He sank back into his desk chair and commanded the
computer, "Send this analysis to the chairman of the research
division at the University of Valparaiso."

The computer replied dispassionately, "Sent."

Then he got to his feet again, slightly surprised that his legs
supported him.

"Administrator Waxman," he said to the computer. "Connect me to him. Urgent!"

"Connecting," said the computer.

Gomez stood there impatiently, realizing that the difference
between intelligent humans and intelligent computers is that
computers didn't *care*. A sneeze was just as important to the machines as the end of the world.

Waxman's handsome, dark-bearded face appeared on the
screen, smiling, unruffled, at ease. "I'm not available at the moment. I'll call you back—"

Gomez interrupted, "Mr. Waxman, this is Tómas Gomez.
I've found steel! At the bottom of the ocean! Steel!"

Waxman's image on the screen flickered and disappeared, replaced by the man's actual face.

"What's that you say? Steel?"

"Steel!" Gomez shouted. "A scrap of steel at the bottom of the sea!"

"Steel," Waxman repeated, his sculpted features looking puzzled.

"Steel doesn't exist in nature," Gomez babbled. "It's artificial. It was created by intelligent creatures!"

"Are you sure . . . ?"

"Yes! Yes! It had to be made by intelligent natives of Uranus."

"But Uranus is barren. Dead."

"It wasn't always that way! It was *alive*! It was populated by intelligent people who manufactured steel."

Waxman seemed uncertain. "Are you certain?"

"Yes!" Gomez replied, beaming. "The sample is at the docking port. The submarine dredged it up, together with a ton or so of other stuff."

"Steel."

"It's not natural. It can't be natural!"

"Maybe it's from one of the earlier vehicles that our scientists put into the ocean," Waxman reasoned.

"No, no, no!" Gomez countered. "It's native to the planet. It has to be."

Waxman looked unconvinced. "That's a big claim, Dr. Gomez. A huge claim."

"Yes, yes, I know. And I know Sagan's old line, 'Extraordinary claims require extraordinary evidence.' But there it is! We scooped it up from the sea bottom. Steel!"

"Come over to my quarters, please," Waxman said. "We've got to proceed very carefully about this."

"I'll be there in three minutes!" Gomez replied.

*   *   *

Steel, Waxman thought as Gomez's fevered image winked out on his living room's wall screen. This could change everything.

As he got up from his compact little desk, he thought, If that damned Latino is right, it will mean a horde of scientists descending on us. It will turn Umber's haven for refugees into a mecca for scientific research.

He stood uncertainly in his living room, silently imagining: This habitat will be crawling with scientists. And engineers. Rocket people. Submarine people.

And news people! Waxman's handsome face pulled into a scowl. News people will come roaring out here, poking their quirky little noses into every corner of the habitat.

That could ruin our Rust trade. Make it impossible to carry out business as usual.

This "discovery" that Gomez has made has got to be stopped, discredited, buried.

Then he thought: Or maybe not. Maybe this could make an ideal cover for the trade. While the scientists are flocking here, I could be doing business as usual—with a few new wrinkles here and there.

By the time Gomez appeared at his door, Waxman was actually smiling.

Business as usual, he was telling himself as he opened his front door and graciously invited the young astronomer into his apartment.

Alicia saw Raven enter the cafeteria and look around for her. She got to her feet and waved. Raven spotted her and made a beeline for her table.

As Raven slipped into the chair opposite her, Alicia leaned toward her and said quietly, "Evan sent me to your place to sprinkle some Rust in your refrigerator."

Raven's eyes went wide with shock. "What!"

"Don't worry," Alicia went on. "I dumped the crap down your disposal."

Raven let out a breath of relief. But then, "He'll expect . . ."

"He'll expect you to be under the influence, I know. And me too, I guess."

"He'll want to party."

Alicia's gaunt features turned grim. "That's why we've got to figure out what we're going to do."

"I'm not going to party!" Raven snapped. "I've had enough of that. I'm through with it."

"Me too," Alicia said.

Raven looked at Alicia's ice-blue eyes. She seems to mean it, she thought. She's not fronting for Evan, she's telling me the truth.

"So what are we going to do?" Alicia asked.

With a shake of her head, Raven replied, "I wish I knew."

"He won't let us go, you know."

"It's a shame you flushed the Rust. We could've used it on him."

Alicia said, "He wears those damned nose filters all the time he's in the office, I'm pretty sure."

"Oh."

The two women sat in mutual discontent, silent, unhappy, wondering and worrying about the future.

After several moments, Raven asked, "Could you get your hands on more Rust?"

"That won't be easy," Alicia responded.

Raven felt her lips curling slightly.

"Is something funny?" Alicia asked.

"Not funny," Raven replied. "I was just thinking of something I read in my history sessions. It's from the American Revolution, if I remember it right."

Alicia's eyebrows rose a few millimeters.

"'Tyranny, like hell, is not easily conquered,'" Raven quoted.

"That's comforting."

"I forget the rest of it."

"Who said it?"

Raven shrugged her shoulders.

Alicia's expression soured. "Well, we're pretty much in hell, true enough."

"And facing tyranny, for sure."

"But what can we *do* about it?" Alicia challenged.

"I wish I knew."

Raven's wrist phone vibrated. She looked down at it and her eyes widened. "It's Evan!"

Alicia glanced up at the ceiling. "He can see us together!"

"Don't get excited." Raven held her wrist close to her mouth and said, "Connect."

Waxman's face took shape on the phone's minuscule screen.

"Raven. Sorry to bother you so late in the day. Could you come over to my quarters, please?"

Raven glanced at Alicia's fear-stricken face. "Now?" she asked.

"If you don't mind. Dr. Gomez is here. He's made what appears to be an important discovery."

"Oh. Yes. I can be there in a few minutes."

"Good." The wristwatch's screen went blank.

"He didn't see me, did he?" Alicia asked, almost breathless.

"No, I don't think so."

Raven got to her feet. "How difficult would it be for you to get a sample of Rust?"

Alicia pushed her chair back and stood up also. "Without Evan knowing about it?"

"Preferably."

"I think I can swing it. Maybe."

"Good enough," said Raven. "I'm going to Evan's place. I'll call you when I get back home."

Uneasily, Alicia said, "Okay."

Leaving Alicia standing by the table, Raven walked quickly toward the cafeteria's exit, thinking, She's terrified of Evan. Maybe I should be, too.

Waxman was all smiles. He let Tómas explain to Raven what he'd found, as he poured snifters of brandy for the three of them.

"If this discovery is valid," Waxman said as he handed the drinks to Raven and Gomez, "we have a world-shaking event on our hands." Then he amended, "Worlds-shaking."

Sitting on the sofa next to Raven, Gomez took a perfunctory sip of the brandy, coughed, then laid his snifter on Waxman's coffee table.

"Mr. Waxman is being very cautious," he wheezed. But he smiled as he spoke.

As he eased himself down onto the sling chair opposite the coffee table, Waxman replied, "I'm sure the Astronomical Association back on Earth will be equally cautious, Tómas. After all, extravagant claims require extravagant evidence."

Raven could not suppress a grin. "That's a quote I've heard before, somewhere."

"Carl Sagan," Gomez said. "Twentieth-century astronomer."

"Ah," said Waxman.

"So where do we go from here?" Raven asked.

"Good question," said Waxman. "We must do everything we can to eliminate the possibility that the scrap of steel that Tómas has discovered was inadvertently dropped onto the ocean bed by one of the earlier exploratory vessels our own scientists put into Uranus's ocean."

"One of our own vessels?" Raven echoed.

"Our scientists put dozens of submersibles into that ocean, back when we first reached Uranus," Waxman explained. "It took them a long time to admit that the planet was sterile."

"And they were wrong," Gomez snapped.

"It's sterile now," Waxman said.

Gomez countered, "But it wasn't always."

"Maybe," Waxman said. "But we've got to do everything we can to rule out the possibility that your sample of steel was left by one of our own exploratory vessels, years ago."

"How in the world can we do that?" Raven asked.

Waxman focused on her. "You, my dear, are going to have to scan through the logs of every mission our people sent into that ocean. You're to look for any mention of releasing metal into the water."

Gomez objected, "That's more than fifty years of missions! You can't expect—"

"We've got to do it," Waxman said firmly. "We've got to eliminate any possibility of a mistake."

"Mistake," Gomez grumbled.

Pointing a finger at the astronomer, Waxman said, "You don't want to announce your discovery and then have it turn out that you simply misidentified a scrap of our own material. That would ruin your reputation, Tómas."

Reluctantly, Gomez nodded. "I suppose you're right."

But Raven objected, "How can we go through all the expeditions that our scientists sent into the ocean? It'll take years!"

Waxman smiled at her. "No it won't. Computers can scan the logs of each expedition in microseconds. It will be a big job, I know, but I doubt that it will take more than a week or two."

"I've already sent the announcement to the University of Valparaiso," Gomez said.

"That's all right," Waxman replied calmly. "It's fine. Just contact them and tell them your announcement was preliminary, not for public release until we confirm it."

Raven saw that Tómas was not happy, but he didn't object to Waxman's decision.

dogwork

Raven spent the next week and a half staring at the desktop computer screen in Tómas's living room. She had asked the computer to review the logs of all the missions sent into Uranus's ocean and highlight any mention of jettisoning anything from one of the subs.

Nothing. As far as the computer records showed, each submarine mission into the ocean refrained from throwing anything overboard. Even the waste gases from the propulsion systems were kept inside each submarine until it surfaced and rejoined the orbiting spacecraft it had been launched from.

As far as the submarines' logs were concerned, Uranus's ocean was as pristine and unbefouled as it had been the day humans from Earth first reached the planet.

Gomez sat beside Raven for long hours, but instead of staring endlessly at the computer screen as Raven did, he spent most of his time holding his personal computer to his lips and whispering into the machine.

Late one afternoon, Raven pushed herself back from the desk they were using and got slowly to her feet. She could feel tendons popping along her spine as she stretched.

"I feel like I'm turning to stone," she muttered.

Gomez, sitting beside her chair, didn't respond. He was

intent on his PDA, whispering to the computer like a lover murmuring into his darling's ear.

Raven shook her head at his intense concentration.

Leaning slightly toward him, she said loudly, "I'm going to the cafeteria for a few minutes, Tómas. Can I bring you something?"

He jerked erect and looked up at her. "Huh? Oh, nothing. I'm okay."

Curiosity getting the better of her, Raven asked, "What are you doing?"

He held his PDA in one upraised hand. "Checking on the varieties of steel each of the submersibles was made of."

"Each submersible?"

"All those that were sent into the ocean. And their consumables, too."

"Must be a long list."

"Yeah. But so far, none of the steels they carried had the exact same composition as our sample."

Raven sat down again, next to him. "None of them?"

"That scrap of steel we found didn't come from any of our submarines," Gomez said firmly. "It's a local product, made by inhabitants of Uranus."

Evan Waxman was sitting before Reverend Umber's handsome desk.

"They're going to send a shipload of investigators here, Kyle," Waxman said.

Umber's brows knit slightly. "Investigators?"

"Scientists."

"Oh."

"Gomez's discovery has stirred up the scientific establishment back on Earth."

"I see. Understandable. If Uranus was once populated by intelligent creatures, naturally our scientists would be interested. Aren't you?"

Waxman hesitated a moment before answering, "I'm just concerned about how it might affect our operations here."

"I'm sure we could continue as we have been. How many people are they sending?"

"A couple of dozen, I believe, to start with. If Gomez's suppositions turn out to be correct, there'll be hundreds more."

"Could we house them on *Haven II*?"

"I hadn't thought of that. Perhaps we could. Or we could ask them to remain on the ship that's carrying them here. Keep them completely separated from our people."

Umber's round face puckered into a frown. "That wouldn't be very hospitable, would it?"

"No, I suppose not. But do you really want them mingling with our people?"

"Why not?"

Waxman suppressed an annoyed sigh. Patiently, he explained, "Kyle, most of our people are very lower class—"

"We have no class distinctions here!"

"I know, but, well—our people are mostly uneducated, lower class. They're refugees, for God's sake!"

"We're educating them," Umber insisted. "We're training them. We're creating a new society for them."

"Yes, I know. But how would they mix with a group of astronomers . . . scientists, PhDs, highly educated men and women."

Strangely, Umber's roundish face eased into a quizzical little smile. "Think of this as a test, Evan. It will be interesting to see how your educated scientists interact with our unwashed masses."

"You can't be serious."

"God works in mysterious ways."

Waxman shook his head slowly. "This is going to cause problems, Kyle."

"Of course," Umber replied, his smile unwavering. "And problems arise to be solved."

Pigheaded idiot! Waxman said to himself. But as he said it, he made a smile for Reverend Umber and got up from his chair.

"I think it's a mistake, Kyle. But if this is what you want . . ." He shrugged and turned toward the door.

Umber watched him leave, then turned to the small frame hanging on the wall behind his desk. He had to squint to make out the faded words printed over the photo of the statue:

"Give me your tired, your poor,
"Your huddled masses yearning to breathe free,
"The wretched refuse of your teeming shore,
"Send these, the homeless, tempest-tost to me,
"I lift my lamp beside the golden door."

His eyes misted over as Umber whispered to himself, "*I lift my lamp beside the golden door.* That's a calling worth a man's life."

reception center

Tómas Gomez stood in Haven's main reception center, his innards twisting and throbbing uncontrollably. In a few minutes, he knew, he would be greeting the team of astronomers arriving from Earth.

He had spent the night in his darkened bedroom studying their resumés on his handheld computer. Fourteen men and women with impressive curricula vitae; not the top people in their fields, but eager young up-and-comers who had flown to Uranus to evaluate Gomez's discovery.

To pick it apart, Tómas told himself. To tell me I'm wrong, I'm dreaming, I'm trying to make a mountain out of less than a molehill.

We'll see, he said to himself as he stood waiting in the reception center, unconsciously drawing himself up to his full height and squaring his shoulders like a soldier facing a firing squad. I've got the evidence, let them try to deny that!

Tómas's eyes were fixed on the hatch where the new arrivals would enter the habitat. Fourteen of them. And their leader, Professor Gordon Abbott, chairman of the Astronomical Association's planetary studies committee. Big brass. His fourteen associates might be small potatoes, but Abbott is a major force in the Association. He's the one I've got to convince, Gomez told himself.

At last the hatch swung inward and the team of astronomers entered the reception center, Gordon Abbott at their head. The team members were youngish, not much more than Tómas's own age, he figured. Their heads swiveled as they took their first look at the habitat's interior.

Gordon Abbott did not waste his time ogling.

My god! Gomez said to himself. He looks like a general out of some old army campaign.

Abbott was a big man, close to two meters tall, broad in the shoulders and thick in the waist. The creases on his light tan trousers and loose-hanging safari shirt looked razor sharp. Silver-gray hair shaved down to a buzz cut. Bushy moustache drooping past the corners of his mouth. He strode into the reception area as if he were marching at the head of a parade. Gomez thought, all he needs is a swagger stick.

Sucking up his courage, Gomez walked up to Abbott and put out his hand, suppressing an urge to snap off a military salute.

"Professor Abbott," he said, trying to keep his voice from shaking. "I am Tómas Gomez."

Abbott grasped Gomez's proffered hand in a crushing grip.

"Ah! Dr. Gomez! The man who's raised all this fuss."

Wringing his throbbing hand, Tómas replied, "Yes, I discovered the relic—"

"We don't know yet whether it's actually a relic, do we? That's what we're here to determine."

"Yes, of course, sir."

"Good. Let's get on with it."

Tómas led the little group through the automated inspection machines, noting that when Abbott smiled toothily at the facial identification screen there was a significant gap between his two upper front teeth.

"Family distinction," Abbott said cheerfully. "Some damned

gene that keeps cropping up every generation or so. My father had a gap you could drive a lorry through."

Gomez made a weak smile.

"You keep Greenwich time aboard this habitat, of course," Abbott said as the others of his group made their way past the identification screens. "That's good. We'll settle into our quarters for a bit and meet you for dinner at nineteen hundred hours."

Seven o'clock, Gomez realized.

"Fine," he said. "I'll be at your door—"

"No need for a native guide," Abbott said, smiling broadly. "We'll see you at the dining hall. Thank you."

Gomez realized he was being dismissed. "Well," he managed to say, "welcome to *Haven*."

"Yes, of course."

Gomez stood there and watched the team troop toward the escalator that led down to the living quarters.

When Gomez entered the dining hall, he saw that Abbott and his crew had already appropriated one of the long tables. And there was an empty chair waiting for him at Abbott's immediate right.

He sat down, selected his meal from the menu displayed on the tabletop screen, then turned to Abbott, who introduced each and every member of his team. Tómas forgot their names almost as soon as Abbott pronounced them, but he smiled and nodded at each of the astronomers in turn.

As soon as he finished the introductions, Abbott fixed Gomez with a cocked eyebrow as he asked, "Whatever gave you the idea of coming out here to search the ocean of Uranus, my boy?"

"The anomaly," Gomez answered immediately. "The other

three giant planets have thriving biospheres in their oceans. Uranus was apparently sterile. That didn't seem to fit."

"H'mm," Abbott murmured. "You were flying in the face of the common wisdom."

"New knowledge, new discoveries, often fly in the face of common wisdom," Gomez replied. "Common wisdom often turns out to be wrong."

A hint of a smile played across Abbott's face. "True enough," he said. "True enough."

One of the astronomers across the table from Gomez, a long-faced, lank-haired young woman, challenged, "Do you really believe that this one little specimen you've turned up is evidence of an ancient civilization?"

Gomez glanced at Abbott, who sat with his hands clasped beneath his chin, the food before him ignored, eager to hear his response.

"Steel is not a natural metal. It is produced by intelligence."

"Or dropped by one of the submersibles that investigated this ocean decades ago," the woman retorted. "What you've discovered is most likely the result of an accident."

"We've scanned the logs of all the submersibles that entered the ocean. No record of offloading a scrap of steel."

The woman's lips curved into a slight smile. "Maybe the people operating the sub had an accident that they didn't want to report."

Abbott broke in with, "That's a possibility, don't you think? Remote, perhaps, but a possibility."

Gomez suddenly realized that they were testing him. "The submersibles were controlled robotically. There were no humans aboard, nobody to attempt covering up evidence of an accident."

"Or incident," said the young man sitting next to the woman.

Gomez continued, "We've scanned the logs of every sub that

was in the ocean. There is no record of offloading anything, not even a bubble of gas."

Abbott broke into a chuckle. "I'm afraid he's already covered your hypothesis, Theresa." Looking down at the dish in front of him, he said, "Come on now, let's eat. The soup's getting cold."

dOUbLE ChECKiNG

Abbott took over effective command of Gomez's investigation. His first step was to review every part of Tómas's work.

Raven suddenly had nothing to do. Abbott's team of professionals was tracing her work, and they did not want her in their way or looking over their shoulders.

"Good!" said Evan Waxman when she told him what was happening. "You can come back to work with me."

Raven—wearing nose plugs wormed into her nostrils—replied, "I'll come back to work with you, but that's all. No fun and games. No Rust or other junk."

Waxman leaned back in his desk chair and studied her face for a long, silent moment. Then, "You mean that, don't you?"

Standing in front of his desk, Raven felt like a schoolgirl who'd been sent to see the principal. But she clenched her fists and said, "Yes, Evan. I mean it."

"Alicia never sprinkled the Rust I gave her into your refrigerator, did she?"

Raven made her eyes go wide. "Rust? In my refrigerator?"

Waxman almost smiled. "Come on, Raven. I can see that you and Alicia have become friends. And become enemies of mine."

"I don't know what you're talking about, Evan," Raven lied.

"Oh, yes you do." Waxman leaned forward and jabbed an index finger in her direction. "Never try to fool me, Raven. You're beyond your depth, out of your league."

Raven stood there and said nothing.

"You're fired, Raven," Waxman said, quite calmly. "I don't want to see your face again. Just clear your office out. And don't expect to get anything more than the minimum compensation from now on. You're on your own."

"All right."

"I expect you'll make out all right. Selling yourself, as usual."

"No, Evan. I'm not going back there."

"Sooner or later," he said, with a smirk. "Sooner or later."

She made an about-face and strode angrily out of his office, past Alicia who sat rigidly at her desk, silent and unmoving.

Once Raven reached her own cubbyhole of an office and started cleaning out her desk, a thread of memory played in her mind. Something about a guy in the Bible who was fired from his job, wondering what he was going to do next: "To dig I am unable, to beg I am too proud."

But what will I do? she asked herself. What will I do? One thing she was certain of, she was not going back to her old way of life.

The habitat gives everybody a subsistence payment, she knew. It's not much, but it's better than starving.

She remembered Alicia's dream of running a store for women's wear. Maybe I can work there.

Maybe.

Then she realized, I'm already working for Tómas! Maybe he can give me a salary. It doesn't have to be much.

But what would he expect in return? she asked herself.

With some trepidation, Raven phoned Gomez as soon as she carried the meager contents of her desk back to her apartment.

Tómas's broad-cheeked face appeared almost instantly on the wall screen in Raven's living room. He seemed flustered, upset.

"*Hola!*" Raven said, forcing a smile.

Gomez looked startled for a moment, then he smiled back—a little tiredly, Raven thought—and answered, "Hello, Raven."

Behind him Raven could see a trio of astronomers intently scanning a viewscreen filled with alphanumeric symbols.

Keeping her smile in place, she asked, "How's it going, Tómas?"

His lips twitched into a bitter grimace. "They're tearing all my work apart. I feel like a criminal who's being investigated by the police."

"That bad?"

"Worse."

Trying to stay cheerful, Raven said, "Would you like to have dinner with me tonight?"

He sighed. "I'm having dinner with Professor Abbott and his crew."

"Oh."

His face brightening, Gomez said, "You could join us, though. Why don't you?"

She suppressed the frown that threatened to break out and said instead, "Okay, sure. Where and what time?"

"Seven o'clock at the main restaurant."

"I'll be there."

Gomez broke into a genuine grin. "Great!"

dinner for seventeen

As usual, Professor Abbott sat at the head of the long table. Gomez was several seats below, but Raven saw that he had kept the chair next to him empty for her.

She sat down and nodded greetings to the others. They nodded back and smiled at her.

How much do they know about me? Raven wondered. About my background, my past life? Those records are supposed to be kept private, but . . .

"And how are you, Ms. Marchesi?" Abbott asked from the head of the table.

"Fine, thank you," Raven lied.

"I believe we've just about concluded the first phase of our study," Abbott went on, smiling enough to show the gap between his front teeth.

Raven saw Tómas stiffen in his chair. "And?" Gomez asked.

Still smiling, Abbott said, "No news is good news, my boy. We haven't found anything that invalidates your conclusion."

"The sample didn't come from one of our own vessels?" asked one of the astronomers, sitting across the table.

Abbott shook his head slowly. "Apparently not. At least, we haven't been able to find any evidence that it did."

The astronomer—young, blond, husky—countered, "Absence of proof is not proof of absence, Professor."

"I quite agree, but we have run into a blank wall. That scrap of steel is real, and—as Dr. Gomez has told us many times—its composition does not match any of the types of steel used in our own submersibles."

Raven saw that Tómas was trembling. "Then it's from here, from Uranus," he said.

Abbott fingered his moustache thoughtfully before answering, "That's the best hypothesis we have at the moment. It might be wrong, mind you, but we haven't found any evidence that proves it's wrong."

The table went absolutely silent. Raven could hear threads of conversation from the other tables in the dining room: laughter, the clink of tableware, murmurs and mumbles from across the big room. But the astronomers' table was absolutely silent.

Yet she knew what was going through the minds of the young astronomers: the scrap of steel that Tómas found was manufactured here on Uranus, by intelligent Uranians. Yet the planet has been sterilized, wiped clean of their existence.

Gomez broke their silence. "So what do we do now?"

"We scan the seabed. We use your submarine to start scanning in the region where your scrap of steel was found. And I intend to ask the Astronomical Association to send digging equipment and a crew out here as soon as possible."

Tómas sank back onto his chair. His face looked halfway between stunned and unutterably satisfied.

The dinner turned into a celebration. Fourteen astronomers, plus Abbott, Tómas and Raven ate, laughed, made jokes, offered toasts until the dining room emptied out almost completely, except for their table. The robot servers waited with inhuman patience by the restaurant's rear wall as the men and women reveled with unrestrained delight.

Through all the merriment, Gomez marveled, They're not against me. They didn't come here to tear me down. They like me!

He basked in the newfound warmth, even as Abbott warned, "What we're facing now is a task that will be far from easy. We're astronomers, not miners—"

The husky blond fellow across the table suggested, "Maybe we could recruit some of the Rock Rats from the Asteroid Belt. They're miners."

But Abbott shook his head. "Not the type we need, not at all. It's one thing to tear up an asteroid and extract the minerals that have a high market price, it's quite another to search for scraps of what might be relics buried in a seabed full of worthless rocks and sand."

The blond young astronomer nodded his reluctant agreement.

"No," Abbott went on, "we have before us a task of the most grueling kind. We're going to need patience, skill, and a fairly sizeable amount of luck."

That's a cheerful note, Raven thought. She saw that Tómas looked sober, thoughtful, as if from an old story of the American Wild West about a gunslinger facing a challenger.

The dinner broke up at last and the group headed for the restaurant's doors. Raven noticed that several of the astronomers paired off; romance was in the air.

Abbott seemed to pay no attention to the apparent couplings. Then Raven realized that Gomez was walking beside her, silent. But his eyes were focused on her face.

While the rest of the group headed down to the quarters

that had been assigned to them, Raven walked with Tómas past her own apartment. And his.

"Where are we going, Tómas?" she asked.

"To the observation blister down at the end of this passageway," he said, almost in a whisper.

"Why?"

He shrugged his husky shoulders. "I want to say goodnight to the universe."

She saw that he was smiling shyly. And she wondered what else he had in mind.

He opened the observation blister's hatch and gestured Raven inside. It was noticeably cooler inside, even though the blister's glass bubble was opaqued.

Before Raven could say anything, Gomez touched the control button next to the hatch and the bubble immediately became perfectly transparent. Raven felt as if she were suddenly standing among the stars, vast clouds of swirling dots of light looking down at her, with blue-gray Uranus hanging to one side, huge and silent.

Raven shuddered at the beauty of the universe.

"You're cold?" Gomez asked, stepping closer to her.

She shook her head. "It's just so . . . so . . ."

"Magnificent," he said.

"Yes," she agreed. "Magnificent."

He slid his arm around her shoulders and for several moments they stood together, silent, awestruck.

"I come here often," Gomez said softly. "I need to remind myself of what I'm dealing with."

Raven forced herself back to reality. It wasn't easy, with the heavens gazing down at her, but she made an effort of will.

"Tómas, Mr. Waxman fired me. I don't have a job anymore."

"I know."

"You know?"

"He called and told me. He said you'd come crawling to me now."

Sudden anger surged through Raven's veins.

Before she could say a word, though, Gomez told her, "I can hire you as my assistant. You've been doing the work, why shouldn't I pay you for it?"

"Tómas, I can't—"

"Of course you can't," he said, in a near whisper. "I don't want you to. I don't want to buy your love, Raven. I want you to love me, really love me."

In the light of the stars, she saw that his eyes were gleaming.

"I don't know if I can, Tómas. I don't know if I know how to!"

"Time will tell, Raven. Time heals all wounds, so they say."

"So they say," she echoed.

He let his arm fall away from her shoulders. Turning toward the blister's hatch, Gomez said, "Come on. I'll walk you home."

Raven walked alongside him toward the hatch, thinking, I don't deserve him. I don't deserve him.

But as they stepped back into the long, curving passageway that led back to the habitat's living quarters, she saw that Gomez was smiling happily.

maneuvering

It took more than four weeks for the Astronomical Association to put together a digging team and send it, with its equipment, to Haven.

Abbott's team of astronomers had little to do but wait. Several of them left the habitat and returned to Earth. Abbott himself jaunted back to Earth for more than a week, then returned on the same vessel that brought the digging team.

During the weeks of waiting, Raven and Alicia worked on the idea of opening a women's clothing shop.

"Evan is absolutely against it," Alicia told Raven over dinner in her quarters. "He doesn't want us to become independent."

Sitting across her narrow kitchen table from Alicia, Raven said, "Then we'll have to go over his head."

Alicia blinked. "Reverend Umber?"

"Reverend Umber," Raven confirmed.

"You're serious!"

"He's the only one who can trump Evan."

"But what makes you think he'll agree with us? What makes you think he'll go against Evan?"

"He's worried about Evan," Raven answered. "Besides, who else can we turn to?"

Alicia had no answer.

*   *   *

"It's good of you to see me, Reverend," said Raven.

She had seated herself in front of Umber's handsome desk, wearing the standard gray uniform of the habitat, feeling like a nun or a novice come to beg a favor from the head of a medieval holy order.

Umber made a small gesture with his right hand. "Not at all, Raven. Your well-being is important to me, as is the well-being of all our people."

Trying to look penitent, Raven said, "What I've come to ask you is out of the ordinary, I know."

Umber's brows rose noticeably. "Really?"

"You know Alicia Polanyi?"

"She's Evan's assistant, isn't she?"

"Part of Evan's harem."

She saw Umber's head snap back as though she had slapped him. For an endless moment, the reverend said nothing. Then, tiredly, "I've tried to show Evan the error of his ways, but he just nods and goes right ahead doing what he wants."

"Alicia and I want to break free of him."

"Evan told me he fired you."

"Yes, he did."

"Whatever for?"

"For refusing to have sex with him."

"Ah."

"He used Rust on me. Got me to do things . . ." Raven let her voice trail off into silence.

Umber's red, round face settled into a forbidding scowl. "I've tried to get him to stop that kind of behavior."

"He won't stop. He enjoys it."

"Yes, I know. I'm afraid he's damning himself, his soul."

"And dragging others down with him," said Raven.

With a sad shake of his head, Umber admitted, "There's no way I can control him, bring him to God's grace. God knows I've tried, but he ignores me. He laughs at me!"

"There is one thing you can do, Reverend. It's just a little thing, but you can help free Alicia Polanyi and me from Evan's control."

"Free the two of you?"

Raven bit her lip, then plunged ahead. "Alicia and I want to open a women's clothing shop."

Umber's eyes went wide for a moment. Then he leaned forward in his capacious desk chair and asked, in a voice heavy with skepticism, "A women's clothing store? How in the world could that make a difference here on *Haven*?"

Raven took a deep breath, then began to explain.

Raven's throat felt scratchy, sore, by the time she finished telling Reverend Umber of the hopes that she and Alicia had built.

Umber's chunky face went from scowling disbelief to puzzled wonderment, to nodding understanding. By the time Raven finished her description he seemed to grasp what she was driving at.

But once she stopped talking, he slowly shook his head. "I'm not sure it's such a good idea, Raven. We don't want to set up distinctions of dress among our people. We don't want that kind of competition among them."

"But it's natural!" Raven countered. "Why should everybody dress the same? Let the women express themselves. They'll be happier for it, and so will the men."

"It will set them in competition against one another. That's something we should avoid."

"Some competition is natural, Reverend," Raven pleaded.

"You think the women of this habitat don't compete against one another?"

Umber hesitated, then replied, "I . . . I don't know. I suppose I've never given it much thought."

"Well, they do. It's natural. And healthy, I think."

A long silence. Raven thought she could see wheels turning inside Umber's head.

"Most of the women already alter their uniforms," she argued. "Just in small ways, perhaps, but they try to make their uniforms a little bit different, distinctive. It's quite natural, actually."

"But if you give them the chance to buy completely different outfits it will set up competition, rivalries, resentments among our women."

With a shake of her head, Raven countered, "It will allow the women of the habitat a measure of self-expression that's denied to them now. Our boutique wouldn't offer the kind of outrageous outfits you can buy on Earth," she insisted. "But something more stylish than these uniforms we're forced to wear would be welcome, I think."

"It's true that many of the women alter their uniforms, at least a little," Umber admitted.

"Of course they do," Raven said. "Why should we all dress exactly alike? It's not natural."

"Not natural," he muttered.

"Let us open the boutique and see how the women react to it," Raven pleaded. "If you're unhappy with the results, you can shut us down easily enough."

"I suppose that's possible."

"Then you'll do it? You'll let us open a shop?"

For an endless moment, Umber remained silent. At last he said, "On a temporary basis. A trial run. If it causes dissension, disharmony, I'll have to close it down."

Raven jumped up from her chair. Suppressing an urge to lean across the desk and kiss the reverend, she extended both her hands and grasped his. "Thank you, sir! Thank you! From both of us!"

Umber looked more embarrassed than pleased. But he managed to say, "Good luck with your endeavor."

Raven practically ran out of his office, not willing to give the red-faced Umber a chance to change his mind.

the miners

There were only four of them—three men and a heavyset, deeply tanned woman. And Professor Abbott, of course, marching alongside a fifth person, a much smaller dark-skinned man with tightly curled black hair, wearing a wrinkled jumpsuit of faded blue.

They were an undistinguished-looking group, Gomez thought as he stood in the reception area, except for Abbott, striding along as if he were leading a parade.

Abbott trooped them to where Gomez was standing.

"Tómas Gomez," he boomed, by way of introduction, "meet Vincente Zworkyn, the best product ever of Italian-Russian collaboration."

Zworkyn grinned, put out his hand and said, "Hello." Gomez took the hand in his own. "Welcome to *Haven*, Dr. Zworkyn."

The man barely came up to Abbott's shoulder. Even Gomez was a good three or four centimeters taller. His face was swarthy, squarish, with a strong chin and slightly hooked nose. His hair was thick and dark.

"I don't have a doctorate," Zworkyn said, without a trace of embarrassment. "I'm a mining engineer."

Gomez glanced at Abbott, then stumbled, "Oh! I'm sorry . . . that is, I apologize . . ."

"No need to apologize," Abbott said. "Vincente is the top man in his field. He doesn't need a PhD, do you, Vince?"

Zworkyn shrugged good-naturedly, "I've never found the time to acquire one."

Gomez realized that his mental image of miners was of dirt-encrusted men shoveling rocks in some deep, dank underground cavern. These people are engineers, he told himself: they don't go down into mines, they direct machinery that does the labor.

Abbott introduced the other three miners, then led the little group through the computers that registered their arrival while they scanned their bodies, leaving Gomez standing there, suddenly alone.

"See you at dinner, Tómas," Abbott called to him as he hurried the miners to the hatch that led into *Haven*'s interior.

Gomez felt more than a little shaky as he walked alone toward the habitat's main restaurant. I'm getting accustomed to having Raven as my dinner companion, he realized. But for the past few evenings, Raven had been busy with Alicia Polanyi, planning the shop they were going to open.

All right, Gomez said to himself as he pushed through the doors of the restaurant's main entrance. I don't need her. I can stand on my own feet.

Still, he missed her.

The restaurant was crowded, but the human maître d' led Gomez directly to the circular table where Zworkyn and his four colleagues were sitting with Abbott and a half-dozen of his astronomers. There was one empty chair, between Abbott and Zworkyn. A robot came up and held it out for Gomez.

"Ah, here at last," Abbott said, with a big gap-toothed grin.

"It's still a few minutes before seven," Gomez protested.

"Yes, yes. We started ahead of you."

Gomez saw that each of the men and women around the table had drinks at their places. He ordered a margarita.

"With salt?" asked the robot.

"Of course."

"Of course," echoed Abbott. Gomez wondered how much he'd already had to drink.

Zworkyn leaned forward slightly and asked Gomez, "What on Earth ever possessed you to search for evidence of life here on Uranus?"

Gomez shrugged. "All the other major planets in the solar system have biospheres—extensive biospheres. It seemed odd that Uranus was sterile. It didn't fit."

"Good thinking," said Abbott. "Go after the anomalies. Find out why they're anomalies."

Zworkyn nodded. "And you found this piece of steel."

"It's not natural," Gomez said. "And it didn't come from one of our own submersibles."

"That's not one hundred percent assured," Abbott corrected.

"Close enough," said Gomez.

Nodding again, Zworkyn agreed. "Close enough to get us sent out here to help you explore the region."

"Yes," said Gomez.

Tugging at one end of his luxurious moustache, Abbott asked the miner, "So when do you start digging?"

With a tight smile, Zworkyn replied, "Once we find something worth digging for."

"Explain, please," said Abbott.

"First we'll have to install our scanning equipment in your submarine, Dr. Gomez—"

"Please call me Tómas."

Zworkyn dipped his chin minimally. "Tómas, then. And I am Vincente."

Abbott smiled benignly at the two of them.

"We will survey the area where you found the relic," Zworkyn continued, "scanning that region of the sea bottom for similar metal. Penetrating radar and isotopic scanners should let us see at least a hundred meters below the seabed's surface. Once we have a picture of what's sitting down beneath the surface, then we can start digging."

"But what if there isn't any other steel down there?" Gomez asked.

With a shrug of his narrow shoulders, Zworkyn replied, "Then we'll have to expand our search."

"Poke around in the dark," said Abbott, "in the hopes of finding something."

One of the other miners chipped in, "Playing blind man's bluff, down at the bottom of the ocean."

"What we're looking for might be buried deeper than our instruments can scan," Zworkyn admitted.

Gomez muttered, "If that's the case . . ."

"If that's the case," Zworkyn said softly, "then we're out of luck. You could be sitting atop a gold mine, but if it's buried too deep for our instruments to detect it, we'll never know that it's there."

Abbott shook his head. "Doesn't sound terribly encouraging, does it?"

Gomez didn't reply aloud, but he thought, They don't expect to find anything. They think they've been sent here on a fool's errand, and I'm the fool who's responsible for it.

Patience . . . and anticipation

Raven was running through a long list of women's fashions when her phone buzzed. Glancing at the corner of her screen, she saw that it was Tómas calling. Again.

I've been neglecting him, she realized. She looked over at Alicia, busily conversing with the image on her screen of the contractor who was turning one of the habitat's empty storage areas into their shop.

Leaning closer to her own screen, Raven said softly, "Phone answer."

Tómas's face filled the screen. "Raven! Hello!"

"Hello, Tómas," she said.

"How's it going?"

She smiled "We're aiming to open the shop in two weeks."

"That's good."

"It'll be good only if we can get a thousand and one details squared away in that time."

"Oh. You must be pretty busy."

"Very," she said. "Extremely."

Gomez looked disappointed. "I guess you don't have time to go to dinner, then."

Raven hesitated. Tómas looked disappointed, forlorn.

She asked, "Would you mind if I brought Alicia along?"

It was his turn to hesitate.

"She's been working awfully hard," Raven said. "I think a pleasant dinner would be very good for her."

Gomez nodded, but it seemed clear his heart wasn't in it. "Okay, I guess."

Raven smiled her brightest. "You're a dear."

"Seven o'clock? In the main restaurant?"

"Can you make it eight o'clock? We have so much work to get through."

"Eight o'clock, sure," said Gomez. Then he added, a bit more sullenly, "Dinner for three."

Alicia objected that she didn't want to be a third wheel at dinner.

"It's you he's interested in, not me."

"I know," Raven admitted. "But I don't think I want to let him get too close. Not yet. Not now."

Alicia studied Raven's face for a long, silent moment. At last she said, "All right. I'll be your chaperone."

"Thanks," said Raven. Yet somehow she didn't really feel grateful.

Once she and Alicia had seated themselves at the table with Gomez, Raven asked, "How's the search going, Tómas?"

"Zworkyn and his people have just started scanning the area," Gomez replied, noticeably less than enthusiastic. "Nothing's turned up so far."

"Patience," Alicia counseled. "You've got to be patient."

Gomez tried to grin at her, failed.

Raven said, "They've just started, after all."

Gripping his salad fork hard enough to bend it, Gomez said,

"I wish I could go down there myself and dig through the rubble."

"Rubble?" asked Raven.

With a shrug of his shoulders, Gomez replied, "The seabed's covered with rocks, all shapes and sizes. And a lot of sand. Like somebody's pounded everything into wreckage."

Alicia's brows knit. "There's a word for that . . . for when you see what you expect to see, instead of what's really there."

Raven suggested, "Hope?"

"No, it's something else," Alicia said. "I remember reading it somewhere."

"Anticipation," said Gomez.

"Yes, that's it," Raven said. Then she cautioned, "But you mustn't let your anticipation blind you to what you're actually seeing."

Alicia giggled. "Like the two of us are doing with this shop we're going to open."

Raven glared at her.

"Well, look at us," Alicia explained. "We're working night and day to set up our boutique. But suppose once we open it, nobody comes to buy? What if the women in this habitat don't care about what we offer them?"

Gomez gave her a lopsided grin. "The Japanese have a word for that."

"They do?"

"Sure. Hara-kiri."

The three of them walked slowly along the passageway that led to their living quarters.

Still thinking of Tómas's "hara-kiri" joke, Raven wondered what he would actually do if the search of the sea bottom turned up nothing of interest. How will he react? she asked herself. What will he do?

They reached Alicia's quarters and bade her goodnight, then Raven and Gomez walked slowly onward. His unit was next, then hers, several doors farther along the passageway.

"You're awfully quiet," he said as they strolled along.

"I've got a lot to think about," Raven replied. "A lot of things to do."

Gomez studied the flooring as they walked. "I've got nothing to do. Nothing but waiting."

"They'll find something, Tómas. I know they will."

He made a tiny smile. "As my Jewish friends say, 'From your mouth to God's ear.'"

"You'll see," Raven insisted.

They reached the door to his apartment.

"Would you like to come in?" he asked. "For a nightcap?"

"Tómas, I shouldn't," said Raven. "I can't."

"You could if you wanted to."

"I do want to. But I shouldn't. Please try to understand."

He shook his head. "I'll never understand women."

Raven pecked at his cheek. "Patience, Tómas. Please."

"And anticipation," he added softly. Reaching for her arm, he said, "Come on, I'll walk you home."

Scanning

††

††††††††††††††††††††††††††††

Tómas Gomez sat in the stuffy observation center between Zworkyn and Abbott, staring at the viewscreen that covered one entire wall of the crowded room.

The observation center was built like a miniature theater. All four of Zworkyn's assistants were sitting tensely at the bottom level, eyes focused on the viewscreens they were monitoring. Gomez, Zworkyn and Abbott sat at the next higher level, then a half-dozen of Abbott's astronomers sat in the next tier, above them.

The submersible that Gomez had originally used—now packed with deep-scanning sensors—was slowly coasting a few meters above the sea floor. A pencil-thin beam of blue-green laser light angled upward, toward the ocean's surface, a precariously slim pencil beam of communication.

The observation center's wall screen showed a full-color view of the seabed, nothing but rocks and sand. No fish, no fronds of vegetation, no sign of life whatsoever.

"Good imagery," Abbott said.

"We're lucky," replied Zworkyn. "The sea's very calm today, very clear. Yesterday the *verdammt* laser beam was so scattered by turbulence that we had to get the sub to send up message drones."

"Today is better," Gomez half whispered, as if fearful of breaking their good luck.

"Much," Abbott agreed.

Zworkyn muttered, "Scan twenty meters deeper."

One of his assistants replied, "That would be nearly at the equipment's limit. We can't scan much deeper."

"Do it," Zworkyn said.

The image on the wall screen changed minimally. Rocks and sand. Sand and rocks.

"No steel," muttered Abbott.

"No metals of any kind," Zworkyn agreed. Somehow, Gomez thought, the man sounded just as disappointed as he himself felt.

A curved line slid into their view. Zworkyn's brows hiked up. "What's that?" he asked.

The one woman among his assistants looked down at an auxiliary screen set into her desktop. "Strontium eighty-seven," she said.

"Follow it."

The man beside her spoke into the microphone perched just above his lip. The big wall screen followed the curved line.

Zworkyn glanced at Gomez, the beginnings of a smile slightly bending his lips. Before Tómas could ask a question, he explained:

"Strontium eighty-seven is formed when rubidium eighty-seven decays radioactively. Its half life is some fifty billion years, within an error of roughly thirty to fifty million years."

"But that's on Earth," Gomez objected. "We're looking at Uranus."

Zworkyn's smile broadened. "The atoms don't know that. They behave the same way no matter where they are."

"Oh." Pointing at the big screen, Gomez said, "So we're following a curve that originally contained a fair amount of rubidium."

"Precisely," said Zworkyn. "Clever lad."

"But it might be natural."

"There was a trace amount of rubidium—and strontium—in the sample you picked up."

"And your sensors are picking up a trace of strontium!"

Nodding, Zworkyn replied, "Indeed they are. And smooth, precise curves like this one could hardly be natural. Not at all."

The observation center fell silent. For several minutes all the people in the cramped room stared at the wall screen. The curve went on and on.

"It's huge," Gomez breathed.

The woman at her screen called out, "Diameter, seven hundred meters, plus."

"Keep following it," Zworkyn commanded.

For long breathless minutes the screen kept tracking the curve. Until a straight line angled off from it.

"A-*hah!*" shouted Zworkyn.

Gomez felt his heart thump.

Grinning fiercely, Zworkyn exclaimed, "Curves exist in nature. But straight lines don't. They are made by intelligent creatures."

Intelligent creatures! Gomez echoed silently. Straight lines are made by intelligent creatures! He expected the crowded little room to erupt in cheers, celebration. But it was deathly, inhumanly silent. Every eye was focused intently on the straight line that angled away from the mammoth circle.

"Follow that line!" Zworkyn snapped.

Straight as an arrow's flight, the line extended through a maze of stones and sand. Until it connected with another broad circle.

"Diameter seven hundred meters, plus!"

"Identical," Zworkyn muttered.

Gomez sagged back in his chair. Two identical circles, connected by a straight line.

"That's not a natural formation," said one of the astronomers sitting behind Gomez, his voice hushed with awe.

"Can't be," agreed the woman at her console, below them.

Zworkyn turned in his chair and extended his hand toward Gomez. "Congratulations, my boy. You've discovered the remains of intelligent life."

Tómas sat there, feeling stunned. Someone clapped him on the back. All three of Zworkyn's assistants had turned their chairs around and were grinning up at him. The astronomers in the rear of the chamber got to their feet, applauding lustily.

Zworkyn stood up. "All right! We can celebrate tonight. But right now, we've got to get this data to the Astronomical Association back on Earth. You're all going to be heroes!"

They cheered mightily.

"Well don't just sit there," Zworkyn said, tugging at Gomez's arm. "We've got to tell Waxman the good news."

Tómas shook his head, as if to clear it, then rose shakily to his feet. Like a man in a trance, he followed Zworkyn out of the monitoring center, down along the curved passageway, toward Evan Waxman's office. Even with the observation center's doors closed they could still hear the cheering and applause.

The two of them barged past the woman who'd replaced Alicia as Waxman's assistant and breezed directly into Waxman's office.

"We've found unmistakable evidence of an ancient civilization on Uranus!" Zworkyn announced grandly.

Waxman looked up from his desktop screen, his expression a mixture of surprise and disbelief.

"Unmistakable? Really?"

Turning to Gomez, Zworkyn said, "Tell him, my boy."

"Buried in the seabed," Gomez chattered. "Circles. A straight line connecting them."

Despite himself, Waxman asked, "A straight line?"

"Yes, sir."

Waxman looked stunned, shocked. "I'd like to see your evidence."

Still half-disbelieving what he himself had seen, Gomez nodded and commanded Waxman's desktop computer to show the scenes that had appeared in the monitoring center.

Tómas saw Waxman's frame stiffen with astonishment.

His eyes widened. "By God, that . . . that's remarkable!" he exclaimed.

With a soft chuckle, Zworkyn said, "More impressive than a single twist of steel, eh?"

Waxman nodded, his cobalt-blue eyes focused on Gomez. "You've made a tremendous discovery, Tómas. You too, Mr. Zworkyn. Both of you. Congratulations."

For the first time, Tómas felt an inner glow of triumph. He paid no attention to the flat, strained tone of Waxman's praise.

CELEBRATION

+++

+++

The party began slowly, with zworkyn's people and Abbott's staff, but it quickly grew to fill half the main dining room as news of the discovery spread through the habitat.

Tómas Gomez sat at the center of the growing crowd, basking in the warmth of their congratulations. But as he scanned the new arrivals he did not see Raven. She's not coming, he told himself. She's avoiding me. The warmth he had felt inside him slowly faded and turned to ice.

He accepted the crowd's increasingly raucous congratulations with a grin and a nod, but inwardly he wanted to get away from their noise, their cheers. He wanted to be with Raven, or bitterly alone.

Zworkyn was grinning broadly as he climbed up atop one of the dining tables and silenced the crowd with shushing motions of both his hands.

"We have a lot to celebrate—"

The people roared and cheered. Zworkyn waited patiently for them to quiet down, then continued, "I don't expect much work out of you tomorrow—" Laughter. "But the day after tomorrow our real work begins. Who were the creatures who built this city at the bottom of the sea? How did they die away? What happened here to extinguish all life on the planet?"

One of the younger men in the crowd shouted, "Where are we going to put the six zillion researchers who'll come flocking out here as soon as they hear the news?"

Standing back at the fringe of the crowd, where the robots were busily picking up the discarded dinnerware, Evan Waxman frowned at the thought of hordes of newcomers arriving at *Haven*.

We won't be able to accommodate them, he thought. Even if we finish the second module and let them have it, this is going to change everything. Ruin everything. A horde of scientists roosting here for God knows how long. Poking into everything.

But then a slow smile crept across his handsome face. A horde of new customers, he told himself. I'll have to increase production.

Umber won't like having a tide of newcomers descending on us, he realized. He set up *Haven* to be as far away from Earth as possible. He wants to keep this area for his refugees, his sick and lame and stupid poor people. He'll want to refuse to let the scientists make a base here for themselves.

Well, I'll have to change his mind about that. Or move him out of my way.

"Aren't you going to join the celebration?" Alicia asked.

Raven looked up from her desktop screen's view of the crowd in the main dining room. "I suppose I should," she said, her tone far from celebratory.

"You don't want to?" Alicia looked surprised.

"I do, but . . ."

"But you're afraid you'll wind up in bed with Tómas."

"Yes."

"Well why not? He's a hero, the darling of the scientists. He's made a great discovery."

"And I'm his reward?" Raven asked.

Alicia stared at her. "It's just a one-night fling. Why not?"

"Because it would mean more to Tómas than a one-night fling. He's very serious."

"And you're not."

"I don't know!" Raven burst. "I like him, but . . ."

"But what?"

"What will he do when he finds out about what I was on Earth?"

"You don't think he knows?"

"I don't know!"

Raven felt Alicia's pallid blue eyes boring into her like twin ice picks.

At last Alicia said, "You're in love with him."

"No! Don't be silly."

With a shake of her head Alicia insisted, "You're in love with him, but you're afraid to admit it to yourself."

"That's ridiculous!" Raven objected, with some heat. "I can't be in love with anybody—especially not him."

"It happens," Alicia countered.

"Not to me."

"Even to you, honey."

Raven felt tears welling up. "I don't want to hurt him."

"And you think you're not hurting him by staying away?"

"He'll forget about me, sooner or later."

A trace of a smile curved Alicia's lips slightly. "Maybe. But will you forget about him?"

"Yes I will."

"Then why don't you go to him and give him a night he'll remember? You know how to please men, why not please him?"

Raven's self-control shattered. She burst into tears.

slowly, like a woman heading toward a guillotine, Raven made her way along the passageway toward the main dining room. she could hear the noise of thumping Latino music and the crowd's celebration long before she reached the dining room's closed doors.

She opened the main door and slipped in, a wall of music and laughter and dozens of shouted conversations assailing her ears.

And there was Tómas, standing on a tabletop with Professor Abbott on one side of him and the smaller, darker Zworkyn on the other.

All eyes seemed to be on Tómas; he looked somewhere between astonished and abashed by the adulation. But the instant his eyes met Raven's, he jumped down from the table and pushed through the crowd toward her.

"Raven! You're here!"

And Raven felt that this was where she wanted to be, with him, with this man who loved her.

"Congratulations, Tómas," she shouted into his ear. "You've made a great discovery."

"You're my discovery," he answered, taking her in his arms.

Raven let him swirl her away through the crowd, dancing to the heavy beat of the music.

Nothing else matters, she told herself. Only Tómas. Only his happiness.

She awoke the next morning in Tómas's bed, curled next to him as he snored softly, a contented smile on his lips. Raven realized that she had hardly ever seen Tómas smile: he was always so serious.

She lay there beside him and studied his face. It was a handsome face, she decided. Strong. Capable. Serious. And she realized that she was serious, too. Despite everything, despite her past and her unknowable future, she wanted to be with Tómas for the rest of her life.

But a voice in her head asked, Will he want to be with you? Once he knows what you were, will his love dissolve and disappear like a beautiful dream burned away by the morning sun?

Then she remembered Alicia and the boutique. I've got to get to work, she told herself.

As gently as she could, she eased herself away from Tómas's arm and began to slip out of bed.

"Good morning," he mumbled drowsily.

"Oh! I didn't mean to wake you. I'm sorry."

Half covered by the twisted bedsheet, he turned and squinted at the bedside clock. "I ought to get up. Work to do."

"Yes," said Raven, sitting up on the edge of the bed. "Me too."

As casually as a man seeking travel directions, Gomez asked, "Will you marry me?"

Raven stared at him. "Marry? That's . . . that's a big step, Tómas."

Lying there with a soft smile on his lips, Gomez replied, "It's not an unusual step."

Raven fought down an urge to cry. "Tómas, you don't know anything about me . . . who I am, really . . ."

"I know I love you." Before she could reply, he added, "And you love me."

"One night in bed together isn't love!"

"Isn't it?"

The tears were threatening to burst out. "Tómas, I was a whore! Back in Naples—"

"I know," he said, reaching out to grasp her arm. "Waxman told me."

"He told you? And you still . . . ?"

"Raven, you *were* a whore. Were. You're not a whore now. You're never going back to that. I'm here for you. I'll protect you."

She collapsed into his arms, sobbing softly, and for long silent moments they clung to each other as Raven said to herself, I love him and he loves me. This is wonderful. Nothing else matters. Nothing. Nothing.

Evan Waxman was sitting before Reverend Umber's ornate desk, spelling out the future.

"I have no idea how many scientists will want to come here, but it will be considerable. Hundreds. Maybe thousands."

"Thousands?" Umber's round face went pale.

"This is a momentous discovery, Kyle. Uranus was once populated by an intelligent species, and now they're gone. Eradicated."

"God's will."

Waxman huffed. "Well, there are going to be a horde of investigators coming here to try to figure out how and why God wiped out a whole intelligent species and every other living creature on the planet."

"We can't allow them into *Haven*," Umber said firmly. "They'd ruin everything we're trying to accomplish here."

With a slow nod, Waxman replied, "I suppose we could house them in *Haven II*."

"No! That's for more refugees. We already have contracts with the social agencies on Earth and the transportation corporations."

"The Astronomical Association can invalidate those contracts."

Umber's face settled into an unhappy scowl.

"And," Waxman continued, "they can commandeer *Haven II* as a shelter for the incoming scientists."

"And set our work back for how long? Months? Years?"

Waxman shrugged. "I think you should sit down with this man Abbott. He sits pretty high in the Association's pecking order."

"I don't want them here in *Haven*," Umber said firmly. "I've thought it through time and again. I don't want them mixing with our people here in *Haven*."

"Neither do I," Waxman agreed. "But there's no way we can keep them from taking over *Haven II*."

Umber shook his head unhappily.

bOOk FOUr

THE INVESTIGATORS

Gordon Abbott

+++
++++++++++++++++++++++++++++++++++

Gordon Abbott tugged at one end of his extravagant moustache as he repeated in his mind a few lines from Kipling:

> *"You may talk o' gin and beer*
> *"When you're quartered safe out 'ere,*
> *"An' you're sent to penny-fights an' Aldershot it . . ."*

"Penny-fights," he muttered. "That's what I'm doing. Penny-fights."

With an exasperated sigh, he gazed up again at the wall-sized viewscreen that displayed the habitat *Haven II*: a huge spoked wheel riding in orbit alongside the original *Haven* space station. Dozens of teams of workmen and robots crawled across the habitat's skin. To Abbott they seemed like maggots infesting a corpse.

His superiors at the Astronomical Association's headquarters on Earth had sent another "reminder" this morning. Abbott scanned it quickly and suppressed the urge to delete it and send it to electronic oblivion.

The message told him that the construction of *Haven II* was still behind schedule—a fact that Abbott was well aware of—

and asked when it would be ready for the groups of scientists who were champing at the bit for their chance to investigate the extinct civilization of Uranus—a question to which Abbott had no reliable answer.

Trying to use the man-and-woman power of the refugees living on the original *Haven* habitat to build *Haven II* had been—at best—a long shot. The Reverend Umber had hatched the idea and insisted on it; his administrator, Waxman, had reluctantly bowed to the lamebrained concept.

Uneducated, for the most part, and unskilled, the immigrants were doing their best, and actually learning to control and command the robot workforce, but it wasn't good enough, fast enough, polished enough for the deskbound bureaucrats Earthside.

Abbott pointed out to his superiors that the task of organizing an experienced construction team and sending them a few billion kilometers out to Uranus was extremely expensive. Use the local talent. Train the uneducated. Teach the beggars. Besides, Umber insisted on it, and without his cooperation nothing could be accomplished.

But the Earthside bureaucrats saw only the original timetable of the construction task and the fact that Abbott's amateurs were lagging behind their preset goals.

There's only one way to ease the pressure they're putting on me, Abbott knew. It was a course he did not really want to take, but when one's career is on the line, a certain amount of risk is called for.

"Memo to Harvey Millard, Interplanetary Council Executive Director," he dictated. As he spoke, his words appeared on the viewscreen.

"Harvey: We're working as hard as we can to prepare the habitat *Haven II* for the scientists who want to come here to

Uranus. But we're behind schedule, and the Astronomical Association is putting a lot of pressure on us. Do you think it might be possible to send a small group of the scientists here, sort of an advance guard? We can house them in the portion of the habitat that we've finished and let them get started on their investigation. Then we can add more groups as the work on the habitat progresses. Do you think that's a reasonable course of action?"

Abbott leaned back in his chair and studied his words. Yes, that sums up the problem and the potential solution very neatly. Harvey can take it from there. He'll get the credit for solving the problem, of course. But I'll get the pressure off my back.

With a satisfied nod, Abbott told the computer,

"Send."

That should do it, he said to himself.

The Reverend Kyle Umber rose from his knees slowly. His left knee throbbed with a sullen pain. Praying and arthritis don't go together well, he told himself.

With great reluctance, Umber had canceled the shipment of two hundred more refugees from Earth. Waxman had told him he had no choice, the Astronomical Association had commandeered the vessel, stranding the poor people in a makeshift shelter so that a team of astronomers and other scientists could fly out here and disturb everything.

Well, they're not going to disturb this sanctuary, Umber told himself firmly. They'll occupy *Haven II* for a while, but they won't set foot in *Haven* itself. As far as I'm concerned, those scientists will be living completely separately from us.

Waxman has apparently agreed with that decision, Umber thought. But I'll have to watch him closely. Evan smiles and nods and then goes off and does what he wants to. Well, that's going to end. I'm going to step up to my duties as the spiritual head of this community. Even if it means a conflict with Evan.

He stumbled to his desk, his knee aching, and sat down heavily in his sculpted chair. The knee's throbbing eased, but did not stop altogether.

OPENING SHOP

Raven and Alicia stood side by side in the entry of their boutique. Behind them hung rows of women's clothes, outfits of bold colors and striking styles, displays of shoes, blouses, underwear.

Alicia was staring at her wristwatch, counting off the seconds. "Eight . . . seven . . . six . . ."

Raven peered through the blinds that covered the shop's front door. She couldn't see anyone out there. All the work we've put in, all the advertisements we've put on the video network, and nobody's come to our opening? She felt a surge of bitter anger. The clods. The stupid clods.

". . . four . . . three . . . two . . . one . . ."

Raven unlatched the door and swung it open. Out in the passageway one lone person was walking past, a middle-aged man.

"Hi!" he said, with a shy wave.

"Hello," said Raven.

The man looked less than handsome: his hair was peppered with gray, his belly strained the front of his light tan shirt.

"This the new shop?" he asked.

"Yes."

"You sell joolery?"

Before Raven could answer, Alicia said from behind her, "Yes, we do. Come on in and see."

"Uh, no. Not now. Gotta get to work. How late you open?"

"Until six," said Raven and Alicia, in unison.

"That's gonna make it tough. I wanna bring my sugar to look over your joolery. She wants some kinda ring."

"We could stay open later," Alicia said.

"Seven, seven thirty?"

"Sure."

"Okay. See you then." And he walked away.

"Our first customer," Raven said.

"Maybe."

"We really don't have much of a selection of jewelry, do we?"

Alicia grinned. "We have the best selection in the habitat. The best selection this side of the Earth-Moon system."

The day wore on slowly. Several women came into the shop during the morning, poked around among the dresses and blouses, bought nothing and left.

Raven went to the nearest cafeteria at noontime and brought back a pair of prepackaged lunches. As they were sitting behind the counter, chewing morosely on their sandwiches, two young-ish women came into the boutique and started thumbing through the dresses hanging on display.

"You got anything my size?" asked one of them. She was tiny, only as tall as Raven's shoulder and elfin slim.

Raven quickly put her sandwich down and stepped around the counter. "The smaller sizes are over here," she said, leading her deeper into the shop.

It took nearly an hour, but the diminutive young woman finally picked a short-skirted dress and a pair of shoes to go with it. Her companion smiled as she studied herself in the mirror.

"Andy will love it," the companion approved.

The woman nodded and, with a shy smile, extended her arm

for Raven to record her credit account from her wristwatch. Alicia wrapped the dress and Raven boxed the shoes and the two women left the boutique chattering happily.

"Tell your friends about us!" Raven called to their departing backs.

"We will!"

As Raven turned back toward the counter, Alicia breathed, "Our first sale."

"The first of many," said Raven.

Then they both said, giggling, "From your mouth to God's ear."

Evan Waxman stared at his desktop screen. "You're coming here?"

The man on the screen wouldn't hear the question for more than two hours, Waxman knew. He frowned inwardly at being so stupid.

The man was saying, ". . . so I talked Millard into appointing me as the official news representative to accompany the first team of scientists going out to your cabin in the sky."

His name was Noel Dacco. He was a news reporter with the Central African Journalism Organization (CAJO). A big-shouldered black man with lustrous dark eyes and an infectious laugh, his head shaved bald, his chin rimmed with a sparse beard, he was Waxman's chief link with the international high-society celebrities and VIPs who were a significant part of the market for Rust.

Waxman frowned at his desktop screen. Noel can't come here! I need him on Earth, handling my contacts with the wholesalers and distributors.

As if he could read Waxman's mind even over the interplanetary distance that separated them, Dacco smiled widely and explained in his deep, rich baritone voice, "Everything is fine at this end, Evan. Everything is going as smoothly as clockwork. I thought it would be fun to ride out there and see your operation firsthand. I *am* a newsman, after all. I won't get in your way, I promise. This is going to be like a vacation for me."

Vacation, Waxman grumbled inwardly. There's more to this than a vacation. He's coming all the way out here for a reason. Are the distributors on Earth trying to move in on me? Take over the production end, as well as distribution and sales?

Waxman stared at Dacco's smiling image on his desktop screen. This is going to be trouble, he told himself. I've got to be prepared for him.

VINCENTE ZWORKYN

Zworkyn felt a surge of fatherly pride as he gazed at the wall screen. It showed segments of four extensive circles, linked by straight lines. All buried beneath nearly a hundred meters of stones and sand.

"It's a city," said Tómas Gomez, sitting beside him, his voice hushed with awe.

"It *was* a city," Zworkyn agreed. "Or whatever the Uranians' equivalent of a city might have been."

The two men were sitting side by side on the sofa in Zworkyn's makeshift office, which was crammed with computers and analytical sensors.

Gomez nodded without taking his eyes from the image. "How old is it? When was it destroyed? What destroyed it?"

"Good questions," said Zworkyn. "Let's hope we can find some answers."

"The first gaggle of astronomers will be arriving here in a week," Gomez said. "Will we be able to accommodate them on *Haven II*?"

Zworkyn nodded guardedly. "Waxman says they'll have a section of the station prepared for twenty arrivals. The incoming ship is carrying eighteen people: seven astronomers, five geologists, and six mining engineers. Plus their equipment."

"And they won't be allowed here, in *Haven*?"

"Strictly off-limits, as far as Reverend Umber is concerned."

Gomez looked troubled. "Umber expects them to stay on *Haven II* all the time?"

"That's what he wants. No contact with them for the inhabitants here in *Haven*."

"That's going to be sticky."

"I've seen worse," said Zworkyn. "Boring through the ice on Europa, *that* was a hassle and a half, let me tell you. The locals were mining the ice and they didn't want a bunch of snotty scientists and engineers from Earth bothering them."

Nodding, Gomez said, "Well, at least we don't have locals to interfere with our work."

"Not yet," said Zworkyn.

The first team of scientists arrived and Professor Abbott supervised their transfer from their ship to *Haven II*, together with the massive loads of equipment they had brought with them.

Gomez goggled at the excavators and retrievers that were loaded into three separate cargo bays of *Haven II*. The geologists and engineers were all strangers to him, of course, but Gomez was disappointed to find that he didn't know any of the astronomers, either. And they were all so *young*! I'm only a few years out of grad school, but these guys are just children!

Very bright children, he quickly learned. Professor Abbott had personally picked this advanced guard of investigators. Gomez felt outclassed.

Still, he stood in the reception area aboard *Haven II* as the newcomers arrived. Abbott was already there, hands clasped behind his back as the newcomers trooped into the reception area.

Abbott strode to the first of the newbies and swept up her hand in his. For an instant Gomez thought he was going to bend over and kiss it. But the instant passed as the rest of the new arrivals crowded into the reception area.

There was one additional member of the incoming crew. It turned out that he wasn't a scientist, but a newsman: Noel Dacco.

Dacco went straight to Gomez as the scientists made their way through the identity-checking computer systems of the ship's reception area.

"You're Tómas Gomez, aren't you?" Dacco said, as he put out a meaty hand. "You're going to be a very famous man, you know."

He was the blackest man Gomez had ever seen. His shaved scalp gleamed almost purple beneath the overhead lights. He was big, heavy-shouldered, with a wide, bright, toothy smile.

Gomez accepted his offered hand as he asked, "And you are?"

"Noel Dacco, with the CAJO news outfit. It's a pleasure to meet you, Thomas."

"Tómas," Gomez corrected, his hand still in Dacco's iron grip.

"Tómas," Dacco repeated, with a slight dip of his chin.

"You're a newsman?"

"Yes. I'm going to make your name a household word, my man."

Gomez finally pulled his hand away from Dacco's as he smiled weakly. "I'm an astronomer, not a dishwasher soap."

Dacco laughed, a deep, bubbling sound. "Good one! I can use that."

Suppressing a frown, Gomez asked, "Would you like me to show you to your quarters? It's not far—"

"That would be fine," said Dacco. With a grand gesture, he boomed, "Lead the way."

As they started toward the hatch that led to the habitat's main passageway, Dacco asked, "Whatever made you come all the way out here?"

Gomez smiled a little and repeated the answer he had given so many times that he knew it by rote.

From his office in *Haven*, Evan Waxman watched Dacco and Gomez walking side by side through the passageway in *Haven II*. The walls were unfinished in places, open spaces that showed wiring and sensors behind them. Still a lot of work to finish up, Waxman said to himself.

Neither man paid any attention to the gaps in the walls as they passed. Gomez was chattering away and Dacco was nodding, grinning, giving every appearance of enjoying the astronomer's discourse.

"There's something wrong about him," Waxman muttered to himself. "I wouldn't trust that toothy smile of his for a nanosecond."

dinner

‡‡

waxman fumed and fidgeted in his desk chair as he watched Dacco and the astronomer Gomez walk along the passageway that led to the quarters prepared for the new arrivals. Gomez was doing most of the talking, with Dacco nodding and asking a question here and there. It was difficult to make out their words, since they were amidst the other newbies, and the new arrivals' chatter nearly drowned out the conversation Waxman wanted to hear.

"Doesn't really matter," Waxman muttered to himself. "It's astronomical talk. Gomez never talks about anything else."

Still, Waxman watched intently as Gomez and Dacco stopped at a door that bore a handwritten *N. Dacco* sign. Dacco tapped out the entry code and the two men stepped into the apartment.

There were no listening devices inside the private quarters, of course. One of Reverend Umber's restrictions: no snooping on private behavior. Stupid rule, Waxman thought, making a mental note to bug Dacco's quarters as soon as he could.

But within a few minutes Gomez re-emerged from Dacco's quarters and started back along the passageway, alone.

And Waxman's phone buzzed.

"Phone answer."

Sure enough, Dacco's gleaming dark face appeared on

Waxman's desktop screen. The newsman smiled broadly. "Well, I'm here," he said.

Waxman forced a smile back at him. "We're neighbors."

"Yes we are."

"Why don't you come over here, Noel. We have a lot to talk about, I think."

Dacco's smile didn't alter a millimeter. But he said, "I'm afraid I've already committed myself to dinner with Dr. Gomez. He said he'd bring two charming young ladies."

Waxman's smile winked off. "We have a lot to talk about," he repeated.

"Can't it wait until tomorrow? I'd like to meet the ladies. After all, I am supposed to be on vacation."

"We both know that's not true."

"But it is, Evan! All work and no play makes Noel a dull boy."

He's toying with me, Waxman realized. He's having fun at my expense.

"Let me check my schedule for tomorrow," he said, calling out, "Tomorrow's schedule, please."

His desktop screen split in half, one side showing Waxman's schedule.

"Lunch tomorrow," he said flatly. "One P.M. Come to my office."

Still grinning, Dacco said, "Hearkening and obedience."

The desktop screen went dark. Waxman stared at it for several wordless moments, then muttered, "He's full of confidence. Hasn't a care in the world. Well, I'll have to teach him otherwise."

"He's a newsman," Gomez was explaining as he walked with Raven and Alicia toward *Haven*'s main restaurant. "Something of a character, I think."

"And he's come all the way out here?" Alicia asked.

"Yes. I think—" Gomez recognized the burly form striding along the passageway toward them. "There he is."

Noel Dacco smiled widely as Gomez introduced him to Alicia and Raven.

"You passed the restaurant's entrance," Gomez said, pointing to the open doorway. People were streaming into the place.

"Yes, I know. I saw you, Tómas, with these two beautiful ladies, and came up to greet you."

Alicia smiled minimally and Raven reached for Gomez's hand. The four of them entered the restaurant and were quickly seated.

A robot waiter rolled up to their table and took their drink orders. Dacco asked for lime juice.

"Are you a Moslem?" Raven asked.

"Very observant!" said Dacco. To Gomez, he added, "You have a very bright young lady here."

Tómas's face reddened. He nodded but said nothing.

Before either of the others could speak, Dacco told them, "You'd never believe the difficulty I had getting here from *Haven II.* Is this habitat in some sort of lockdown situation?"

"Lockdown?"

"There was no connection between this wheel and Number Two, where I'm quartered. I had to call Evan Waxman and get him to provide me transportation. I arrived here in a dinky little shuttlecraft."

Alicia smiled a bit and said, "Reverend Umber doesn't want the residents here to mix with the visiting scientists."

"Why not?"

"He wants the residents to be free of all their old associations with Earth."

"Ah! And he's afraid I'll contaminate his flock?"

Her smile broadening, Alicia said, "Something like that."

Dacco swung his gaze across the crowded, bustling restaurant. "You mean all these people are refugees from Earth?"

"Émigrés," said Alicia. "This is their home."

"And Umber doesn't want them contaminated by people like me."

"By people who can return to Earth," Alicia corrected. "All of us here have given up our former ways of life. We're going to live here for the rest of our lives."

Dacco blinked several times. Gomez said, "Why don't we order some dinner?"

"Why not?" said Dacco, his toothy grin returning. "That's what we're here for, isn't it?"

Halfway through their appetizers, Raven asked, "You said you had to get Evan Waxman to provide you transportation between here and *Haven II*."

"That's right," Dacco answered, as he deftly speared a stalk of asparagus from his salad plate.

"Do you know him personally?"

Dacco's smile stayed fixed on his face, but somehow Raven thought he looked suddenly less than happy.

At last he answered, "Yes, slightly. He personally approved my request to come here."

Raven caught his hesitation. *He's lying,* she said to herself. *I wonder why.*

Waxman and Dacco

Precisely at 1:00 p.m., Waxman's new assistant called over the intercom, "Noel Dacco to see you, sir."

Looking up from the report he was reading, Waxman said, "Send him in. No interruptions while he's here. And order luncheon for two, please."

"Yes, sir."

His office door slid open and Dacco stepped in, smiling, broad-shouldered, nimble as a ballet dancer.

As Waxman got up from his chair, Dacco stepped to the desk and stuck out his hand. "It's a pleasure to meet you in person, Mr. Waxman."

Taking the black man's hand in his own and smiling tightly, Waxman said, "It's good to meet you face-to-face, Noel." Gesturing to the two upholstered chairs in front of the desk, he said, "Why don't you sit down? Lunch should be here shortly."

Dacco seated himself in the chair to his left. Is he left-handed? Waxman asked himself.

Easing back into his own commodious chair, Waxman asked, "So how is everything going back on Earth?"

"Very well," said Dacco, still smiling. "Sales are steadily increasing. You might give some thought to raising your production goals."

"That good?"

Nodding, Dacco said, "The habitats in Earth orbit are a strong market. So are the stations orbiting Jupiter."

"And the Rock Rats?"

"A reliable market. It's all in the reports I've sent you."

Waxman nodded. "Your latest report mentioned some problem at the power complex on Mercury."

"A little argument over paying for the Rust they've ordered. It's being straightened out."

"No pay, no Rust," said Waxman. "They pay up front."

"That's our policy, I know. But we've found that letting the customer have a sample before he plunks down his money makes it much easier to get him to pony up the whole amount a little later."

Waxman shrugged. "A distribution problem."

"It's being handled. No worries."

Waxman's phone buzzed. He glared at the tiny console. "I said no interruptions!"

His assistant's voice replied timidly, "Your lunches are here, sir."

"Oh. Bring them right in."

"Yes, sir."

The office door slid open again, and Waxman's assistant carried in a sizeable tray loaded with a pair of lunches and drinks.

"On the conference table," he told the woman.

Dacco eyed her appreciatively. She was tall, willowy, with reddish-blond hair and a doe's provocative eyes. Slim figure, but long legs—almost hidden by a floor-length black skirt that was slit from the hip.

She set out the two lunches on the corner table and left the office without a word.

"She's a refugee from Earth?" Dacco asked, once the door slid shut behind her.

"War casualty. Lost her right leg in the fighting in Tasmania."

"Pity."

"She does very well with her prosthetic leg."

"In bed?"

Waxman smiled thinly. "Or on a trampoline."

Dacco's look of surprise made Waxman want to laugh. But he suppressed the urge.

Nearly an hour later, as the two men sat at the circular conference table with the scattered crumbs of their lunches between them, Dacco said, "I had dinner last night with a woman who told me she used to be your assistant."

Waxman almost uttered Alicia's name, but he held himself back at the last instant. No sense letting him know I can watch him without his knowledge of it.

"My assistant?"

"Alicia Polanyi."

"Oh, her." Waxman forced a chuckle. "She's opened a women's clothing boutique. She and a former whore. They'll go broke in a month or so."

"Really?"

Waxman nodded as he reached for his cup of coffee.

"She seems quite determined to make a success of her establishment," Dacco said.

With a careless shrug Waxman replied, "They'll be out of business very soon."

"Pity."

"The iron laws of economics."

"The dismal science."

Waxman asked, "Did you find her attractive?"

"A little too skeletal for me," Dacco replied. "The other one was much sexier."

"Raven Marchesi. She ought to be sexier. She was a whore, back on Earth."

"Not here?"

With a sly grin, Waxman answered, "Almost."

For several silent moments, Dacco seemed to mull Waxman's reply in his mind. Then he said, "She seems attached to the astronomer."

"Gomez? Really?"

"Looked that way to me."

"Raven and Tómas Gomez," Waxman mused. "That's interesting."

"So she's not available?"

Waxman studied Dacco's face and saw desire burning in his dark eyes. He asked himself, Can I bind him to me with Raven? It's worth a try.

"She can be made available," Waxman finally answered, with a knowing smile.

BOOK FIVE

THE ENGINEER

the hospital

vincente zworkyn lay on the hospital bed glaring down at his left leg. It was covered by a plastic bandage from just above the knee down to the ankle. It didn't hurt much, but it *itched* maddeningly.

Damned fool, he told himself. Damned stupid, overeager, moronic idiot. Jetbike racing. At your age. Trying to show the youngsters that you're just as good as they are. Reckless irresponsible asshole.

His hospital billet was screened off for privacy, but his team had squeezed in to visit him and offer their apologies for the accident. The four young men and one woman crowded around his bed, all looking as sheepish as children who had been caught raiding the cookie jar.

"Wasn't your fault," Zworkyn told them, trying to smile despite his foul mood. "I should have known better."

It had seemed like a good idea, a bit of fun to break the monotony of their dedicated work. A race around the circular passageway of the *Haven II* habitat on jetbikes borrowed from the recreation center on the older wheel. Zworkyn had sped into the lead as they zoomed along the kilometers-long passageway, past teams of robots working on the construction details. Fun to feel the wind in your face and know you were ahead of the kids,

But it only took one discarded hammer lying on the passageway's flooring to flip Zworkyn's bike into the air and send him flying ass over teakettle into a newly installed section of paneling, badly bruising his back and breaking his kneecap and the slender fibula below it.

The hospital's medical staff had welcomed him with barely hidden glee: they seldom got to deal with such interesting fractures.

Now he lay on the hospital bed, waiting for the stem cell injections to repair his bones. He felt little pain: even his injured back was quickly healing, thanks to modern electrotherapy.

But his leg *itched*. Zworkyn imagined he could feel the microscopic stem cells knitting his broken bones together. No, the chief of surgery explained to him, gently, patiently. The itching was psychosomatic. Had to be.

His team mumbled apologies and good wishes and shuffled out of his narrow space. Alone now, he glared at the bandaged leg, wishing that he could reach down and scratch the damned itch.

His bedside phone buzzed.

"Yes?"

"Professor Abbott wishes to visit with you," the phone replied.

"He's here?"

"He's in the waiting room."

"Send him in!" Maybe, Zworkyn thought, Abbott could get his mind off the insidious itch.

Zworkyn raised the bed to a sitting position as Abbott pushed through the curtains that surrounded his narrow berth.

"Well, well," said Abbott, extending his hand. "How are you doing, Vince?"

Zworkyn made a grin. "Not too bad. They tell me I ought to be out of here tomorrow."

Pulling up the enclosure's only chair to the edge of the hospital bed, Abbott said, as he sat down, "Really? That's remarkable."

"Stem cells."

"Ah."

"How's everything in the uninjured world?"

Abbott tilted his head slightly. "Your people and my people are working together rather nicely. They've been scanning images we've gotten from the sub, trying to reconstruct the city down there."

"So? Have they come up with anything?"

"It's a hard slog, I'm afraid," Abbott said, unconsciously tugging at one end of his moustache. "The city's been thoroughly flattened. It's almost as though some angry god smashed it all with a superhuman hammer."

Zworkyn nodded.

"And the dating is all out of whack," Abbott went on. "Uranus was smashed by a sizeable planetoidal object back during the time of the Late Bombardment, some four billion years ago. Yet all the radioactive dating we're getting from the city's remains are much younger. *Much* younger. Something's badly out of whack."

Almost smiling, Zworkyn muttered, "That's what makes science interesting, don't you think? The unanswered questions."

Fingering his moustache again, Abbott replied, "I wish it wasn't so damned *interesting*! I want to find out what happened down there."

With a heartfelt sigh, Zworkyn agreed, "So do I, Gordon. So do I."

Raven tried to suppress a frown as she looked at Noel Dacco's grinning face on the viewscreen of the boutique's computer.

"A date?" she asked. "You want to take me to dinner?"

"I find you very attractive," Dacco replied.

"I'm afraid that won't be possible, Noel. I'm practically engaged to Tómas Gomez."

Dacco's smile didn't diminish by as much as a millimeter. "Practically?" he asked.

"He loves me."

"And you love him?"

Raven's breath caught in her throat. Then she answered, "Yes, I do."

Waggling a finger at her, Dacco said, "You had to think about it."

"I love him," Raven said, more firmly.

"Wouldn't you like to have a fling with me? It doesn't have to mean anything. Just fun. One last fling before you tie the knot with Tómas."

Raven shook her head. "I'm afraid not."

Dacco's smile evaporated. He said, "From what Waxman tells me, you weren't so reserved before you came here. And you've slept with *him* often enough."

"That's over!" Raven snapped.

"Really?"

"Really."

With a careless shrug, Dacco said, "Okay. You can't blame a man for trying. You're a very delectable dish. But you already know that."

With a hand that trembled slightly, Raven tapped the screen's OFF button. That's not the end of it, she told herself. Waxman's pointing him at me, like a hunter unleashing his dog to chase down a rabbit.

Well, I'm no rabbit, she thought. And wished it were true.

the Late bombardment

Vincente Zworkyn lay back on his bed in his darkened compartment, his eyes closed as he tried to will himself to sleep.

But in his mind he saw the Late Bombardment.

Some four billion years ago, back in the early days of the solar system's existence, countless chunks of rock and ice hurtled through the newly formed planets, blasting out continent-sized craters whenever they smashed into a fledgling world.

Zworkyn saw the turmoil, the havoc, the mayhem as thousands, millions of worldlets zoomed through the young solar system.

Four billion years ago, he said to himself. The craters that those cataclysmic collisions gouged out of the young Earth's red-hot crust were erased in time, smoothed away by four billion years of weathering: wind and rain and continental drift. But the young Moon, airless and waterless, kept the evidence across its cratered surface. When human explorers reached the Moon, they dated the craters that blanketed its bleak surface.

Four billion years ago, Zworkyn repeated to himself. While the Earth and Moon were being pummeled, Uranus was hit by a truly massive planetoid, smashed so hard that the planet was knocked over sidewise, its poles pointing to the Sun, unlike any other world in the solar system.

That cataclysm scrubbed Uranus clean of all life. All life. Down to amoebas and even microscopic chains of DNA. Not just the city we're exploring. All life. Destroyed.

Zworkyn stared at the darkened ceiling above him, clean and white. He listened to the monitors clicking and chugging away behind him at the head of his bed.

All life. Wiped out. Four billion years ago.

But why does the evidence we've pulled up from that destroyed city date it at only a couple of million years old? Two million years ago. That's about when the last ice age began on Earth. It's practically yesterday afternoon, in the history of the solar system.

Zworkyn closed his eyes and tried to let go of the puzzlement that bedeviled him. But instead of drifting to sleep he kept thinking about Uranus, lifeless, scoured clean of every living organism that once inhabited it. From the creatures who built that city down to the molecules that formed the basis of life. All gone. Destroyed. Wiped out.

His eyes flashed open. What if the cataclysm that knocked over Uranus's spin didn't happen during the Late Bombardment? What if it happened only two million years ago?

Then it would all fit! The planet was knocked over sideways. The city down there was flattened. All life on Uranus—*all* life, down to the molecular level—was eradicated.

What could have caused that? he asked himself. Then he shivered as a wave of cold swept over his healing body.

Not *what* could cause that, Zworkyn realized. *Who* could cause that? Who destroyed all life on Uranus?

Gordon Abbott frowned down at Zworkyn's body on his hospital bed as the two doctors finished their examination of the patient.

The male doctor straightened up and smiled at Zworkyn. "You're fine. Kneecap and fibula are both completely repaired. You're free to go."

The woman doctor nodded. "All indices in positive territory. You can get up and leave whenever you're ready."

Abbott thought, Physically, Vincente is healed. But mentally . . . ? I wonder.

As the two medics left his narrow stall, Zworkyn sat up on his bed. "Gordon, that's got to be the answer. Uranus was battered over sideways a scant two million years ago, not during the Late Bombardment!"

Abbott shook his head. Softly, almost pityingly, he said, "That's absurd, Vince. You can't believe—"

"Where's the evidence that Uranus was knocked sideways during the Late Bombardment? It's all conjecture! Why couldn't it have happened two million years ago instead of four billion?"

"Where's the evidence for that?" Abbott snapped.

"Down at the bottom of the ocean! That smashed city. The radioactive dating tells us it was smashed two million years ago. That's real, hard evidence, not conjecture."

"The Late Bombardment isn't conjecture."

"Yes, I know. But there is no actual evidence that Uranus was whacked sideways at that time. That idea *is* conjecture! Truly!"

Abbott was frowning. "Two million years ago there weren't big protoplanets whizzing through the solar system. How do you explain Uranus being smacked sideways? What caused that?"

"Not what," Zworkyn replied. "Who."

"Who?"

"What happened on Uranus wasn't natural, Gordon. Not a cataclysm that erases all life on an entire planet, down to the molecular level. It was a deliberate act of destruction."

"That's crazy."

"So was Wegener's idea of continental drift," Zworkyn countered. "But it turned out he was right."

"You can't be serious."

"I am. Damned serious."

Abbott's face was turning red. "You can't seriously believe that some interstellar invader wiped Uranus clean of life. That's the stuff of fantasy!"

"So were airplanes and rockets and colonies on Mars, not so long ago."

The look on Abbott's face was more of sorrow than anger. He shook his head slowly. "Vincente, my friend, you're going off the deep end. Maybe you need a bit more rest here in the hospital."

"No," Zworkyn barked. "We need to excavate the ruins down there at the bottom of the sea and find out what they have to tell us."

Abbott started to reply, caught himself, then began over. "Well, that's something I can agree with. When in doubt, study the evidence."

"Right," said Zworkyn.

"But if I were you, Vincente old friend, I wouldn't spout your E.T. invasion idea to anybody. Not until you have some real evidence to back it up."

Zworkyn nodded. "I suppose that's right."

"You bet it is."

Searching

+‡+ ‡+

"Can you keep a secret?" Tómas asked.

He was sitting beside Raven on the sofa in her living room, watching the Zworkyn team's report on the latest samples they had dredged up from the ruined city at the bottom of the sea.

Raven nodded easily. "Keep a secret? Sure."

"No," Tómas said, turning to face her. "I mean *really* keep a secret. Not tell anybody else. Deep and dark."

She saw that he was totally serious. "If you want me to."

"It's something Zworkyn told me. In total confidence. But it's so crazy, I've got to tell somebody about it or burst."

"I'll keep your secret, Tómas. I promise."

"Well . . ." He hesitated, then plunged ahead. "Zworkyn thinks that the city they've found was wiped out by aliens."

Her eyes widening, Raven asked, "Aliens? Like extraterrestrials?"

Tómas nodded solemnly.

"Wow!"

"I don't know if he's gone off the deep end," Tómas said, almost wistfully. "Maybe that jetbike accident has rattled his brain."

"Does he seem okay? I mean, has he done anything weird?"

"No, but this afternoon he told me what he thinks about the city down on the seabed. It sounds crazy to me."

"Did he give you any reason for what he believes?"

Tómas quickly ran through Zworkyn's reasoning. Raven followed it, just barely.

Touching Tómas's arm, she asked, "Does any of it make sense to you?"

"I learned about the Late Bombardment in undergraduate school. Everybody thinks that's when Uranus got knocked over sidewise."

"Do you think so, too?"

He nodded, but said, "Zworkyn pointed out that there's no real evidence that Uranus got knocked sidewise at that time. It's mostly conjecture. But it does add up, really. I mean that's when the Late Bombardment took place."

Raven murmured, "If everybody else thinks that's when it happened . . ."

"Everybody but Zworkyn."

"And he's not really a scientist, is he? He's just an engineer."

Tómas almost frowned. "Engineers have brains, you know."

Raven smiled at him. "Not like yours, Tómas."

Noel Dacco smiled handsomely at Evan Waxman. "As far as I can see, Evan, you're running a smooth operation."

Dacco was sitting in one of the guest chairs in front of Waxman's desk. Waxman smiled back at him, but he was thinking, This man is making a nuisance of himself. He's obviously been sent here to check on my operation. Maybe the distributors back on Earth want to ease me out of the Rust production operation, put their own person in to replace me. Maybe I should send this black blowhard back to them in a fancy coffin.

"I'm glad you approve of the way I'm running things," Waxman said, keeping his smile in place.

"One thing, though," said Dacco, his face growing serious.

"Oh?"

"Raven."

"Raven?" Waxman repeated.

"She's being coy with me. Is there anything you can do to . . . uh, loosen her up?"

"She's no longer in my employ. She's attached herself to that young astronomer from Chile."

"Gomez."

"Yes. The one who's stirred up this hullabaloo about the destroyed city down at the bottom of the sea."

Just a hint of frown lines appeared between Dacco's brows. "I'm supposed to be doing a major piece about him for CAJO."

Waxman thought, Honest work? How unusual.

"About Raven," Dacco reminded.

"Ah yes. Raven," Waxman temporized. "Very independent woman."

"I know that. But you promised me that you could, ah, break through her defenses."

Waxman nodded. "I'll take care of it, don't worry."

"But I do worry, Evan. I can't stay here much longer. I have obligations back Earthside, you know."

"And the article you have to write about Tómas Gomez."

"Yes. That too."

Waxman drummed his fingers on his desktop for a few moments. "I'll get Raven for you."

"When?"

"Tomorrow night."

Dacco's beaming smile returned. "Tomorrow night. Good."

Waxman smiled back. Bind him to you with hoops of steel, he told himself. Send him back to Earth happy and satisfied.

Vincente Zworkyn stood on his two legs without a tremble. The legs felt fine, quite natural, completely healed. In the privacy of his hospital alcove he dressed quickly in the clothes that he'd been wearing when his accident occurred. They were stained and dusty but, thankfully, untorn.

Only one of his team was waiting for him at the hospital's discharge lobby, the chunky, heavy-featured Leeanne Russell. The instant Zworkyn pushed through the lobby's door, she jumped up from the chair she'd been waiting in.

"They wouldn't let me in," she said apologetically.

"That's all right, Lee," Zworkyn replied. "It was good of you to come and collect me."

She grinned at him. "Where do you want to go?"

"Back to work. We've got a hypothesis to prove."

HOOPS OF STEEL

Raven stared at the viewscreen in her living room. She had finished breakfast and was just about to leave for the boutique when Waxman's call came through.

Despite the early hour, Waxman appeared to be in his office, dressed for a working day, all business.

"How's your shop doing, Raven?" he asked, with a pleasant smile.

He's not calling about the boutique, Raven told herself. He gets our sales information automatically. What does he really want?

"Sales are moving upward," she said to the screen. "We'll have to order more merchandise next week."

"Really?"

"Really. But you could see that in the daily files we automatically send you."

Waxman's smile thinned just the tiniest bit. "Do you really think you can make a success of your little shop?"

"Look at the sales record," Raven replied. "The trend is upward."

"It's not a very steep climb."

"But it's better than a downward spiral. Word's spreading

throughout the habitat, Evan. Women are coming in, looking at what we have to offer, and buying."

He conceded the point with the barest of nods. But then, "My computer calculates it will take at least six months for you to reach a break-even point. Even if your sales keep climbing at their present rate."

"But they're not climbing at our present rate," Raven countered. "They're accelerating."

"Slowly."

Raven's patience ended. "Look, Evan, I've got to get to the shop. Are we finished?"

"Not quite," he said, his smile evaporating. "There's the matter of Noel Dacco."

"Noel Dacco? I'm not interested in him."

"But he's interested in you."

So that's it, Raven realized. "And you're pimping for him."

Waxman's eyes flashed angrily. But he quickly took control of his temper. "What a pleasant way to put it."

"Aren't you?"

For a long moment Waxman said nothing. Then, "It would be good if you spent an evening with Dacco. He's very interested in you."

"And you've told him about my life in Naples."

"Of course. Why do you think he's interested in you? For your intellect?"

Raven gritted her teeth.

"It won't hurt you to spend a night with the man."

"I spend my nights with Tómas."

Waxman broke into a grin and pointed an accusing finger at her. "Not true. Gomez sleeps in his own quarters most nights."

"Not every night."

With a careless shrug, Waxman said, "You can spend a night with Dacco. If you don't, I'll have to shut down your boutique."

"You can't do that!"

"Can't I? Just try me."

"I'll tell Reverend Umber!"

"Hah! Our beloved minister. What do you think he'd do, once I've told him that you've been whoring here in his precious *Haven*?"

"That's not true!"

Waxman smiled thinly. "It doesn't have to be true, Raven dear. It just has to be believable. And I'll make him believe me."

Raven stared at the viewscreen, trying to think of something to say, some way to get out of this trap. I don't want him to close the shop; that would destroy Alicia and everything she's dreamed of. But if I do what he wants and Tómas finds out . . .

Then she realized that if she did what Waxman wanted, he'd have that to hold over her forever. Tómas would leave her. She'd be right back where she was before she came to *Haven*.

Waxman understood her silence. "You should go to the shop now. Call me this evening, when you get back home."

Raven nodded wordlessly.

"The bastard!"

Alicia's eyes blazed with fury.

Raven sat with her partner behind the boutique's counter. It had been a slow morning, yet it wasn't until nearly noon that the shop went empty enough for Raven to tell Alicia of her conversation with Waxman.

"I'll never get him off my back," Raven whispered, surprised at how weary, how desperate she felt.

"He'll be pulling my strings as long as I live," she added, close to tears.

Alicia stared at her in silence for several moments. Then she said, "As long as *he* lives."

Raven's eyes went wide as she realized what Alicia was thinking.

"No," she said softly. "We can't go that way."

"Why not? You, yourself, were all for it a few weeks ago. He's trying to kill you, isn't he?"

"Not murder."

"Justice," said Alicia.

"No."

"I'll do it. Gladly."

Raven leaned toward her friend and slid her arms around Alicia's shoulders. "Don't talk that way. That's not the way to go."

"How else are we going to get free of him?"

Raven straightened up and looked into Alicia's ice-blue eyes, murderously cold.

"I don't know," she admitted. "I don't know."

Alicia shook her head pityingly. "Reverend Umber's really changed you, hasn't he?"

Before Raven could reply, the shop's front door slid open and a trio of women strode in, their eyes goggling at the displays of clothing.

EVIDENCE?

TÓMAS GOMEZ SAT IN THE LIVING ROOM OF HIS QUARTERS, STARING FIXEDLY AT THE WALL SCREEN, HIS MAKESHIFT LABORATORY JAMMED WITH ANALYSIS EQUIPMENT, SENSOR receivers, and computers of half a dozen different types.

He ignored the mug of chilled *malteada* that he had made for himself. The drink rested on his cluttered coffee table, unnoticed.

Gomez studied the readouts from the analyses of the battered debris recovered from the seabed. Every reading of their age centered around the two-million-year mark.

Can Zworkyn be right? he asked himself. Was that city destroyed only two million years ago?

He leaned back in his sofa and rubbed his eyes. Two million years ago. Was Uranus knocked sideways *then*, not during the much earlier Late Bombardment? Could that be possible?

Taking in a deep breath, Gomez pushed himself to his feet. All around him, display screens showed scraps of metal, chips of stone, bits and pieces of the ruined city from the bottom of Uranus's worldwide ocean. The city was destroyed two million years ago, he told himself. That's what the evidence says and that must be what had happened.

But is that true? Could it be true? If it is, it flies in the face of all we've told ourselves about the history of the planet—of the whole damned solar system.

Yet that's what the evidence shows.

With a dogged shake of his head, Gomez stepped past the accumulation of sensors and computers and headed toward his bedroom. Get yourself cleaned up and then call Zworkyn. Talk it over with him. And then—maybe—face Abbott with your evidence.

Briefly he thought about calling Raven. Then he decided against that. I've bothered her enough with this problem. She listens, but this is way above her level of understanding. I'll talk to her tomorrow, when we have dinner.

Twenty minutes later, showered and dressed in clean clothes, he started for Zworkyn's quarters, in *Haven II*.

For one of the rare times in her young life, Raven felt nervous about going out on a date.

Dacco had called her at the boutique and asked to take her to dinner. Raven knew that the man had much more than dinner in mind, but she also understood that Waxman would shut down their boutique if she refused Dacco.

To the man's image on the shop's desktop screen, she had said carefully, "Yes, I'll go to dinner with you. But please don't expect anything more."

Dacco had smiled toothily. "Dinner at seven P.M."

"In the main restaurant here in *Haven*," Raven had said.

"Fine. I'll call for you at your quarters at six forty-five or so."

Before Raven could reply, he cut off the connection.

Raven said nothing about her dinner date to Alicia. They closed the store at 5:00 P.M.—actually shooing out a pair of women who'd been browsing through the skirts and blouses for the better part of an hour.

"Time wasters," Raven muttered as she and Alicia turned off the display lights.

"Oh, they'll be back," Alicia said, with a smile. "Sooner or later."

"To waste more time."

"Patience. You have to be patient. And remember that the customer is always right."

Alicia's smile was infectious. Raven grinned back at her. "Whether she's right or wrong."

"Exactly."

Raven rushed home and changed into one of the boutique's outfits: a sleek pale pink dress with knee-length skirt and round-necked bodice, attractive without being overtly seductive. You want to keep Noel happy, she told herself, but not salivating.

Dacco rang her door buzzer precisely at six forty-five, wearing a one-piece form-fitting outfit of white and gold.

His eyes brightened when Raven opened the door.

"You look beautiful!" he said, then amended, "You *are* beautiful."

"And you look dashing," answered Raven, as she closed the door behind her. "Very handsome."

Dacco offered his arm. Raven took it, smiling sweetly, and together they walked to the restaurant.

"Do you really think so?" Zworkyn asked.

Gomez shrugged. "I don't know. All the evidence we've dug up so far leads to the conclusion that Uranus was clobbered only a couple of million years ago. But . . ."

Gomez had ridden over to *Haven II* and gone straight to Zworkyn's quarters. Despite the piles of equipment arrayed from wall to wall, the engineer's living room was as tidy and precisely arranged as a military barracks. Everything in place, neat and well-ordered. Even the coffee urn that Zworkyn had brought in from the kitchen seemed to be polished and standing at attention.

Now they sat on the living room sofa, side by side, frustrated and unhappy.

"But?" Zworkyn prompted.

"But it's kind of fantastic to think that some alien invaders wiped Uranus clean of life."

"That's what the evidence is telling us."

Gomez shook his head slowly. "Maybe that's what we want the evidence to say, and we're fooling ourselves."

Zworkyn stared at the younger man. "Maybe," he conceded.

"We should try to come up with an alternative scenario," Gomez mused.

"Like what?"

Gomez shrugged elaborately. "Damned if I know."

"There *isn't* any other possibility!" Zworkyn shouted, startling Gomez. "It happened two million years ago, not four billion."

Staring into space, Gomez muttered, "Aliens entered the solar system—"

"About two million years ago," Zworkyn added.

"And they found an intelligent civilization on Uranus."

"And wiped it out."

"Why?"

"That's not our problem," Zworkyn said. "Our problem is to prove that our dating is correct."

Gomez nodded wearily. But suddenly he brightened. "Wait a minute. If I remember my classroom studies correctly . . ."

He got up and threaded his way through the rows of equipment, heading for Zworkyn's desk. "May I use your desktop, Vincente?"

With a gracious nod, Zworkyn replied, "Be my guest."

Sitting at the engineer's desk, Gomez tapped the computer's ON button and said, "History of Neptune's moons, please."

Zworkyn got up from the sofa, puzzlement showing on his face. "Neptune?"

It took a few minutes of jiggering the program that the desktop brought up, but at last Gomez leaned back in the desk chair and gestured at the computer's screen.

"I thought I remembered this from my history lessons."

Zworkyn bent over Gomez's shoulder and stared at the screen.

"Display system of Neptune's moons, please," Gomez commanded.

"Thirteen moons," Zworkyn read off the computer's monitor. "Only one big one, Triton. The rest are just little chunks of rock."

"Show history of Neptune system," Gomez commanded.

The screen blinked once, then showed the planet Neptune with a retinue of twenty-five tiny moons, bits of irregularly shaped rock and metal too small to pull themselves into spherical bodies.

Then a much larger body—perfectly spherical—swung through the system, tossing the tiny moonlets into a wild jumble of looping, asymmetrical orbits. As the two men watched, twelve of the moonlets were hurled out of the picture entirely, while the rest settled into new orbits around Neptune. As did the much larger body.

"That's Triton," Zworkyn said, awed.

"Right," Gomez agreed. "According to present thinking, that interaction happened during the time of the Late Bombardment."

"Some four billion years ago," said Zworkyn.

"But what if it happened only two million years ago? What if this cataclysm forced a much larger moon into a collision with Uranus?"

"But the analysis doesn't show a big moon."

"That doesn't mean there wasn't a major-sized moon in the system. A moon big enough to knock Uranus sideways."

Zworkyn reached for a chair and dropped into it. "Orbital analysis might be able to prove the dating."

"Maybe," said Gomez.

"And if the dating shows it happened two million years ago . . ."

"We've proved my theory," Gomez said.

For several moments Zworkyn remained silent, staring at the mayhem that the computer screen was still displaying.

Then he said, "We've got to show all this to Abbott. First thing tomorrow morning."

truth

++
+++++++++ +++++++++++ +++++++++++++++++++++++++++

Raven was growing more nervous with each step as she and Dacco strolled leisurely along the passageway toward her quarters.

Dinner had been pleasant enough. Noel chattered endlessly about himself, especially about the interview he was planning with Tómas.

"Interesting fellow," he was saying.

Raven nodded absently, thinking about how she could get rid of Dacco at her door.

Smiling contentedly, he pointed. "That's your place, isn't it?"

"Yes," said Raven.

They walked up to the door. Raven turned toward Dacco, her back to the closed door, got up on tiptoes and gave him a peck on the lips.

"Goodnight, Noel."

"Aren't you going to invite me in?"

"I'm afraid not."

"You expect me to go all the way back to *Haven II*, alone and forlorn?"

"I really can't ask you in."

His smile fixed on his face, Dacco said, "You could if you wanted to."

"Noel . . . I'm practically engaged to Tómas."

"Practically."

A youngish couple ambled past them, smiled hello, and continued on their way.

"Young love," sighed Dacco, following them with his eyes.

"Goodnight, Noel."

His smile disappeared. Looking down at her, Dacco said, "No, Raven. That's not the way this evening is going to end."

"Noel . . ."

He reached past her and tapped out her entry code on the door's control panel. Almost silently, the door slid open.

Tómas Gomez stepped through the shuttle's hatch and back into the empty reception area of the *Haven* habitat. Alone, he trudged past the silent ID computers and made his way through the hatch and into the passageway that led to his quarters.

Glancing at his wristwatch, he saw that it was past eleven o'clock. I wonder if Raven's still awake? he asked himself. Without any real deliberation, he started for her quarters.

Dacco pushed Raven into the living room of her apartment. The front door slid shut behind them.

Raven glared up at him. "Noel, this isn't going to work. I'm not going to bed with you."

"Oh, yes you are," Dacco said, grinning at her. "Just pretend you're back in Naples, on the job."

"No!"

He smacked her in the face. Not too hard, just enough to make her understand who was in charge. Hardly left a mark on her cheek.

"Be reasonable, Raven," he said, calmly, placatingly. "If you don't come through Waxman will close up your little shop."

Growing angrier with each breath she took, Raven hissed, "Waxman can go to hell. And you with him!"

Dacco let out a mournful sigh. "Do you want me to get rough with you?"

"I want you to leave!"

"Come on, Raven. I'm not so terrible. And you're not in a position to turn me down. What will your friend Alicia do when Waxman closes up your boutique?"

"Get out!" Raven screamed.

Dacco's smile turned sinister. "Some like it cold," he misquoted, "some like it hot . . ."

Raven glanced around the living room, looking for a weapon, a tool, an ornament, anything that she might use to defend herself. She backed away from Dacco, her eyes searching.

"Would you like some Rust?" Dacco asked, drawing a slim plastic bag from his pocket. "It'll make it easier for you."

"Go away! Leave me alone!"

Instead, Dacco grabbed her and ripped her dress down off her shoulders. Then he swept her struggling form up in his arms and headed for the bedroom. She kicked the empty air so hard that one of her shoes flew off; she struggled to free her arms, pinned to Dacco's chest, to no avail.

Gomez arrived at Raven's door and hesitated. She's probably asleep, he told himself. You don't want to make a nuisance of yourself.

But his left hand was already tapping out the entry code on Raven's door pad.

The door slid open with barely a sound. Gomez looked in. The living room was empty, but its lights were on.

She's not asleep yet, Gomez told himself. He stepped into the living room. The door to the bedroom was open and he heard Raven shout, "Stop it! Get off!"

Tómas dashed to the bedroom door. Raven was on the bed, struggling fruitlessly, Dacco atop her, pinning her down.

Without an instant's hesitation Tómas raced to the bed and slammed his right fist into Dacco's kidney. His spine arched and he yowled with pain. Tómas grabbed at him with both hands and pulled him off Raven.

Dacco fell off the bed. The expression on his face was murderous.

"You're gonna pay for that," he growled, climbing slowly, painfully to his feet.

Tómas backed away a couple of steps, both fists raised. He saw Raven sit up on the bed, the bodice of her dress torn from her shoulders, her chest heaving, eyes wide as she stared at Tómas.

He quickly returned his eyes to Dacco, who was stepping toward him, his hands raised in a karate posture, bloody fury blazing in his eyes. Dacco was several centimeters taller than Gomez, and bulkier in the shoulders and arms.

Dacco lunged at Tómas, who ducked under his arm and rammed his head into Dacco's midsection. The breath gushed out of Dacco's lungs. Tómas kicked at Dacco's knee and the black man crumpled to the floor.

Raven swung off the bed, the phone console from the night table in both hands, and smashed it onto the back of Dacco's head. He slumped over, facedown, onto the carpet.

Raven looked up at him. "Tómas," she breathed.

"Are you all right?"

"Yes. . . . I think so."

He saw that the side of her face bore the red imprint of Dacco's fingers. Looking down at the unconscious form, he muttered, "I should kill the bastard."

Raven tossed the phone console onto the bed and rushed into Tómas's arms. "He was going to rape me!"

"I should kill him," Gomez repeated.

"No!" Raven snapped. "No. Just call the security team. Let them deal with him."

Without taking his right arm away from Raven, Tómas spoke into his wrist phone. At their feet, Dacco groaned and began to stir.

Raven slipped out of Tómas's protective grasp and sank wearily onto the bed. He stood beside her, looking down at Dacco's writhing form.

"You broke my knee," Dacco moaned.

"I should have broken your damned neck," said Tómas.

Dacco touched his knee lightly. It looked swollen, beneath his trousers.

"Where did you learn to fight like that?" Raven asked.

Tómas came close to smiling. "You grow up in the slums of Santiago, where I did, you learn to fight. Or you die."

"I'll get you for this," Dacco muttered, rubbing his knee.

"When you can walk again, come and see me," said Tómas.

A uniformed security team—one lanky, leggy young man and one elfin, dark-haired young woman—appeared at the bedroom doorway. They stared at Dacco, still sitting on the floor.

"What the hell happened here?" the young man asked.

"They attacked me!" Dacco snarled.

Raven, holding her tattered dress up to her shoulders, pointed to Dacco and said, "He tried to rape me." Gesturing toward Tómas, she went on, "My fiancé saved me."

The woman called for a medical team. Once they arrived

and carted Dacco off to the hospital, together with the security team, Tómas stared in wonder at Raven.

"You told them I'm your fiancé," he said.

"Yes, I did."

"Am I? I mean, really?"

Raven smiled warmly. "Yes, Tómas darling. Really and truly."

"This proves nothing," said Gordon Abbott.

Zworkyn and Gomez were sitting before Abbott's spotlessly clean desk. Nothing on it but a phone console, a fancy pair of pens and an ancient wire in-basket, conspicuously empty. The viewscreen that covered the wall to their right showed a display of Uranus and its moons.

"Nothing?" Gomez bleated. "It shows that Uranus was knocked into its present orientation two million years ago, not four billion!"

"By mysterious alien invaders," said Abbott, irony dripping from his lips.

"It's what the available data shows," Zworkyn said calmly.

Abbott shook his head. "It's all conjecture, Vincente."

"Conjecture?" Gomez screeched.

"Nonsense," Abbott insisted.

"It's what the available data shows," Zworkyn repeated.

Abbott shook his head. "It's conjecture, pure and simple. You started with a premise and you've arranged the available evidence to make things work out the way you want them to."

"No," Gomez countered. "That's what the available evidence shows."

"It couldn't have taken place only two million years ago. That's ridiculous."

"It's what the evidence shows!"

"It's what the evidence *you've selected* to deal with indicates," Abbott insisted. Unconsciously tugging at his moustache, he added, "Good heavens, man, you're flying in the face of established astronomical fact."

"Not fact," Gomez insisted. "Conjecture. Blaming everything on the Late Bombardment is where the conjecture lies."

"And what is inventing an alien invasion of the solar system? Where are the facts supporting that piece of fantasy?"

Zworkyn said mildly, "I recall hearing a line that some twentieth-century astronomer spoke: 'Just because an idea is crazy doesn't mean it's wrong.'"

"It doesn't mean it's right, either," Abbott snapped.

The office fell silent. Zworkyn and Gomez sat on one side of the desk, Abbott on the other, glaring at one another.

At last, Abbott asked more moderately, "Do you have any evidence that proves your hypothesis? Anything that undeniably shows you're right and the rest of the astronomical community is wrong?"

Zworkyn shifted uneasily in his chair. "Well . . ."

"Undeniably," Abbott emphasized.

"I think I can get it," Gomez said.

"You can?"

His hands trembling excitedly, Gomez said, "If we can use Big Eye—"

"The lunar Farside telescope?"

"Yes. The moons that were ejected from Uranus's orbit, if we can locate one of those moons, would that satisfy you?"

Abbott stared at the younger man for a long, silent moment. Then he murmured, "And the data shows that its current position agrees with the idea that it was tossed out of Uranus orbit only two million years ago. . . ."

Brightening, Gomez added, "If it was ejected during the Late Bombardment, it'll be too far away even for Big Eye to pick out."

"It's a long shot," Zworkyn murmured.

"But if it works, it'll prove we're right," said Gomez. Then he turned to Abbott. "If we can get a few hours on Big Eye."

Abbott started to frown, but eased into a slow grin instead. "I'll get Big Eye for you . . . if you come up with a reasonable approximation of where your errant moon should be."

Gomez nodded enthusiastically. "I will! Or bust a gut trying."

trial <2>

Kyle Umber wore his usual spotless white suit as he entered the conference room. Raven, Gomez and Waxman got to their feet as the minister went to his chair at the head of the oval table.

"Where's Mr. Dacco?" Umber asked, as he sat down.

"He should be here," Waxman said, his brows knitting. "He was released from the hospital earlier this morning."

The conference room was small, almost intimate. Its walls were smooth, bare, gray floor-to-ceiling viewscreens, all blank at the moment. The ceiling glowed with glareless lighting.

Umber's usually smiling face pulled into a frown. "We can't hold this hearing without—"

The door that connected to the passageway outside slid open and Noel Dacco limped in. He leaned heavily on a cane and his head was swathed in bandages.

"Sorry I'm late," said Dacco as he hobbled to the empty chair at the foot of the table.

Waxman asked, "How are you, Noel?"

With a rueful grin Dacco said, "I'm one of the walking wounded. The medics said my knee will heal in a few days. My concussion is only a slight one, nothing to worry about."

"You could have been killed," Waxman said.

Gomez, tense as a hunting cat, muttered to himself, "He should have been."

From the head of the table, Umber said in a carefully modulated tone, "Now that we're all here we can begin. We are here to determine what happened two nights ago that led to Mr. Dacco's injuries."

Waxman said, "Violent assault."

Umber seemed to ignore the comment. Looking down the length of the conference table, he said, "Mr. Dacco, you are accusing Ms. Marchesi and Dr. Gomez of attacking you."

Dacco nodded, wincing.

Turning to Raven, Umber continued, "And Ms. Marchesi, you are accusing Mr. Dacco of sexual assault."

"He would have raped me if Tómas hadn't intervened."

Dacco objected, "We were engaging in some bedtime fun when he"—pointing at Gomez—"burst in and attacked me."

"He was trying to rape me!" Raven cried.

"You can't rape a whore," said Dacco, smirking.

Tómas bolted up from his chair.

"Sit down!" Umber commanded, in a voice of sudden thunder.

Tómas stared at the minister, but dropped back onto his chair, his face red with anger.

Patiently, Umber listened first to Dacco's version of the night's happenings, then to Tómas's.

Turning to Raven, he asked gently, "And what do you have to say, Ms. Marchesi?"

Her face still bearing a slightly bluish bruise, Raven replied, "I had dinner with Noel at Evan Waxman's request. He said he would shut down the boutique Alicia Polanyi and I had just recently opened if I didn't."

"I never said that!" Waxman objected.

Ignoring the remark, Raven continued, "Noel walked home

with me from the restaurant. I said goodnight to him out in the passageway, in front of my door. But he forced his way into my quarters, pawed me, tore my dress and carried me into the bedroom. I tried to fight him, but he was too strong, too powerful. If Tómas hadn't come in, he would have raped me."

Umber turned to Gomez. "You just happened to pop into her quarters."

His voice trembling, Tómas answered, "Raven is my fiancée, sir."

"Utter bilge!" Waxman exploded. Jabbing a finger toward Raven, he went on, "She's got him wrapped around her little finger! He'll say anything she tells him to!"

"Quiet, Evan," Umber said. Returning his focus to Gomez, he asked, "What did you see once you entered Ms. Marchesi's quarters?"

With a murderous glance at Dacco, Tómas replied, "He was on top of her, on the bed. She was struggling and shouting. I pulled him off her."

"He dislocated my knee and she gave me a concussion," Dacco grumbled.

Umber closed his eyes momentarily. When he opened them he looked down the table toward Dacco. "Unfortunately, we have no visual or even audio record of what took place inside Ms. Marchesi's quarters."

Waxman smiled slightly and cocked a brow at Dacco.

"But we do have this," Umber continued. Raising his head slightly, he spoke to the sound system built into the ceiling, "Show passageway security camera record."

The wall screen behind Waxman glowed to life. He and Dacco both turned in their chairs to look at it. On the other side of the table, Raven and Gomez also stared at the screen.

From a camera built into the ceiling of the passageway that went past Raven's quarters they saw and heard Dacco and Raven.

The two of them walked up to Raven's door. She turned toward him, her back to the closed door, got up on tiptoes and pecked at his lips.

"Goodnight, Noel."

"Aren't you going to invite me in?"

"I'm afraid not."

"You expect me to go all the way back to *Haven II*, alone and forlorn?"

"I really can't ask you in."

His smile fixed on his face, Dacco said, "You could if you wanted to."

"Noel . . . I'm practically engaged to Tómas."

"Practically."

A youngish couple ambled past them, smiled hello, and continued on their way.

"Young love," sighed Dacco, following them with his eyes.

"Goodnight, Noel," Raven repeated, more firmly.

His smile disappeared. Looking down at her, Dacco said, "No, Raven. That's not the way this evening is going to end."

"Noel . . ."

He reached past her and tapped out her entry code on the door's control panel. Almost silently, the door slid open. He pushed Raven into the apartment and stepped in after her. The door slid shut.

Umber's face seemed set in stone. "She didn't invite you into her quarters, Mr. Dacco."

Dacco shrugged. "Not in so many words. . . ."

"Where did you get the door's entry code?"

His eyes shifting momentarily to Waxman, Dacco admitted, "Evan told me."

Waxman sat in silence, his eyes staring straight ahead.

Umber's gaze was locked on Dacco's face. He repeated, "Ms. Marchesi did not invite you into her quarters."

Again Dacco muttered, "Not in so many words."

Kyle Umber seemed to relax, although his facial expression remained grave. For long moments the conference room was absolutely silent, except for the faint whisper of the air circulating system.

At last Umber made up his mind. "Mr. Dacco, I personally find your conduct reprehensible. If I allowed this case to go before a jury I'm sure you would swiftly be found guilty of sexual assault and sentenced to our habitat's prison. Therefore, I strongly recommend that you leave *Haven* on the next departing vessel. Return to Earth as quickly as you can, and try to mend your ways."

Dacco stared back at the minister. "I'm supposed to interview Dr. Gomez. . . ."

"I don't think that will be possible now," Umber said, his voice cold and hard.

"Totally impossible," Tómas confirmed, through gritted teeth.

"Go back to Earth," Umber repeated. "Try to find God's mercy and forgiveness."

"And if I refuse?"

"You will be placed under arrest, put on trial, found guilty, and put in jail."

Looking alarmed for the first time, Dacco glanced at Waxman, who refused to return his gaze.

"Well?" Umber demanded. "What is your decision?"

His shoulders sagging, Dacco said mildly, "I'll leave. I'll return to Earth."

"Good," said Umber. "And I'll pray that God brings you to His path." Glancing at the others around the small table, he added, "This hearing is ended. Praise God."

Raven reached for Tómas's hand as she echoed, "Praise God."

Waxman, Abbott, and Dacco

The Reverend Kyle Umber remained in his chair, hands folded as if in prayer, while the rest of the group got up from the conference table and headed for the door.

"Evan," he said, as Waxman went past him. "Please wait. Sit down."

Waxman hesitated, then turned around and took the chair at the minister's left. The others stepped out into the passageway. The door slid shut.

For a nerve-tightening few seconds, Umber stared into Waxman's face, as if searching for something, some sign, some expression.

Impatiently, Waxman said, "Well, what is it, Kyle?"

"You gave Dacco the combination to Ms. Marchesi's door control?"

Waxman's eyes shifted away from Umber's face. "I don't know. I may have."

"You did."

With a shrug, Waxman said, "What if I did? He was taking a whore to dinner. What happened afterward was only to be expected."

"She's not a whore. Not anymore."

Waxman laughed. "She comes to my bed when I want her to."

"Because you threaten to close the shop she and Ms. Polanyi have opened."

"That's just her excuse. She's a whore, plain and simple."

Umber stared at him, his face a frigid mask. Then, "I want your resignation, Evan. It pains me to say it, but I don't see how we can continue with you heading this habitat's administration."

For a moment Waxman looked surprised. Then his face broke into a wide grin. "My resignation! You want me to resign. That's rich. Kyle, you're really very funny."

"This is not a laughing matter."

"Yes it is," Waxman retorted. "It's ridiculous. You think you have the power to fire me? That's beyond ridiculous. It's ludicrous. It's—"

Calmly, Umber interrupted, "And this drug trafficking has to stop, as well. I won't have it."

"You won't have it? Hah! You've got it, Kyle. You're stuck with it! How do you think we keep this home for runaway bums and prostitutes running? By prayer? It's the money we take in from Rust and other narcotics that keeps *Haven* afloat financially. Cut that off and you'll be out of business in less than a year."

"God will find a way to keep us going."

"God's already found the way, and I'm administrating it. Open your eyes, Kyle!"

"I won't have it."

"You've got it. And I've got the Council. Try to oust me and they'll laugh in your face. Maybe they'll vote to kick *you* out of *Haven*."

"They wouldn't do that."

"Oh no? Don't be so sure. You're just a figurehead, Kyle. We could find another one easily enough."

"You wouldn't!"

"Don't tempt me."

Umber sagged in his chair. Waxman stared at him, gloating, for a few moments, then got up and walked out of the conference room, leaving the minister sitting there, alone and silent.

Tómas Gomez walked Raven to her door. She tapped out the entry code on the door's keyboard and gestured him to enter.

Glancing up at the passageway's ceiling, Tómas said, "I think I'd better not, Raven."

With a smile, she replied, "Not even for lunch?"

Obviously torn, Tómas said, "I have a lot of work ahead of me. An enormous amount."

"You can tell me about it over lunch."

He broke into a sheepish grin. "All right. But it's all astronomical stuff."

"Tell me about it. Teach me."

Tómas nodded, smiled and followed Raven into her quarters.

The clock on Abbott's desktop computer read 1:45 as Tómas came through the door. Vincente Zworkyn, sitting in front of Abbott's desk, turned to greet the new arrival.

From his chair behind the desk, Abbott asked, "How'd the hearing go?"

Striding to the empty upholstered chair in front of the desk, Tómas answered, "Reverend Umber ordered Dacco to clear out."

"Really?"

"Really," Tómas replied. Hunching forward in his chair, he said, "Now let's get down to work."

With a nod, Abbott said, "You've put yourself into a lovely trap, my boy."

"Trap?"

"Yes indeed. Vincente and I have been going over the available data, and it looks awfully slim."

Zworkyn said, "The estimates of the moons ejected from orbits around Uranus are nothing more than that: estimates. They're based on theoretical conjectures, not observational facts."

Tómas nodded. "But they're all we've got to go on."

"Yes," said Abbott. "And you want to use these guesses to—"

"They're more than guesses," Tómas objected. "They're based on backtracking the orbits of Uranus's existing moons."

"Not much better than guesses," Abbott said.

Zworkyn said nothing.

His back stiffening, Tómas said, "Well, it's the best we've got. We'll have to work with that."

Smoothing his moustache with a finger, Abbott said, "I was afraid that would be your response."

"It's better than nothing," Zworkyn offered.

"Not by much," said Abbott.

Tómas asked, "How much time can we get on Big Eye?"

"That depends on when we want the time," Abbott replied. "It varies from twelve to maybe twenty-four hours."

"*Hours?*" Tómas gasped.

Abbott nodded. "Time is a precious commodity."

"Hours," said Zworkyn. "That means we'll have to have a pretty damned precise estimate of the moon's location before we ask the Big Eye people for some time."

"Hours," Tómas muttered. "Hours."

Abbott commiserated. "It's going to be like asking a blind man to find a penny in a dark alley."

"Worse," said Zworkyn.

Abbott shook his head. To Tómas he said, "You're going to need an incredible amount of luck, my boy."

"Luck, *mi trasero*," Tómas growled. "We're going to need to work our tails off. And then some."

His healing leg propped up on the bed of his stateroom, Noel Dacco repeated to his visitor, "I don't want any slip-ups."

His visitor was wearing the sky-blue uniform of one of *Haven*'s security police, a sergeant's chevrons on its sleeve, the name JACOBI lettered on an ID card pinned to his jacket's chest. He nodded knowingly. "There won't be any slip-ups. We've done this kind of thing before. Plenty times."

"For what I'm paying you," Dacco went on, his voice low and hard, "I want the job done right."

Jacobi was slight of build, his face all bones and glittering eyes, his hair shaved down to a thin fuzz. "It'll be done right. Just as you said."

"Break his leg, fracture his skull. Maybe pop some ribs for good measure."

"Look," Sergeant Jacobi said, "my people know what they're doing. We control our whole section of the habitat. Somebody gets out of line, we bring them back where they belong."

Dacco stared at the man. "Make it look like an accident. But make sure he knows who did it to him."

"He'll know. I'll tell him myself."

"Good."

The overhead speaker announced, *"Departure in fifteen minutes. All visitors must return to the habitat."*

Jacobi got to his feet. "Gotta go."

Dacco nodded. "His name is—"

"Tómas Gomez," said Jacobi. "You already told me,"

"Let me know when it's done."

"Right."

Jacobi left the narrow stateroom. Dacco stared at the closed door for long minutes. Give the snotty little bastard what he deserves, he told himself. Break him up real good.

neeDLe in a haystack

"These are *estimates*, Tómas," said Zworkyn, his voice edging close to exasperation. "Not much better than guesses."

The two men were sitting side by side in Zworkyn's quarters, staring at a wall screen that showed the planet Uranus surrounded by dozens of tiny moons.

Without taking his eyes from the screen, Gomez muttered, "When you're given a lemon, make lemonade."

Zworkyn sighed dramatically. "I just don't see how you're going to get anything useful from these wild-ass guesses."

Gomez turned in his chair to look at the engineer. "They're more than guesses, Vincente. They're based on backtracking the orbits of the moons now in orbit around Uranus."

"With error bars on the estimates that are bigger than the orbits themselves."

"That's what we have to work with. We'll have to project these estimates and see where they lead us."

Zworkyn shook his head. "You have nothing to offer but blood, toil, tears and sweat."

Gomez smiled thinly. "Not much blood, but plenty of toil and sweat."

Smiling back at the younger man, Zworkyn said, "I understand. You're telling me to stop crabbing and get to work."

"Sort of. The computers will do most of the actual work. All we have to do is to program them correctly."

Zworkyn puffed out a sigh. "All right. Tell me what you need me to do."

Sitting behind the boutique's central counter, tapping out the command to close the shop's blinds, Alicia asked Raven, "How's Tómas?"

Raven was straightening up a rack of dresses that had been pawed through by several customers. She shrugged her slim shoulders. "I haven't seen much of him this past week. He looks tired, but kind of happy."

"Like I feel," Alicia said, leaning back in her padded chair. It had been their busiest day ever; from the moment they'd opened that morning the shop had been filled with eager, chattering women fondling through the merchandise on display.

"How'd we do today?" Raven asked.

Pointing at her computer screen with a happy smile, Alicia said, "Best day ever. We're going to need to restock our inventory sooner than we thought."

"Wonderful!"

"But Tómas," Alicia asked again. "How is he?"

"Like I said," Raven replied. "Tired but happy."

"Have you set a date for the wedding?"

Raven shook her head. "Not yet. He's too busy with his astronomy work to even think about a wedding."

"But you do plan to get married, don't you?"

"He insists on it. Says we're living in sin and he wants to make an honest woman of me."

Alicia couldn't help giggling. "He must have been raised Catholic."

"What else?"

Suddenly Alicia's expression changed. Her smile faded. Her eyes misted over.

Raven stared at her friend. "What's the matter?"

Getting up from her chair, Alicia answered, "Nothing much. I'm jealous, that's all."

"Jealous?" Raven came away from the clothing rack, stepped around the counter and embraced her friend.

"Alicia, there must be at least three or four men to every woman in this habitat . . ."

"I know," said Alicia. "But look at me. Skin and bones. A recovering drug addict. Who'd want me?"

Raven held her by both shoulders and stared into her eyes. "You've got good bones. And a pretty face. All you need is to put on a few kilos and you'll be stunning."

With a forlorn nod, Alicia said, "My parents never married. I don't think their parents were married, either." She shook her head. "But there it is. Wedding bells. I'm like a teenager."

"It's natural," Raven said.

"But not for me."

"Don't be so sure."

"Easy for you to say."

Raven smiled at her friend. "You do have to make an effort. You can't sit in this shop and then go straight home."

Smiling back faintly, Alicia said, "And then get up the next morning and come straight to the shop."

"We need to find somebody to make a foursome out of us."

"I don't want to tangle up your relationship with Tómas."

"Nonsense. We'll get started on this right away."

"But—"

Raven placed a fingertip on Alicia's lips. "No buts. You allowed me to join you here at the shop. The least I can do is help you to find a little happiness."

ᚱᛖᚢᛖᚾᚷᛖ

"It's useless," Tómas moaned. "we're using data that was assumed to be some four billion years old. nothing more than an educated guess."

Sitting across her kitchen's narrow table from the astronomer, Raven asked, "The data isn't good enough?"

Tómas shook his head wearily. "It's all guesses. Theory. Hot air."

"But you said you thought the moons were scattered two million years ago, not four billion."

"That's a guess, too. My guess."

"Isn't there any way to prove that?"

He stared at her. "Raven, what do you think I've been trying to do for the past two weeks? Zworkyn and I have been going through the numbers backward and forward and upside-down! Nothing works!"

"What about the big moon, Triton? Could you backtrack its orbit or something?"

"Pah! You don't understand. You just don't understand anything!" Tómas pushed his barely touched plate of dinner away and got to his feet.

"Where are you going?" Raven asked.

"Back to Zworkyn's place. At least I can talk to him. He knows what we're up against."

And he stormed out of the kitchen, through the living room, and left Raven sitting at the table alone.

In *Haven*'s surveillance center, Sergeant Jacobi sat in front of a spare monitor screen. Three other men, all in security department uniforms, hunched behind him.

"There he is now," said Jacobi, pointing to Tómas Gomez's figure as the astronomer left Raven's quarters.

The men nodded. "Shouldn't be much trouble," said one of them, a chunky, dour-faced Asian.

"Get him when he's alone. No witnesses. Plain clothes."

"Sure." Straightening up, the Asian turned to his two companions. "Come on, our shift's just about over. Let's get out of these uniforms."

"Hoodies," said Jacobi. "The surveillance cameras won't be able to identify you."

The Asian nodded. He left with the two others following him.

Jacobi turned back to the monitor screen, a grim smile creasing his face. He whispered, "You're in for a surprise, smart boy."

As he stared at the computer's latest imagery, Vincente Zworkyn shook his head.

Turning to Gomez, perched tensely beside him on the edge of the sofa, Zworkyn said mournfully, "Another dead end, Tómas." He pointed at the screen. "See? The trajectory data disappears into the noise."

Gomez nodded. "Let's go on to the next one."

"What for?" Zworkyn demanded, his voice rising. "We've tracked six of the moons and their paths all get swallowed up in gibberish. It's hopeless!"

"We still have a half-dozen more moons to track."

"And their trajectories will all end up in the noise, too! Admit it, we're defeated."

His jaw settling into a stubborn scowl, Gomez said, "The information is there, Vincente. I know it is."

"No," Zworkyn countered. "You *think* it is. You hope it is. That doesn't mean that it's really there."

"It's *got* to be there!"

"Why? Because you want it to be? The universe doesn't play favorites, Tómas. You've got to know when to fold 'em, buddy."

Never! Gomez said to himself. But he slowly got up from the sofa and, without a word, left Zworkyn's quarters.

Out in the empty passageway, Tómas debated whether he should go to his own quarters or ask Raven if he could spend the night with her.

If she'd have me, he said to himself. I treated her pretty shabbily at dinner. He glanced at his wristwatch: almost midnight. She's probably already asleep.

Still, he walked to the embarkation center where the shuttle was moored.

There was only one person at the center, an elderly white-bearded clerk sitting comfortably behind a semicircular desk, intently watching a motion picture of some sort on his desktop screen.

He looked up as Tómas approached. "Evenin', Doc. Workin' late again, huh."

Tómas nodded and gave him a half-hearted smile.

"You're in luck, Doc," said the clerk. "We got one bird all primed and ready to go."

"Thanks," said Tómas. He ducked through the hatch and entered the shuttle's passenger deck. It was empty, except for him.

"Bon voyage," called the clerk.

Tómas made a half-hearted wave for him.

The shuttles were automated, no crew aboard. Tómas took a seat, the hatch swung shut, and within less than a minute he felt the subtle surge of acceleration. Five minutes later the shuttle made a little lurch that meant it had docked at *Haven*.

I wonder if Raven will open her door for me? Tómas asked himself as he stepped through the shuttle's hatch and into the empty reception area. I wasn't much fun for her at dinner.

Still, he walked through the reception area and out into the passageway that led to Raven's quarters. The passageway was empty, except for a trio of kids in hoodies lounging a few dozen meters up ahead. Tómas paid them no mind.

Until, as he passed them, one half whispered, "Hello, Doc."

Slowing his pace, Tómas asked, "Do I know you?"

"Naw. But we know you."

They weren't kids, Tómas realized as the three of them surrounded him. Two grabbed his arms and the third smashed a paralyzing blow to his nose. Tómas's head snapped back. He struggled to free his arms. A punch to his kidney collapsed him and he sagged to the ground.

One of his assailants pulled a hammer from his jacket. "Compliments of Noel Dacco, pal." He smashed Tómas's left leg just below the kneecap. The pain was shattering. Then another crushing blow to his head and Tómas blacked out.

When he regained consciousness he was lying on the passageway floor, bleeding, his leg broken and his skull fractured. As if from an incredible distance he could hear the sound of a trio of footfalls running away.

book six

THE SAINT

ƘƳLƐ UMbƐr

Ƙƴle umber always insisted that he was not a saint.

"You have to be dead before you can be made a saint," he would say, with that boyish smile of his. "I'm still alive and kicking."

Now, though, as he knelt alone in his private quarters, the memory of that little piece of self-serving humility bedeviled him. The arrogance of it. The self-important smugness. Here we have several thousand migrants from Earth—the poor, the hopeless, the lost—and I joke about being worthy of sainthood.

He had been on his knees for the better part of an hour, vainly seeking a path out of the trap he'd built for himself. You don't run this habitat, he realized. Evan Waxman does. And you let him do it! You stood aside, content to be admired by the poor souls arriving here, and let Evan take up the controls of the habitat.

Rust. Narcotics. God knows what else is taking place in that tower Evan's built, right under my nose. And I've been too vain, too conceited, too stupid to take notice of it.

Fool. Blind, arrogant, trusting fool.

I've let Evan place me on a pedestal. And now I don't know how to climb down off it and take control of *Haven* back into my own hands.

Pride, Reverend Umber told himself. The sin of pride.

Umber remembered the words of St. Augustine: It was pride that changed angels into devils.

Pride. Blind, stupid, self-glorifying pride. The sin from which all others arise.

Slowly, painfully, Umber struggled to his feet. All around him lay the trappings of power, the ornaments of selfish pride. His quarters resembled a scene out of ancient royalty: luxurious damask draperies and silken bed linens, bejeweled chandeliers and fine graceful furniture.

All the embellishments of wealth and power. Useless. Vain, self-glorifying, self-defeating pride.

I wanted to create a new heaven, here among the distant worlds, far from the corruption and temptations of Earth. And all I've accomplished is to create a center for drugs, narcotics, lustful sin. I've built a modern hell, not a new heaven.

Tottering before his handsome desk, surrounded by lush foliage and exquisite furniture, Umber cried aloud, "Lord, show me the way!"

But he heard no answer.

Raven was undressing for bed when the phone buzzed.

It must be Tómas, she thought. For an instant she hesitated. After the way he behaved at dinner, why should I talk to him? But she was already leaning across her bed, reaching for the phone. He's under tremendous stress, she told herself. I shouldn't get frosty with him.

The face in the phone screen was obviously a nurse. Tómas has been hurt. Badly. Raven pulled her discarded clothes back on and ran to the hospital.

He was stretched out on the bed, one leg encased in a cast and raised in traction, a big bandage hiding one side of his face, his skull wrapped in more bandages.

The doctor standing beside Raven, a plump red-haired woman, was saying in a whisper, "It's the concussion that worries me most. They almost killed him."

"They?" Raven asked, tearing her eyes away from Tómas's unconscious form. "Who?"

The doctor made a small shrug. "We don't know. He was found unconscious on the floor of the passageway. Surveillance video shows he was accosted by three young men."

Raven stared down at Tómas's battered face. Who would do this? Why?

The astronomer's eyes fluttered open. Bloodshot, unfocused, blinking. Then they stopped at Raven's form standing beside the bed.

He made a groaning sound.

She flung herself onto his prostrate form, cradling his bandaged face in her hands. He winced deeply.

"Tómas!" she sobbed.

He croaked, "Raven. I'm sorry."

"Who did this to you?"

Tómas did not answer. All he could remember was the suddenness of the attack. The pain. His helplessness. But he recognized that Raven was here, sobbing uncontrollably as she lay sprawled across his chest.

He smiled faintly as he slid back into unconsciousness.

The following morning Evan Waxman strolled through his outer domain and into his private office, smiling at his assistants as they sat at their desks, already busy with their morning assignments.

Sliding into his handsome, comfortable chair, he told his desktop computer to present a summary of the week's production figures. He smiled as the numbers showed that sales of various narcotics were climbing nicely.

Then an attention-demanding star flashed in the corner of his screen. With a puzzled frown Waxman told the computer to present the relevant data.

The screen showed the passageway from the shuttle docking area. A man was being viciously assaulted by a trio of thugs wearing gray hooded jackets. Waxman couldn't make out their faces. They swiftly beat their victim and left him sprawled unconscious on the passageway floor as they ran away.

Waxman stared at the scene, his eyes wide with surprised disbelief. A mugging! Here in *Haven*? Outrageous. Unacceptable. Umber will hit the ceiling when he learns of this.

"Phone," Waxman commanded. "Get me the security department. Top priority!"

The screen immediately showed a young woman wearing police blue. Waxman demanded to speak to the chief. The woman swiftly connected him.

Before Waxman could speak a word, the security chief—a grizzled, gray-haired man in a tight-fitting blue uniform—said, "This is about the incident last night, isn't it?"

"Incident?" Waxman snapped. "We can't have that kind of violence here! What the hell happened?"

"We're trying to put the pieces together," said the security chief, his beefy face showing concern, almost anger. "Seems like a random act of violence."

"Random act? You mean those thugs were just having fun?"

"Could be," said the chief.

"Who are they? Have you identified them?"

"Not yet. Those hoods they were wearing hid their faces pretty effectively."

"Well find them!" Waxman demanded. "Find them quickly! We can't have this kind of violence here!"

As reasonably as he could, the chief said, "You've got to expect little outbreaks like this from time to time. After all, this habitat is filled with the dregs of society."

"You let them get away with this and pretty soon the whole damned colony will become a battleground! Find them! Quickly!"

The chief nodded. "Right."

Waxman's screen went blank. He leaned back in his self-adjusting chair, thinking, Umber will go berserk the minute he learns of this. He'll blame me for it!

reactions

++
++

Kyle Umber sat open-mouthed with shock as he watched the video of the attack on Tómas Gomez.

"This is terrible!" he exclaimed.

Evan Waxman, standing anxiously before Umber's ornate desk nodded unhappily. "The victim was one of the astronomers: Tómas Gomez."

"How badly was he hurt?"

"Broken leg, broken nose, fractured skull."

"Good lord!"

"The assailants said something to him, but the surveillance system couldn't make out the words."

"I've got to go to the poor man," Umber said, pushing himself up from his desk chair.

"We're trying to amplify the words, maybe they'll give us a clue as to who the ruffians were."

As he came around his desk, Umber said, "And why they did such a senseless act of violence. Why would they do this?"

Waxman said, "Young thugs. They don't need a reason."

"No," Umber disagreed. "Every human action has a motivation behind it. The motivation might seem farfetched, outrageous, but every action has a cause."

Waxman shrugged. "I suppose so."

"I'm going to the hospital, Evan. Please let me know if you learn anything about this."

"I will."

"Immediately."

"Certainly."

Umber hurried out of his ornate office. Waxman watched him leave, then headed for the meeting that the chief of security had set up for him. With a Sergeant Jacobi.

"Frankly," said Jacobi, "I'm surprised that we haven't seen more of this kind of thing."

Waxman was sitting before Jacobi's desk, a standard-issue gray metal type shoehorned into the sergeant's narrow office; it was nothing more than a closet-sized space partitioned off from the rest of the station by flimsy shoulder-high panels. The area was barely big enough for the two of them, and Waxman could hear the daily chatter of the security people filling the air outside the cubicle.

Through gritted teeth, he said to Jacobi, "You'd better nail these thugs before other would-be vandals start terrorizing the people."

Jacobi nodded. "We're devoting all our resources to it, but there isn't much to go on. Their faces were pretty well obscured by the hoods on their jackets—"

"You have voiceprints of what they said, don't you?"

With a sad shake of his head, Jacobi replied, "Not clear enough for voiceprint ID, I'm afraid."

Waxman stared at the sergeant. "Then what are you doing?"

"Initiating regular patrols along the passageways," Jacobi answered. "The obvious presence of security patrols is the best way to prevent future incidents."

"But what about finding the kids who attacked Dr. Gomez?"

"We're bringing in kids by the carload and questioning them closely. Sooner or later we'll get a lead."

"Sooner or later," Waxman echoed.

"Police work takes time, and patience."

For several moments Waxman simply sat in the uncomfortable straight-back chair, glaring at Jacobi. At last he got to his feet.

"Keep me informed of how the investigation is progressing," he said. Then he turned and left Jacobi sitting at his desk.

Watching his retreating back, Jacobi said to himself, Sure. I'll send you written reports every day for the next week, then weekly, and then I'll stop. You won't pay them any attention and in a few weeks the whole affair will be forgotten.

He smiled knowingly.

Alicia could see how upset Raven was. The morning flow of customers was on the slow side, yet Raven hardly responded to the women's questions and comments.

The crowd thinned to only two shoppers as the noon hour approached. Alicia pulled Raven aside and told her, in a low voice, that she should go to the hospital to visit Tómas.

"And leave you alone here?" Raven objected.

"I can handle things for a while," Alicia replied. "You go and see Tómas."

"You're sure?"

With a smile, Alicia said, "I'm sure."

It wasn't until nearly closing time that Raven returned. She looked worried.

Alicia waited until the last customer sauntered out of the boutique. Then, as she lowered the window blinds, she asked, "So how is he today?"

Raven was obviously tense: her hands clenched into fists, her face looked strained, upset.

"He can't remember very much about the attack," she said. "It's all a blur in his mind."

"I suppose that's typical."

Raven nodded tightly. "That's what the doctor said. She told me he was recuperating normally. But he can't remember what happened! Not any details."

"Nothing to worry about," Alicia said, trying to sound comforting, sure of herself.

"I'm worried," Raven replied.

Alicia went to her and wrapped her arms around Raven's shoulders. "He's going to be fine."

"But who would do this to him?" Raven said, tearfully. "Why? Who would want to hurt him?"

"Some people are crazy," Alicia said.

"But we were all tested during the trip out here," Raven pointed out. "The psychotechnicians weeded out the violent ones."

Alicia pulled up one of the wheeled chairs from the counter and sat Raven on it. Then she went to the water fountain and poured out a cupful.

Handing the cup to Raven, she said, "When I lived back in Chicago, there were plenty of cases of sidewalk violence. You couldn't walk alone in some neighborhoods. People carried guns and knives."

"Not here in *Haven*."

"I hope not," said Alicia. "It would be awful if this habitat sank into that kind of mess."

Frustrations

"It's all a blur," Tómas muttered. "It happened so fast. . . ."

Sitting beside the astronomer's bed, Kyle Umber nodded sympathetically. "But you don't remember what they said to you?"

Tómas started to shake his head, winced with pain, and said merely, "No, I don't."

"You can't think of anyone who would want to hurt you?"

"Only that guy who tried to rape Raven, but he's halfway back to Earth by now."

"Noel Dacco."

"Yes."

Umber sighed. "We've never had an incident like this, not in the three years since we opened *Haven* to immigration."

Through the dull pain throbbing behind his eyes, Tómas thought, It's like he's blaming me for the attack. Like it's my own fault.

The minister leaned over and lightly patted Tómas's uninjured leg. "Well, I'm sure the security chief and his sergeant Jacobi will get to the bottom of this. In the meantime, you relax and get well."

Tómas smiled weakly. "I don't have anything else to do, do I?"

Umber pushed himself to his feet. "God be with you."

"And with you, sir."

Umber left the narrow enclosure. Gomez stared at the door as it slid closed behind him. Then he shut his eyes and drifted to sleep.

He dreamed. He saw the planet Uranus surrounded by dozens of tiny moons whirling around it in hyperkinetic orbits. Then a huge moon came hurtling out of the darkness of space and smashed into the planet. The small satellites were swirled into a frenzy of new orbits, many of them flying completely away from Uranus. The planet itself tilted over on its side as huge clouds of gas and debris erupted from beneath its clouds and spurted into space.

Tómas saw it all clearly. So clearly it hurt his eyes, numbed his soul.

And a voice from deep within him said, "Find the wanderers, Tómas. Find the wanderers."

He asked, "How? How can I find a moon torn loose from its orbit when I don't know what its original orbit was?"

He heard no answer.

Kyle Umber returned to the security department's headquarters and asked the chief to allow him to review the surveillance videos of the passageway where Gomez had been attacked.

The security chief looked surprised. "I doubt that you'll see anything that Sergeant Jacobi and his team haven't noticed."

Umber smiled tightly and nodded. "Probably not. But I would like to try."

With a cocked brow, the chief asked, "You're sure?"

"The Lord helps those who help themselves, you know."

Suppressing a sigh, the chief spoke into his desktop phone and called for an assistant to bring Umber down to the security camera monitoring center.

It was a small, tight circular room, its curving walls covered with monitoring screens that showed every passageway and public space in the habitat. Umber's guide, a petite brunette young woman in a snugly form-fitting blue uniform, showed him to a vacant desk. As he slid into its chair, she tapped the viewscreen built into the tiny table before him.

"It's voice activated," she said. "Just tell the screen what you want to see: call up the list of cameras, pick the one you're looking for. That's all there is to it." Then she added, "Oh, and tell the screen the time you're interested in. Otherwise you'll have to wade through *weeks* of observations."

Umber nodded gratefully. With the young woman standing behind him, he plowed through a diagram showing the locations of the surveillance cameras. He found the one he wanted, then ordered the monitor to start one hour before the attack on Dr. Gomez.

The screen showed an empty passageway. Umber asked for fast-forward.

A trio of young men walked into the scene, ridiculously jerky in the fast-forward mode. Their faces were shaded by the hoods on their dark gray jackets.

"Normal speed, please," said Umber.

The screen went totally blank. Then bright red lettering announced, FOOTAGE UNAVAILABLE. SECURITY INVESTIGATION IN PROGRESS.

Umber stared at the words for a silent moment, then turned to the young woman. "How do I get to see this footage?"

She seemed just as surprised as he. "I guess you'll have to talk to Sergeant Jacobi. He's in charge of the investigation."

SEarChing

His cold gray eyes focused on Reverend Umber, Sergeant Jacobi said, "I'm afraid that footage is being studied by our analysis team. I really wouldn't want to interrupt their work."

"You don't have a copy of the footage?"

"Apparently not," Jacobi answered, straight-faced.

"I see," said Umber. "Could you kindly notify me when it's available for me to see it?"

"Yes, certainly," said Jacobi.

Umber got to his feet. Jacobi rose also.

"This is all very distressing," said Umber.

Nodding, Jacobi said, "We haven't had a beating this serious since the habitat was opened to immigration."

Frowning slightly, Umber asked, "But there have been other . . . incidents?"

With a small shrug, Jacobi replied, "Petty stuff. Kids roughhousing, arguments that got out of hand—that sort of thing."

"But this was a vicious attack. Deliberate."

Jacobi stood behind his desk, perfectly motionless.

The silence between the two men stretched painfully. At last Umber said, "Please let me know as soon as you can."

"Of course," said Jacobi. Coldly.

* * *

As he walked slowly along the passageway back toward his office complex, Reverend Umber thought, There's something out of place about this. A vicious attack on Dr. Gomez. The security people appear to be at a loss in their investigation. That Sergeant Jacobi doesn't seem very upset about the incident. He acts as if it's strictly routine, as far as he's concerned.

But what if this incident is just the start of a new phase of our habitat's development? What if we're going to see more attacks? More violence? That could bring everything I've worked for crashing down around my shoulders.

The following morning, Raven was surprised to see a man enter the boutique. Alone. A few boyfriends and the rare husband had been dragged into the shop by their women, but a lone man was a surprise.

He was compactly built: good shoulders and a flat midsection. Swarthy face and dark wavy hair that curled down almost to the collar of his one-piece zipsuit. He maneuvered through the women pawing through the shop's merchandise and came straight to Raven, standing behind the counter.

"Are you Raven Marchesi?"

Blinking with surprise, Raven answered, "Yes, I am. And you are . . . ?"

"Vincente Zworkyn. Tómas Gomez and I work together."

"Oh! Yes, Tómas has mentioned your name many times."

Zworkyn said, "I went to visit him this morning, but the nurse told me he was in a therapy session and couldn't see visitors until it was finished."

Raven nodded. "Yes, he's able to walk now. The nanomachines are repairing his leg."

"I thought I'd come over and say hello to you. Tómas is quite taken with you."

Raven heard herself say, "It's mutual."

"That's good."

Glancing swiftly at Alicia, talking to a trio of potential customers on the other side of the shop, Raven turned back to Zworkyn and asked, "Do you have any idea of who attacked Tómas?"

With a shake of his head, Zworkyn replied, "I'm afraid I don't. But I hope the security department finds them and pushes them out an airlock."

Raven decided she liked this man.

After a few moments of embarrassed silence, Zworkyn asked, "May I take you to dinner tonight?"

Raven hesitated, then replied, "My partner and I usually have dinner together. At home."

"May I take you both to dinner?"

With a smile, Raven said, "Let's see what Alicia thinks of that."

Zworkyn smiled back, looking somewhere between embarrassed and hopeful.

Raven said, "I believe Tómas told me that you are married."

Zworkyn's smile evaporated. "My wife is back on Earth. Filing for a divorce."

"Divorce?"

Looking uncomfortable, Zworkyn explained, "It's my fault, I suppose. I'm away from home most of the time. Leaving her alone. It's not a happy situation."

"She doesn't travel with you?"

"I've asked her to. But she'd rather stay at home. She has lots of friends there."

"Where is your home?"

"Denmark. Copenhagen."

From the pain that showed clearly on his face, Raven realized she was treading on a sensitive subject. "I'm sorry," she said, in a low voice.

"Not your fault," said Zworkyn. "Nobody's fault but my own."

dinner

++
++++++++++++++++++++++++++++++++++

zworkyn sat patiently—and silently—with Raven until
Alicia brought the two shoppers to the counter.
Both had several colorful skirts and blouses draped
over their arms. They eyed Zworkyn with unabashed curiosity as Raven introduced the engineer to Alicia and her customers. Alicia rang up the sales while Raven wrapped their
purchases and escorted the women to the boutique's door.

"You work with Tómas?" Alicia asked as Raven bid a cheerful
goodbye to the departing women.

"Yes," said Zworkyn. He hesitated for a moment, then said,
"I've invited your partner and you to dinner tonight. Will you
join us?"

Alicia smiled. "It's my turn to cook tonight. Why don't you
come to my quarters?"

Zworkyn smiled back. "I thought dinner at the restaurant
would be a pleasant change for you."

"That's very thoughtful of you."

"Will you join us?" he repeated.

"Has Raven agreed?"

"Yes," he said, stretching reality a bit.

"All right, then. But we'll have to change into something
more fitting for the restaurant."

"Why? You both look fine."

"We'll look better," said Alicia.

As she was pulling on a colorful blouse, Raven heard Alicia ask from the adjoining dressing room, "Who is he?"

"He's a mining engineer. He's working with Tómas . . . that is, he was, until Tómas got hurt."

Raven's tone of voice changed slightly as she said, "He told me his wife is divorcing him, back on Earth."

"Oh? I didn't know. I wonder if that's true, or it's just a line he uses on susceptible women."

Raven felt surprised. Susceptible? Alicia? It's going to be an interesting dinner.

Tómas, meanwhile, was stretched out on his hospital bed. His leg ached from the walking that the nurses had made him do in the hospital's recuperation ward. But I'm walking, he told himself. A few more days and I'll be as good as new.

His narrow compartment had been turned down to sleep mode, dark and quiet. Tómas slid his hands behind his head and closed his eyes. No pain, he realized happily.

Suddenly his eyes popped open and he propped himself up on his elbows.

I don't have to track the moons that were bumped out of orbit around Uranus! he realized. If they were forced out only a couple of million years ago, I should be able to spot one of them with a Schmidt!

Pushing himself up to a sitting position, Tómas ran the problem through in his mind. If the moons were forced away from Uranus a couple of million years ago, one of the wide-field Schmidt telescopes at the Farside Observatory ought to be able to see them. I don't need Big Eye, not until we pick up one of the escaped moonlets and want to get a close-up of it to verify what it is!

He was so excited he started to pull off the bedsheet covering him and swing his legs off the bed. But he hesitated in mid-motion. Try to stand up and fall on your face; set your recuperation back a week or more.

He swung his cast-covered leg back onto the bed and turned to the telephone on the night table.

"Vincente Zworkyn," he commanded the phone.

Almost immediately he heard Zworkyn's recorded voice. "I'm not available at the moment. Please leave your name and I'll get back—"

Tómas snapped, "Phone, locate Mr. Zworkyn. Wherever he is, *find him*. Emergency! Top priority!"

The robot waiter trundled up to their table with three desserts on its flat top. As it began to place them on the table where Raven, Alicia and Zworkyn were sitting, Zworkyn's phone vibrated in his pocket.

Frowning, the engineer muttered, "I instructed the phone not to interrupt us."

The phone buzzed again, softly but insistently.

"Damn," Zworkyn muttered, tugging the phone from his pocket.

He could see the excitement on Tómas's face even in the phone's tiny screen.

Before Zworkyn could say a word, Tómas gushed, "We can do it! We can find one of Uranus's runaway moons! Maybe more than one!"

With a glance at his two dinner companions, Zworkyn said, "I'm in the middle of dinner—"

"We use the Schmidts at Farside," Tómas went on, undeterred. "We figure out the moonlets' exit velocities and search at the distance they'd be after a couple of million years!"

"That's a needle in a haystack approach."

"No, it's the way to find the escaped moons," Tómas insisted. "It'll work, I know it will!"

Zworkyn looked up at Alicia and Raven again as he said, "All right. All right. Calm down. I'll come over and see you first thing in the morning."

"I'll start in on the math. We can estimate the exit velocity of the moons pretty well. . . ."

"Get some sleep, Tómas. I want you bright-eyed and bushy-tailed tomorrow morning."

"Yes. Sure. Of course."

"Goodnight, partner."

"Goodnight, Vincente."

Zworkyn clicked the phone off. "Scientists," he muttered. "They're all a little crazy."

Alicia smiled at him. Raven did not.

abbott

Gordon Abbott could feel his brows knitting into a frown as he asked the image on his office's wall screen, "Use the Schmidt telescopes?"

"Yes!" replied Tómas Gomez eagerly. "The wide-field Schmidts. They can cover the whole sky in a couple of sweeps!"

"Not Big Eye."

Gomez shook his head. "We won't need Big Eye until we've located one of the escaped moons."

Abbott couldn't help noticing that Gomez didn't wince at all when he shook his head. The lad's recuperation is progressing nicely, he thought.

Practically quivering with excitement, Gomez said, "We don't need to have tracking data for the runaway moons. We just estimate how far they've traveled since they left Uranus orbit and scan the sky until we find one!"

"Ingenious," Abbott muttered.

"Can you get us time on the Schmidts at Farside?"

Nodding unconsciously, Abbott replied, "I believe that's possible. In fact, you can scan the sweeps they've already made at that distance. You might find what you're looking for that way."

"Wonderful! How soon—"

Breaking into a reluctant grin, Abbott interrupted, "I'll call Farside today. The director there is an old friend of mine."

"Great!"

Abbott's wall screen went blank. He stared at it for several long moments, thinking that it had been a long time since he'd felt as excited as Gomez about a sky survey. Ah youth, he said to himself. I just hope he actually finds the damned moon. It'd be a major breakthrough. Fine feather in the lad's cap.

The Reverend Kyle Umber was far from joyful as he sat alone in his sumptuous office.

I'm a figurehead, he told himself for the hundredth time. A bloated, pompous, self-important figurehead; all display and no real power. Evan Waxman controls this habitat and he's turned it into a center for narcotics and lord knows what else.

And I let him do it! I sat back and let him handle the habitat's day-to-day administration. He's taken control of everything. Everything I've worked for, hoped for, prayed for—it's all in his hands now.

He looked out from his desk, slowly scanning the trappings of authority and command that surrounded him. All make-believe, he told himself. A narcotic to keep me quietly sedated while Evan turns *Haven* into a drug manufacturing center and God knows what else.

His eyes focused on a faded picture in an old wooden frame hanging on the wall to one side of his desk. It showed a soldier carrying a wounded comrade across his shoulders, slogging painfully through jungle underbrush.

He heard the words of a long-dead political leader: ". . . no matter how long, or hard, or painful the journey may be . . ."

He whispered to himself, "Every journey begins with a single step."

Slowly, Kyle Umber pushed himself to his feet. "The journey begins *now*," he told himself.

But as he stood there behind his handsome desk, he realized that he had no idea of what his next step would be.

Then he remembered that Sergeant Jacobi had promised to send the surveillance camera footage of the attack on Tómas Gomez to him. He leaned over and told the phone to contact Jacobi.

The security chief sat rigidly in his desk chair as he watched Sergeant Jacobi's lean, pinched face on the wall screen.

"He's pushing for something," Jacobi was saying. "He keeps asking me for the footage of the attack on Dr. Gomez."

The chief felt puzzled. "You've gone over the footage of the attack. Is there anything in it that can identify the attackers?"

"Nope. I personally reviewed every millimeter of the footage. It's clean."

With an exasperated sigh, the chief said, "Let him see it, then. He won't be able to meddle with our investigation."

Jacobi nodded. "Yes, sir." A split-second's hesitation, then, "About my promotion . . ."

"All in good time, Sergeant," said the chief. "All in good time."

the force of righteousness

When in trouble or in doubt, Kyle Umber recited silently to himself, run in circles, scream and shout.

He smiled bitterly at the old bit of doggerel as he walked slowly along *Haven*'s central passageway. Doors lined both sides of the broad corridor, men and women strode purposefully along its plastic floor paneling.

Well, I'm walking in circles all right, he said to himself. He had traversed the kilometers-long passageway more than once since he'd started pacing its circular length earlier in the morning.

Everyone he met smiled and said hello to the founder of the community. Umber smiled back, with only his lips, and nodded benedictions to them.

But his mind was far away from this refuge in space. As *Haven* glided smoothly in orbit around Uranus, Kyle Umber was thinking of his younger days back on Earth and how he got the inspiration for developing the habitat and offering it as a refuge for Earth's forgotten, downtrodden people.

Three thousand and some refugees, he thought. Hardly an imposing number. There are millions more back on Earth desperately seeking a way out of poverty and despair. But I won't be able to help them, not unless I can wrest control of this habitat back out of Evan's hands.

How? he cried silently. How can one man stand against Waxman and his minions? He has the Council under his control. He's reduced me to a figurehead. How can I fight against him? How can I win?

Glancing about, Umber realized he had walked completely around the habitat's passageway again; he was back where he had started earlier in the day.

How symbolic, he told himself. Back where you began. You've accomplished nothing. All you're doing is rearranging the deck chairs on the *Titanic*.

But there was something tickling the back of his mind. A hazy thought, a vague idea was prodding him. Yet he could not form a clear picture of it.

Lord, he prayed silently, show me the way.

As he started on his next circumnavigation of the passageway, he listened for God's wisdom.

In vain.

Vincente Zworkyn looked up from his cluttered desk and saw Tómas Gomez standing at his door, grinning uncertainly as he leaned on a silvery cane.

Bouncing up from his chair, Zworkyn beamed a smile at the younger man. "Tómas! They let you out!"

Gomez stepped stiffly into the office/workshop, his free arm outstretched, a wide grin on his tan face. "I am officially released from the hospital."

"Wonderful!" said Zworkyn, ushering Tómas to his desk. "How do you feel?"

"Like I'm a hundred and fifty years old. My leg's not accustomed to walking long distances yet."

"You walked all the way here from the hospital?"

"Yes," said Tómas, as he eased himself into the chair in front of Zworkyn's desk. "Ahh. It feels good to sit."

Zworkyn went back around the desk and sat himself down. "Abbott was as good as his word. I got a call from the Farside Observatory this morning. They're sending the Schmidt data to us. Should be here by lunchtime."

"Good. Then we'll have some work to do."

Zworkyn nodded happily.

Kyle Umber was halfway through his fourth trip around *Haven*'s central passageway when it hit him.

Gandhi! he thought. Mohandas K. Gandhi. The liberator of India, back in the twentieth century.

Umber stopped in his tracks and stood stock-still in the middle of the crowd of men and women walking through the passageway.

"Gandhi," he said aloud. "Nonviolence."

Gandhi was so revered that the Indian people dubbed him "Mahatma": holy one. His campaign of nonviolent protest against the British forces that had occupied India for several hundred years eventually forced the Brits to leave India and allow the Indian people independence and the right to form their own government.

Could it work here? Umber turned around and hurried toward his office, back in the habitat's administrative tower. Gandhi, he kept repeating to himself. Nonviolence.

Once he reached his office he slid into his desk chair and asked his computer to pull up everything it had on Gandhi.

Well past the dinner hour, he was still at his desk, watching ancient newsreel films of the frail, wizened little man who freed his people from British domination.

He saw snippets of Gandhi's description of the nonviolent approach to political freedom.

The term Satyagraha *was coined by me* . . . the computer spelled out over a scene of police beating unresisting Indian men and women in old, grainy, black-and-white newsreel footage. *Its root meaning is "holding on to truth," hence "force of righteousness." I have also called it love force or soul force. . . . I discovered in the earliest stages that pursuit of truth did not permit violence being inflicted on one's opponent . . . for what appears truth to the one may appear to be error to the other. And patience means self-suffering. So the doctrine came to mean vindication of truth, not by the infliction of suffering on the opponent, but on one's self.*

Umber sank back in his desk chair and stared at the words of Gandhi. Eyes wide with discovery, he told himself, That's a form of Christianity! Not by inflicting suffering on one's opponent, but on one's self.

That is the way to deal with Waxman and the people around him. *Satyagraha.* The force of righteousness.

He raised his eyes to the ceiling of his office and his vision seemed to penetrate through it and out into the limitless depths of space.

"Lord, help me in this quest for righteousness."

He heard no reply, but he neither expected to nor needed to. He had found his way and was fully committed to it, mind and heart and soul.

Yet a thin, hard voice in his mind asked, All right, then. What's your first step?

the first step

"Please come in, Reverend," said Raven, gesturing her visitor into her living room.

Reverend Umber stepped somewhat hesitantly into Raven's apartment. Alicia Polyani was already there, sitting on the sofa beneath the view of Uranus turning serenely on its axis.

"Thank you," said Umber. "It's good of you to see me." He went to the sling chair in front of the sofa and lowered himself carefully into it.

Before either of the women could say anything, Umber began, "I've come to ask the two of you to help me organize a cabal, a protest against what Evan Waxman is doing to our habitat."

Raven glanced at Alicia, then turned back to Umber. "A protest?"

"A nonviolent protest that could break Waxman's control of *Haven*."

"That sounds . . . interesting," said Raven.

"It sounds dangerous," Alicia murmured.

"This is like looking for a needle in a haystack," complained Zworkyn.

"It's there," said Tómas, sitting on the edge of the sofa in

Zworkyn's living room. The wall screen across the room showed views of the stars from one of Farside Observatory's wide-field Schmidt telescopes.

"It's there," Tómas repeated, without taking his eyes off the star-littered screen. "We just have to find it."

"A tiny needle in a huge haystack. A minuscule needle in an enormous haystack."

Tómas shook his head stubbornly. "We've estimated what its magnitude should be. We just have to search until we find it."

Zworkyn stared at the younger man. "Look, Tómas. We've set the parameters. We've estimated the range of magnitudes that the moon would show, we've calculated how far from our solar system it would be. And we've found nothing. Nothing even remotely similar to what we're looking for."

Tómas nodded absently, still staring at the screen. "All right, so it's not in this view. We still have six other Schmidt images to look at."

"It's dinner time," Zworkyn grumbled. "Past dinner time."

"Go ahead and eat. I want to look at the next display."

Zworkyn shook his head unhappily, but didn't move from the sofa.

"Passive resistance?" Alicia asked.

"Yes," said Umber. "It's the way to break Waxman's control. It's a hard way, a difficult way. It requires enormous self-control, enormous sacrifice—"

"But you expect the people of this habitat to set themselves down in front of the manufacturing tower and let the security police beat them?"

Umber nodded silently.

Raven murmured, "That's asking a lot from them. Maybe more than they can give you."

"They wouldn't be giving it to me," Umber corrected. "They'd be giving it to themselves. To each other. They'd be winning back control of this habitat."

"You expect them to allow themselves to be beaten to a pulp?"

"Yes," said Umber. "And I'll be the first one in line."

"I don't think it would work," Alicia said. "They'd break and run as soon as the police started hitting them."

Umber sighed. "Perhaps they would."

"I would," said Alicia.

"Umber's been in there for a long time," said Sergeant Jacobi.

The viewscreen in Evan Waxman's living room showed the passageway outside Raven Marchesi's apartment. Occasionally someone walked past. But what was going on inside the apartment?

Feeling frustrated, Waxman wondered, "What's he doing in there with the two women?"

"Getting laid."

Waxman looked sharply at the sergeant. "Not him. I think he's impotent."

"H'mmph."

Waxman got up from his desk chair. "We should have bugged that woman's apartment."

"*Now* you think of it."

Shaking his head disconsolately, Waxman said, "Umber wouldn't let me. He said that people's private quarters should remain private."

"Great humanitarian thinker," Jacobi sneered.

"Well, it's too late—"

"Hey! Here he comes." Jacobi pointed to the wall screen, which showed Kyle Umber leaving Raven's apartment.

Waxman studied the reverend's face as he started up the passageway. "He looks very serious. Very somber."

Jacobi huffed. "He didn't get laid."

PLANNING

+++
+++++++++++++++++++++++++++ ++++++++++++++++

"Let them hit me?"

Raven nodded.

"But that's crazy."

"It's passive resistance," she said. "It's worked in the past, back on Earth."

Raven was sitting on the sofa in the living room of her quarters, Alicia beside her. Sitting on the sling chair facing them was Syon Shekhar, head of the habitat's plumbers guild. Small, thin almost to the point of emaciation, dark of skin, hair and eyes, his face was set in an expression of dismayed disbelief.

"You want me to tell my people to go out and sit on the lawn in front of the Chemlab Building and allow the security guards to beat them?"

Raven nodded, tight-lipped.

"Get real," Shekhar snapped. "That's crazy."

Alicia repeated, "It's called passive resistance."

"It's called lunacy," said Shekhar.

"It originated in your country," Raven coaxed. "Gandhi used it—"

"My country is South Africa," Shekhar interrupted. "For the past eleven generations."

"Whatever," said Raven, undeterred. "Passive resistance can work. It's worked in the past."

Shaking his head, Shekhar objected, "So you expect my people to go out and sit in front of the Chemlab Building and let the security goons split their skulls?"

"I'll let them split my skull," said Raven.

"And mine," Alicia added.

"You're both crazy."

With a slow smile creeping across her face, Alicia coaxed, "You mean you wouldn't be willing to do what the two of us intend to do? You'd let us show more guts than you would?"

"You'll show more guts, all right," Shekhar countered, getting to his feet. "And brains. And blood."

Raven stood up too, barely as tall as Shekhar's thin shoulders. "Will you at least tell your people about it? Will you do that much?"

With a resigned shrug, Shekhar answered, "Sure, I'll tell them. But they're not going to go for it, I can tell you that right now."

"Maybe," Raven admitted.

"So how many do we have?" Kyle Umber asked the two women.

The minister was in his own private quarters, sitting in front of the viewscreen that took up most of the far wall of his living room. Raven and Alicia sat huddled together on the sofa of Raven's living room.

"Not many," answered Alicia.

"Most of the group leaders were surprised when we told them about it."

"Shocked."

Umber bit his lower lip. "This will only work if we have a big turnout."

"I know," Raven replied. "But the idea seems to shock them."

"It's too new. Too different," said Alicia.

"Maybe if I tried to explain it to them," said Umber. "Show them what we're trying to accomplish. . . ."

Raven shook her head. "We can't have you meeting with all the habitat's group leaders. Waxman would catch on to what we're trying to do."

Alicia nodded minimally. "Benjamin Franklin said three people can keep a secret—if two of them are dead."

Umber nodded back at her. "I just hope Waxman's not tapping into our communications with each other."

"No," said Alicia. "I asked the leader of the communications group and he told me no one has asked to read private messages."

"Not yet," breathed Raven.

"Evan would have to bring any such request to the Council for a vote," Umber said. But his voice did not sound certain about the idea.

"Why couldn't you record a speech, Reverend Umber," asked Raven, "so we could give copies of it to the various group leaders."

Umber's expression changed from doubt to a glimmering hint of possibility. "A speech," he said, savoring the idea. "A short, strong speech."

The next morning, Umber sat at the desk in his living room, staring at the viewscreen on the wall opposite his sofa. The screen was broken into half a dozen scripts, quotations from brilliant, successful speeches of the past.

"When you decide to steal," Umber muttered to himself, "steal from the best."

Leaning back in his comfortable desk chair, Umber began reading. *These are the times that try men's souls.* He paused momentarily, then went on. *Tyranny, like hell, is not easily conquered; yet we have this consolation with us, that the harder the conflict, the more glorious the triumph.*

He stopped and stared at the words of Thomas Paine that he had just quoted. They were good enough to rally the upstart American colonists against the world-girdling British Empire, he thought. Maybe they'll help to raise the residents of this habitat against Waxman's tyranny.

He fervently hoped so.

discussion

+++
+++++++++++++++++++++++++++++++++++

When in doubt about what to say, Gordon Abbott always unconsciously tugged at his moustache. He was pulling it now hard enough to make himself wince.

Reverend Umber's image filled his office's wall screen, looking uncertain, worried, almost fearful.

Abbott jerked his hand away from his face and asked, "You want me to contact the Interplanetary Council and ask them to give you a hearing?"

Nodding slightly, Umber replied, "So that we can apply for membership to the Council."

Blinking anxiously at the reverend, Abbott asked, "Why don't you call them yourself?"

His round face showing obvious distress, Umber admitted, "Because my calls are blocked."

"Blocked? By whom?"

"Evan Waxman."

"Your own chief administrator?"

With a lugubrious nod, Umber explained, "Evan has taken control of the habitat's council. *He's* running *Haven*, not me. He won't let me contact Earth under any circumstances."

Abbott pondered that admission for several long, silent moments, consciously keeping his hands folded tightly on his desk-top.

"He's controlling this habitat's government, then?"

"To a large degree, yes."

"I see," said Abbott. He pursed his lips, glanced up at the ceiling of his office, squirmed uncomfortably in his desk chair.

At last he said, "Actually, I'm here at your habitat at your request. I'm not a citizen of *Haven*. I shouldn't get involved in your politics."

"But this wouldn't involve you in our politics," Umber replied. "All you would be doing is sending a message from me to Harvey Millard, the IC's executive director. Let him know that I want to converse with him."

"And you think that Waxman will let my message go through to him?"

"I hope so. He can't be blocking *all* of the habitat's communications with Earth."

"You think not?"

"I hope not."

Abbott stared at Reverend Umber's round, pinkish face. The man seemed sincere enough. More than that. He looked determined, desperate.

"I know Millard," he said. "He's a decent chap."

"Then you'll call him?"

"It might be better if I didn't try to reach Millard directly. I've been sending progress reports to my people Earthside. I'll slip your request into one of them. My next one, in fact. It's due to go out tomorrow."

Umber broke into a grateful smile. "God bless you, Dr. Abbott! God bless you!"

* * *

Syon Shekhar hated it when his meetings broke into a hassle of individual arguments. He stood in front of his twelve local organizers, who packed his living room, taking every chair in his quarters and even sitting on the carpeted floor. Hands on his narrow hips, he watched his subordinates gabbling at one another.

Like a pack of stupid chickens, he thought. This idea has unsettled them all. It's like nothing they've ever heard of.

Despite his distaste, he let them squabble for a full five minutes before calling the meeting to order again.

Standing before them, he said, "There's nothing much to argue about." The twelve men and women looked up at him with expressions of surprise, uncertainty, even outright fear on their faces.

"Just sit there and let them hit us?" cried one of the men.

"We could get hurt!"

"Or killed!"

Shekhar waved them to silence. "You saw Reverend Umber's vid, same as I did. He's asking for our help. Do we give it or not?"

"We can't order our people to let themselves get beaten!"

"No," agreed Shekhar. "It's all got to be completely voluntary."

One of the women, her voice quavering, said, "Just sit there and let them hit us?"

"That's what Reverend Umber is asking of us. He's asking all the people in the habitat. What's our answer going to be?"

"I think it's crazy!"

Another of the women scrambled to her feet. "Listen. The security goons are people like you and me. They're not going to kill us."

"No, they'll just make us wish we were dead."

Shekhar realized this debate could go on indefinitely. Raising his hands, he asked, "All right, all right. Will you tell your people about this? Ask them to show up when Reverend Umber wants us to?"

They reluctantly agreed. Very reluctantly.

SUSPICION

+++
+++++++++++++++++++++++

"I don't like it," said the security chief. He was sitting at his desk, as usual, but the expression on his hard-bitten face as he stared at his office wall screen showed suspicion, doubt, worry.

"They're up to something," the chief muttered.

Sergeant Jacobi, sitting in front of the chief's desk, nodded agreement. "Yeah, but what?"

The wall screen showed a section of the habitat's main passageway filled with men and women walking along. But instead of their usual pairs or individuals, most of them were clustered in groups of five or six or more. They were chattering among themselves, too low for the security microphones set into the ceiling to pick up more than a random snatch of a phrase. Worse, they would occasionally glance up at the cameras and microphones and lower their voices even more.

"They're up to something," the chief repeated, his chiseled features set in a grim, hard expression.

Jacobi suppressed an urge to ask again, But what?

The chief focused his steel-blue eyes on Jacobi. "What have you heard?"

With a shrug, the sergeant replied, "Not a helluva lot. Something's in the wind, that's for sure. But what it is . . ." Again he shrugged. ". . . we don't know yet."

"Your informers haven't picked up anything?"

"I've picked up a few hints about 'passive resistance.' But what the hell that is and how it fits into the situation here is pretty much a mystery."

"Passive resistance," the chief repeated. "Doesn't sound very dangerous."

"Maybe not. But just about everybody in the whole damned habitat seems to be in on whatever the hell they're buzzing about."

"Everybody except us," the chief growled.

"We could pick up a couple people at random and squirt 'em with truth serum."

"And have Umber come howling down on us?" The chief shook his head.

"Maybe if we question the reverend himself . . ."

"On what grounds? We still have to follow the law. We can't start an investigation before we know what we're looking for. This isn't Chicago, for God's sake. Or Hitler's Germany."

Jacobi didn't answer. But he was thinking, Umber knows what's going on. If we could just squeeze him a little, he'd spill his guts.

"So what do we do?" Jacobi asked.

Obviously unhappy, the chief said, "We watch and wait. And lean on our informers."

We follow the law, Jacobi said to himself. The hoi polloi can keep secrets and we have to try to find out what the hell they're up to without stepping on any of their precious goddamn rights.

Raven felt the man's presence, skulking along the passageway behind her. She had put in a full day's work with Alicia at the boutique, trying hard to keep their plan a secret. Many of the women who came into the place wanted to talk about the passive resistance plan. Raven hushed them and told them to talk to their neighbors in the privacy of their quarters.

Now, as she and Alicia walked along the passageway toward their quarters, Raven said quietly, "We're being followed."

Alicia started to turn her head but Raven said, "No! Don't let him know!"

"You're sure somebody's following us?" Alicia whispered.

"He's been trailing along behind us since we left the shop."

With a tight little grin, Alicia said, "Well, let's see what he wants."

"No!" Raven snapped.

"We're not doing anything wrong. Let's ask him why he's following us."

Alicia stopped walking and turned to stare at the man approaching them. He was slim, dark-haired, good-looking except for an oversized nose.

He stopped a dozen paces behind the two women, looking suddenly embarrassed, confused.

Alicia called out to him, "Are you following us?"

He coughed once, glanced down at his shoes, then admitted, "Yes, ma'am. I was."

"What for?" Raven burst. "What gives you the right—"

"Reverend Umber told me to make sure you got home okay. With nobody bothering you."

"Reverend Umber?"

"Yes, ma'am. I'm one of his assistants. He thought that with tomorrow being the big day and all, he didn't want anything to happen to you two."

Alicia admitted, "You frightened us . . . sort of."

"Oh, I'm sorry. I didn't mean to."

"It's all right. We're nearly home," said Alicia.

Raven added, "We can make it on our own from here."

"You sure?" the young man asked.

"We're sure," Alicia said, with a smile.

In the surveillance center, surrounded by the viewscreens that watched every square centimeter of public space in the habitat, Sergeant Jacobi pulled the earphones off his head.

Tomorrow's the big day, he said to himself. But where? What for? I'd better tell Waxman about this right away. And get every able body we have on the force into uniform tomorrow morning, ready for anything.

confrontation

It seemed like an ordinary weekday morning. Instead of opening their boutique, though, Raven and Alicia marched with determination to the grassy open park space in front of the Chemlab Building. But not before leaving a sign in the shop's window advising customers to join them in the protest.

Raven saw a half-dozen men and women already there, sitting on the grass. One was staring intently at the pocket-sized reader she had propped on her folded legs. Another was stretched out on his back, seemingly napping.

"Why don't we sit here?" said Alicia.

Raven nodded her agreement, and the two of them sat down on the grass along the edge of the paved walkway that led into the building.

"Now what?" Alicia asked.

With a tiny shrug Raven said, "Now we wait."

More people were coming to the little park in groups of three and four and sitting down quietly. A few spoke to one another. Most sat tensely, expectantly, some fearfully.

"Not many people," Alicia said.

"It's early," Raven replied. Then she pointed, "Look, here come some more."

Within fifteen minutes, Raven counted forty-three bodies sitting or lying on the grass. A uniformed security guard came out of the building's main entrance, frowning as he looked around, then popped back inside again.

A middle-aged man carrying a briefcase approached the building, found his path blocked by a handful of people, and bent down slightly to talk to them. He didn't seem to be angry or alarmed, just puzzled.

Raven watched their conversation, too far away to hear their words. The middle-aged man pointed to the building's entrance. The younger men and women blocking the path to the entrance said something to him, shaking their heads.

Raven guessed it was, "Sorry, the entrance is closed."

Even at this distance, Raven could see the surprise on the older man's face. Then it turned to anger. He reached into his jacket and pulled out a pocket phone.

"Now it starts," Raven said to Alicia.

In the security department headquarters, Sergeant Jacobi reached across his desk and touched the ANSWER button on his intercom phone.

"Jacobi . . . What? Blocking the entrance? Who is? The entrance to what?"

Evan Waxman had just slipped into his desk chair when his phone buzzed.

"Good mor—What? Blocking the entrance to the Chemlab Building? Who is? . . . Well, clear them out of there! That's what your job is!"

With a snap of his fingers, he silenced the phone. Blockading the Chemlab Building? he thought. So *that's* what they're up to.

Feeling more relieved than alarmed, he commanded his wall screen to show the entrance to the Chemlab Building.

Reverend Umber pushed himself up from his desk chair as he watched the mounting confrontation in the minipark in front of the Chemlab Building. Security police were streaming in from the main passageway, armed with electroshock wands. A gaggle of people—including a trio of the building's security guards—were arguing heatedly, arms waving, mouths yammering.

I should be there, the reverend said to himself. I should have been the first one out there this morning.

Get moving, he told himself. You're supposed to be their leader. Get out there and lead.

He strode purposefully away from his desk, toward the exit of his office domain, heading for the Chemlab Building. He could feel his pulse hammering in his veins.

Sergeant Jacobi hustled down to the locker room and picked up his riot gear, slinging it over one shoulder as he headed for the exit and the Chemlab Building. Shaking his head as he adjusted the strap over his shoulder, he said to himself, riot gear. Never thought I'd have to use this stuff. So that's what they're up to. That's what "passive resistance" means to them. Target practice. They want to let themselves get whacked, we'll whack 'em.

He hurried to the security cruiser waiting in the passageway outside.

Raven and Alicia got to their feet, their eyes fixed on the confrontation in front of the building's entrance.

Three red-faced security guards were arguing heatedly with

a dozen or so of the demonstrators. More of the demonstrators were getting up off the grass, looking uncertain, alarmed. In the distance, more security guards were running toward the entrance area, brandishing wicked-looking black batons.

One of the demonstrators—young, curly-haired, beefy-cheeked—was nose to nose with one of the building's guards, obviously trying to outshout the guard, who was doing the same to him.

The youngster shoved the guard with both his ham-sized hands. The guard staggered backward, then fell onto the seat of his pants.

"Come on!" the youngster shouted to the men and women around him, waving one arm over his head.

"No!" Raven shouted. "Don't move!"

The young man looked surprised as Raven rushed up to him.

"Sit down," Raven commanded, gesturing with both her hands. "Just block the entryway. That's all we want to do."

Looking surprised, perplexed, the youngster sank down onto the paved walkway. As did the handful of men and women around him.

Two other guards hauled the fallen policeman to his feet. Another security guard popped out of the building's entryway, a black baton in one hand. "What the hell's going on here?"

"They're blocking the entrance," replied one of the guards.

"Well, clear 'em out of the way. Now!"

The trio of guards stood uncertainly, looking around at the growing crowd. Raven could see dozens of other people joining the demonstrators, walking into the crowd and sitting down on the pathway and the grassy area.

She also saw several security cruisers gliding to a stop and dozens of guards pouring out.

"Clear the area!" shouted a guard with sergeant's stripes on his blue sleeve, as he loped through the growing crowd from

one of the cruisers to the building's entrance. "That's an order!
Clear the area! *Now!*"

The sitting men and women looked at each other, some puzzled, some grinning. None of them got up. Raven felt a thrill.

Sergeant Jacobi climbed past the sitting protestors and reached the building's entrance.

"You're blocking a public walkway," he shouted. "Disperse. Now!"

No one moved.

"I'm warning you!" Jacobi bellowed, raising the black nightstick in his hand.

The crowd stirred, but did not get up. Raven saw that they were turning to look at a new arrival striding purposefully toward the building's entrance.

Reverend Umber.

Everyone seemed to freeze in place as Umber weaved through the sitting protestors. He was wearing his customary suit of pure white, with the black button of a loudspeaker clipped to the jacket's collar.

Umber stopped in front of Sergeant Jacobi, panting slightly from his exertion. The sergeant let his arm drop to his side.

The reverend pointed to the building's entrance and said, "These people are peaceably assembled to protest an inequity that is being perpetrated inside this building."

His amplified voice carried across the grassy square.

Jacobi said, "They're blocking a public walkway."

"And they will continue to block it until this building is closed permanently," said Umber.

action

For several breathless moments, Jacobi stood in silence, glaring at Reverend Umber. Umber stood as immobile as a statue, hands on his hips, still puffing slightly.

Tapping his truncheon into the open palm of his hand, Jacobi said, "You'd better tell them to disperse, Reverend. Otherwise there's going to be bloodshed."

Umber seemed to draw himself up a little taller. "On your head be it, then."

Jacobi nodded slowly. "No, Reverend, it's gonna be on your head." And he jabbed Umber in the midsection with the end of his baton.

Umber *oofed* and staggered back a couple of steps. The whole crowd of demonstrators clambered to their feet.

"No!" Umber shouted, his amplified voice ringing across the plaza. "No violence!"

The crowd stood uncertainly, shifting on their feet, waiting for the next blow.

Jacobi raised his nightstick over his head, held it there for an endless moment, while Umber squeezed his eyes shut and hunched his shoulders, waiting for the blow.

At last Jacobi opened his fingers and let the bludgeon fall, clattering to the ground.

"The hell with it," he muttered, turning around and walking past the other guards, into the Chemlab Building's entrance.

The crowd stood frozen, unmoving. The remaining security guards slowly retreated toward the building's entrance. When the last one entered the lobby, the glass doors swung shut.

Raven turned to Alicia, standing breathlessly beside her. The two made their way through the crowd to where Reverend Umber stood, looking surprised, dumbfounded.

"They just . . . went away," Umber said, almost in a whisper.

"And we're still here," said Alicia.

Raven turned to the crowd and made a sitting motion with both her hands. "Sit down," she shouted. "This isn't over yet."

Evan Waxman rose slowly from his desk chair, the scene from the entrance to the Chemlab Building filling his wall screen.

"Get back out there, you idiots!" he yelled at the screen. "Get rid of them! Drive that rabble out of there!"

But the security guards remained inside the building, the demonstrators out on the grassy park ground.

Whirling toward his desktop phone, Waxman shouted, "Security chief. *Now!*"

The security chief's hard-edged face appeared on the wall screen, three times larger than life.

"Did you see what just happened?" Waxman demanded.

The chief nodded, tight-lipped.

"Well, what are you going to do about it?"

"Not much I can do."

"I want that sergeant broken, fired, thrown out!"

"And what good would that do?" the chief asked.

"You find somebody who knows how to obey orders!"

The chief shook his head slowly, almost sadly. "Mr. Waxman, think for a moment. My guards are citizens of *Haven*, just like the people you want them to hurt. They're not storm troopers. They're not even Green Berets. They live with those people. They're part of this habitat's population, just like you and me."

"And they can get away with refusing to follow orders?" Waxman bawled.

"Looks that way," said the chief.

Umber was the only person standing. The crowd dotting the little park was sitting, or crouching, their eyes on him.

So far, so good, Umber thought. He could see more people coming into the area and sitting down on the grass or the paved walkway.

He spread his arms and said, "We may be here for quite a while. I suggest you pick people from among yourselves to go out for meals and bring them back here."

"And then what?" a deep male voice called from the crowd.

"And then we wait here until Evan Waxman agrees to shut this narcotics factory down. *Permanently!*" He shouted the last word.

The crowd stirred. No cheering, but they were obviously moved.

Raven turned to Alicia, sitting on the grass beside her. "We're going to be here for a long while," she said.

So that's what he's trying to do, Waxman said to himself as he watched Umber's performance.

Shut down the narcotics manufacturing. Stop producing Rust. Cut off this habitat's main source of income.

He smiled grimly as he stared at his wall screen. So we'll just have to wait him out. Let his followers sit there and twiddle their thumbs. Sooner or later they'll get tired of this charade and go home.

Time is on my side, he told himself.

NIGHTFALL

"This isn't very exciting," Alicia said to Raven.

In the orbiting habitat of *Haven*, the cycle of day and night was artificially controlled. The habitat's lights dimmed to a twilight level at a predetermined time, then went down to evening and finally the darkness of night—all controlled by the habitat's automated lighting system.

The two women were still reclining on the grass in front of the Chemlab Building. The crowd of demonstrators was still sprawled all around them. The lights had dimmed to their twilight level more than ten minutes earlier, but hardly anyone had left the park.

Reverend Umber was sitting with them, gnawing on the last bit of faux chicken meat that one of the demonstrators had brought from the habitat's cafeteria.

"How much longer will we have to stay out here?" Raven wondered.

Umber shook his head. "Until they capitulate."

Alicia said tightly, "Or until our people get tired of this and go home."

Umber frowned slightly. "Several people have already left," he said.

"Can't say I blame them," Alicia replied. "After all, they do have homes. With beds."

"And bathrooms," Raven added.

"Some of them have come back, though," Umber pointed out.

"But our numbers are dwindling," said Raven.

Umber shook his head. "They'll grow again tomorrow morning, you'll see. We'll get stronger."

"From your mouth to God's ear," said Alicia, without a trace of reverence in her voice.

Evan Waxman was still in his office, still watching the scene on his wall screen.

Stalemate, he grumbled to himself. We can't get our technicians into the building; production today has been zero.

But, he reasoned, they can't leave the entrance area. Once they do, we can move in our people and start up the production lines again.

If that idiot sergeant hadn't caved in to those demonstrators this would all have been over and done with hours ago, Waxman fumed.

The security chief studied Jacobi's hard-bitten face as the sergeant stood unhappily before his desk.

"What happened out there, Franco?" the chief asked.

Obviously uncomfortable, Jacobi frowned as he answered. "I just couldn't do it. Whack Reverend Umber? Knock him down? Bloody his head? You try it."

For several long moments, the chief remained silent. At last he said, "So that's how 'passive resistance' wins. It depends on the decency of the people they're resisting."

"I suppose," Jacobi muttered.

"Waxman's pissed with you," the chief said. "Wants you boiled in oil, at least."

Jacobi nodded silently.

"I'm placing you on administrative leave until this mess gets resolved. You'll get half pay. No duties. Just report in every morning."

"Okay." Tightly.

"Stay away from the demonstrators."

"Yeah."

"That's all."

Jacobi half turned toward the door, but quickly spun back again to face the chief. "I just couldn't do it! I mean, Reverend Umber! I couldn't whack the guy! The whole crowd would've swarmed us. It would've been a riot!"

The chief made a reassuring motion with his hands. "I know, Franco. I understand. But Waxman wants your balls pinned to his wall. Give me a couple of days to make him happy again. Cool yourself down. Stay out of Waxman's way."

Evan Waxman, meanwhile, was still at his desk, fuming at the image on his wall screen. Hundreds of men and women were sitting in front of the Chemlab Building, relaxed and chatting with one another, eating and drinking as if they were participating in a mammoth picnic.

The security guards were nowhere in sight. Most of them were still inside the building, cringing like sheep, while the crowd outside showed no signs of dispersing. A few of the guards had picked their way through the protestors and disappeared from view. Cowards, Waxman thought. Miserable weaklings who shrank from doing their sworn duty.

And there sat Kyle Umber, in the midst of the demonstrators, speaking intently, earnestly to those nearest him.

Waxman recognized Alicia Polanyi sitting next to the minister, and Raven Marchesi next to her. They'll pay for this, he told himself. I'll make both of them wish they'd never been born.

His phone buzzed. The screen showed that it was the security chief calling him. A glance at the clock on the screen's face showed it was eleven thirty. Almost time to put the plan into action.

Without preamble, Waxman asked, "Is everything arranged?"

The chief nodded solemnly. "The guards inside the building are armed and ready. Six mobile units are assembling on the edges of the park area."

"Good," said Waxman. "Tell them to be ready."

"Yes, sir."

Waxman killed the chief's image and then reached out and touched the button that activated the habitat's public address system.

"Good evening," he began. "This is Evan Waxman, chief administrator of *Haven*. Those of you now loitering before the Chemlab Building have until midnight to leave the area and return to your homes. At midnight the security guards will forcibly eject anyone remaining in the area in front of the Chemlab Building."

MidNight

"we have until midnight," said Alicia.

"Don't move," Umber told her, his amplified voice carrying across the little park. "We must all stay where we are."

Pointing to a handful of people who had gotten to their feet and were leaving the plaza, Raven muttered, "Tell *them*."

Umber made a philosophical shrug. "The weak are always among us. Let them go in peace."

A tense silence descended across the plaza. Raven saw that most of the protestors were still in place, sprawled across the grass and the walkway. A few had risen to their feet.

Raven glanced at her wrist. Almost twelve o'clock. Several police cruisers glided to a stop on the outskirts of the plaza.

Midnight.

The Chemlab Building's glass doors banged open and a phalanx of guards marched out, helmets on their heads, truncheons in their hands.

"Time's up!" shouted their leader. "Up and out. Now!"

Umber sat with his arms around his knees. No one got to their feet. The few who had been standing dropped to the ground. Raven saw that the crowd of protestors outnumbered the security guards by about five to one.

"Stay where you are," Umber told them, his amplified voice booming across the plaza. "Don't move. Don't resist."

The leader of the guards came up to Umber. "On your feet, Reverend."

Umber looked up and smiled at him. But did not move.

"Haul him up!" the guard leader commanded. Two of the guards hefted Umber by his armpits to a standing position, but as soon as they let go of his arms the minister sank to the ground again.

"Up!" the guard leader shouted, his face reddening. "And get him the hell out of here."

The guards dragged Umber's limp form off toward the edge of the crowd.

"And the rest of 'em," shouted their leader.

A pair of guards grabbed Raven by her arms and hauled her to her feet. She winced at their gruff handling but said nothing. She saw Alicia being hefted too. Side by side, the two of them were dragged toward the edge of the crowd.

One of the guards whispered to Raven, "Hey, you wanna have dinner with me tomorrow night?"

She didn't even turn her head to look at him.

Raven saw that Reverend Umber was dropped like a sack of cement onto the paved walkway that circled the outer edge of the plaza. As the guards who had carried him there walked back into the still-seated crowd, Umber got to his feet and walked back behind them.

Once the guards deposited her on the outer walkway, Raven also got to her feet and headed back toward the Chemlab Building's entrance. Alicia did the same. So did the other demonstrators that the guards had carried away.

It was almost farcical. The guards were hauling away the demonstrators, who got to their feet as soon as they were dropped off and headed back to where they'd been picked up.

Umber smiled and nodded encouragement to the demonstrators. Passive resistance, thought Raven, with a smile. We could keep this going indefinitely.

But it ended suddenly. One of the guards, his face twisted with frustration and rage, smashed Reverend Umber on the side of his head with his truncheon. The minister dropped to the ground, moaning.

For an instant everything stopped. Then the demonstrators who were still sitting scrambled to their feet with an animal roar.

"They've killed him!" a woman's voice screamed.

The unarmed demonstrators leaped at the security guards. Truncheons flashed through the air, striking flesh and bone, but the demonstrators far outnumbered the guards and swarmed over them. The plaza became littered with fallen bodies. Women as well as men attacked the guards with fists and teeth and wild, maniacal fury.

Raven leaped onto the back of the guard nearest her, reaching across his face to scratch at his eyes. Alicia kicked a guard in the groin and smashed both her knees against his back as he fell. Another guard cracked his truncheon into the back of her head and she slumped to the ground, unconscious.

Time lost all meaning. The plaza had turned into a battleground as the demonstrators pummeled the guards, grabbing their truncheons and swinging them against the unifomed men.

Raven struggled to her feet, ducked under a guard's panicked swing, and crawled to Reverend Umber's fallen form. His face was split open from temple to jaw, his eyes glassy, unfocused. But he was breathing. He was alive.

With the guards disarmed, one of the men picked up a discarded truncheon and pointed at the entrance to the Chemlab Building.

"Tear it down!" he shouted.

Howling their fury, the angry mob followed him, surging through the entrance and into the building.

Raven saw Alicia sprawled on the grass, unmoving. She screamed into her wrist phone, "Medics! Medical help needed at the Chemlab Building. Immediately!"

Most of the crowd was pouring through the building's entrance. Raven went to Alicia and lifted up her head slightly. No reaction. Umber was groaning, his legs moving slightly, slowly, his eyes fluttering.

Raven knelt on the grass between Alicia and Umber. She heard sounds of shouting and breaking glass from inside the Chemlab Building. The plaza was littered with fallen bodies. Ambulances were gliding to a stop, white-coated medics scrambling out of them.

This is what a riot looks like, Raven said to herself. Utter confusion. Mayhem. Hell on Earth.

aftermath

+++
++

IT SEEMED TO TAKE HOURS. THE MEDICS BENT OVER THE injured slumped across the plaza's grass and walkways. Men and women tottered out of the Chemlab Building, many glassy-eyed, staggering. Only a handful of security guards were still on their feet, disarmed, dazed by the ferocity of the protestors' attack.

Slowly, slowly order was restored. Most of the protestors stumbled through the carnage and staggered toward their homes. Ambulances carried away the injured, then came back for more.

Reverend Umber had sunk into unconsciousness as the medics lifted him carefully, tenderly, onto a stretcher and bore him to the nearest ambulance.

Raven sat next to Alicia, who hadn't moved at all. She lay on the grass, eyes closed. Raven could not tell whether she was breathing.

A tendril of smoke was twisting out of one of the Chemlab Building's shattered upper windows. Raven looked up at it with bloodshot eyes. Her back felt stiff, sore. Somebody must have hit me there, she thought dully.

Looking across the plaza at the medics carrying the injured to the waiting ambulances, Raven muttered to herself, "I guess we won. I guess we shut down the Rust production."

* * *

The still unfinished *Haven II* habitat orbited around Uranus's huge blue ball alongside the original *Haven*. In its completed section, where the scientists from Earth were housed, Tómas Gomez was roused from a blissfully deep sleep by his phone announcing, "Big Eye imagery has arrived."

His eyes snapped open and he sat up in the desk chair he'd been using.

"On screen, please," he commanded.

The wide-angle views from Farside Observatory's Schmidt cameras had picked up three objects that might be former moons of Uranus, driven out of their orbits around the planet and hurled into the depths of interstellar space. Now the Big Eye telescope's much more detailed view came up on the bedroom's wall screen.

Sitting bolt upright in the desk chair, Gomez stared at the imagery.

Centered in the picture was an irregular, misshapen chunk of rock. The figures on the bottom of the screen showed it was just short of two hundred seventy kilometers across.

Tómas stared at it, goggle-eyed. That's one of them! he shouted silently. That's one of the moons of Uranus that was bounced out of its original orbit and is now coasting through interstellar space!

Glancing around the darkened living room, Tómas asked himself, Where's Vincente? Then he saw that the apartment's bedroom door was shut. He's asleep. In bed, sleeping.

Tómas went to the bedroom door and pounded on it. "Vincente!" he shouted.

Mumbles and grumbles from the other side of the door. A thump and a string of what was obviously swearing.

Then the bedroom door slid open.

Zworkyn's bleary-eyed face stared at Tómas.

"We've got one!" the younger man exclaimed.

Vincente's eyes widened, and he croaked, "You're sure?"

Tómas's excitement evaporated. Very steadily, he replied, "Pretty sure. We've got to get its trajectory parameters and see if they lead back to Uranus."

"Right," said Zworkyn. "Let's get to work."

Raven sat in the hospital corridor outside Reverend Umber's door. The hospital staff had given the minister an entire room to himself. The rest of the hospital was filled to bursting with demonstrators and security guards who had been beaten senseless or breathed in Rust or other narcotic vapors once they started shattering the Chemlab Building's processing glassware.

Doctors and nurses and orderlies were hurrying past Raven's sitting form. Bodies of men and women—unconscious, raving, struggling, or blank-eyed and docile—paraded past her. But all Raven could see was Alicia's dead body, the back of her skull crushed by a truncheon's blow, bits of bone and brain dotting her blood-stained dress.

She's dead, Raven kept repeating silently. Alicia is dead. Killed. Murdered.

As the habitat's lighting system brightened to its full daytime level, Gordon Abbott studied the starry image on his office wall screen, and the alphanumerical symbols running across the screen's bottom.

"The data seem rather convincing," he said into his desktop phone. "That chunk of rock probably did originate in orbit around Uranus."

Tómas Gomez's voice sounded more tired than triumphant.

"Mr. Zworkyn and I agree," he said. "The numbers point to that conclusion."

"This is extraordinary," Abbott said, consciously resisting the urge to tug at his moustache.

"It is," Zworkyn's voice concurred. He sounded much more buoyant than Gomez.

"Two million years ago," Abbott muttered.

"That's when the latest ice age started on Earth," said Gomez.

"Incredible."

In the makeshift analytical laboratory that had originally been Zworkyn's living room, the engineer beamed happily at Tómas. "You've done it, lad. You've proved that the Uranus system was shattered and sterilized two million years ago."

"But how? By natural causes? Or alien invaders?"

Zworkyn smiled. "That's going to keep this entire generation of cosmologists busy for the rest of their lifetimes. And probably their children's, too."

"It's a helluva way to find extraterrestrial intelligence," Tómas muttered.

The engineer's smile faded. "If this wasn't a natural event . . . if it *was* caused by intelligent creatures . . ."

His voice died away.

"If it was caused by aliens," Tómas finished the thought, "they might return some day and do the same to us."

Zworkyn simply stared at Tómas, wide-eyed, suddenly frightened.

CONSEQUENCES

+++
+++++++++++++++++++++++++++ ————————————————————————

Tómas shuddered, like a man trying to forget a nightmare. Looking at the clock numerals in the corner of the computer's screen, he saw that it was well past 7:00 A.M.

"We've worked the night through," Zworkyn said, then yawned. "I need to get back to sleep."

"Do you think you can sleep?" Tómas asked.

With a shrug, Zworkyn replied, "I'm sure as hell going to try."

Tómas nodded as he pulled his pocket phone from his trousers. "I should call Raven."

Zworkyn made a bitter smile. "Ah! True love."

"You should try it some time."

"I did. Wasn't so great."

Raven's face appeared on the phone's screen. Tómas saw the bustling commotion of the hospital in the background.

"What's going on?" he asked. "Where are you?"

"In the hospital," Raven said.

"The hospital?"

"We had a demonstration in front of the Chemlab Building. It turned into a riot. Reverend Umber was beaten unconscious. Alicia . . ." Raven struggled to hold back tears. ". . . Alicia was killed."

She broke into sobs.

"Are you all right?"

"Yes, yes. But Alicia . . . she's dead."

Tómas forgot everything else. "I'll be there as soon as I can get a shuttle. I'll be there, Raven!"

Evan Waxman had turned off his wall screen hours earlier. He sat in his silent office as the habitat's outdoor lights slowly turned up to their morning level.

It's gone, he kept repeating to himself. They've smashed everything. I'm ruined.

I can't stay here on *Haven*, he told himself. Umber will organize a group of citizens and boot me out. Then, with a shudder of comprehension, he realized, But I can't go back to Earth! They'll kill me! I owe them deliveries of Rust that I can't make good! Dacco and his bosses will want me dead!

The hospital had quieted down. Its corridors were crowded with people on stretchers—bandaged, battered, sedated—nurses and orderlies bending over them, administering medications.

But where is Raven? Tómas wondered as he searched through the crowded hallways.

A beefy orderly loomed before him. "I'm sorry, sir, but you can't go roaming through the corridors. We have a lot of work to do—"

"I'm looking for my fiancée," Tómas replied. "Raven Marchesi."

"Is she among the injured?"

"I don't think so. I don't know!"

The orderly fished his pocket phone from his rumpled white trousers. "Ms. Raven Marchesi. You have a visitor—"

Past the orderly's burly shoulder, Tómas saw Raven walking up the corridor toward him, her hair disheveled, her dress spotted with blood, her face tired but still beautiful.

She saw Tómas and broke into a run. He pushed past the orderly and opened his arms to her.

They enfolded each other.

"You're all right?" he asked. "Not hurt?"

"I'm fine," she gasped. "Now."

The orderly broke into a grin. "All right. Will the two of you please clear out of here and let us do our work?"

Arm in arm, Raven and Tómas walked to her quarters. The habitat's passageways seemed strangely empty; the usual clusters of pedestrians were few and far between.

"Everybody's gone home," Raven said softly. "There's been enough excitement. Too much."

Tómas asked, "Alicia?"

Raven had to take in a breath before she could reply, "One . . . one of the guards smashed her head in. It was gruesome. Terrible."

He fell silent for several paces, then asked, "But you're all right?"

Reaching to rub her back, "I've got a pain back here, but otherwise I'm okay."

"You could've been killed."

"But I wasn't."

"Thank God."

She blinked at him. "I thought you were an atheist."

"I am," he said with a boyish grin. "But every now and then I wonder if I might be wrong."

Raven smiled and twined her arms around his neck. They kissed passionately, there in the middle of the empty passageway.

Nearly empty. A teenaged boy came skimming by on a pair of jetskates and made a 180-degree turn as he zipped past them, grinning hugely.

Tómas frowned. "Are they allowed to run on jets in the passageways?"

"Who cares?" said Raven.

QUESTIONS

Reverend Umber was sitting up on his hospital bed, one side of his face covered by a bandage from his temple to his chin.

Evan Waxman stood at the foot of the bed, his head hung low, both his hands clutching the bed's railing as if it were a safety buoy in the midst of a churning, frothing sea.

"They destroyed the Chemlab facilities," Waxman was saying, in a low dismal tone. "Everything's smashed."

Umber started to nod, winced with pain. "So I've been told."

"It's all gone," said Waxman.

"And good riddance to it."

Drawing himself up a little straighter, Waxman said, "There was nothing illegal about it. We have no laws against narcotics here in *Haven*."

"That was my oversight," Umber responded. "I should have had the Council outlaw narcotics."

"I saw to it that none of it was sold here. The local population—"

"Rust was used here, Evan. Don't try to deny it."

Waxman's head sank lower.

Umber said gently, "You know I can't keep you as chief administrator."

"I didn't do anything illegal."

"But immoral."

Waxman raised his head and stared into Umber's eyes. "You didn't care about that as long as I was bringing in the money to keep this habitat going!"

"Yes, that's true enough. I share the responsibility."

"So?"

"So we'll start over. Clean and new."

"And be bankrupt before the year is out."

"The Lord will provide."

Waxman's expression soured. "Kyle, you can't expect people to eat hope. *Haven* is heading for catastrophe."

For a long moment Umber said nothing. Then, in a whisper, "I know it."

"What are you going to do about it?"

"I don't know . . . yet."

"You're a dreamer! A hopeless dreamer!"

"I am a dreamer," Umber admitted. "But I'm not without hope."

Waxman shook his head.

"But what about you? I presume you'll return to Earth."

For the first time, Waxman's face showed fear. "I . . . I don't know. I don't think so."

"I can't give you much of a recommendation."

"They'll kill me!" Waxman burst out. "I owe them a shipment of Rust that I can't deliver now. If I return to Earth they'll have me killed."

Umber's eyes went wide. "Kill you?"

"Yes."

"What kind of people have you been dealing with, Evan?"

With a bitter smile, Waxman replied, "Not your church-going type."

* * *

Gordon Abbott frowned at the image on his office wall screen. It showed Harvey Millard, executive director of the Interplanetary Council, sitting in his office in Copenhagen, on Earth.

He doesn't think the data are conclusive, Abbott almost growled to himself.

The distance between Uranus and Earth made normal conversation impossible. It took more than two hours for light to travel one-way between the two. Abbott fidgeted with impatience as he tried to do some work on the report he was writing while he waited for Millard's response to his message.

In the image frozen on his screen, Millard was smiling slightly. He was a smallish man. Even seated in his desk chair he looked undersized, diminutive: shoulders slim, torso slender, trim little moustache. But the expression on his face was intelligent, inquisitive, with light brown eyes alert and probing.

Abbott knew that one does not become executive director of the IC through family connections or the good will of friends. Beneath his nearly frail appearance, Harvey Millard was a veritable lion.

"Not conclusive," Millard replied at last. "Not entirely. Very suggestive, of course, but the astronomers aren't going to rip up their cherished theories without overwhelming evidence."

"Gomez and Zworkyn are working night and day to provide the evidence," Abbott said, somewhat testily. "They could use some help."

And then the inevitable wait. Abbott had been at this "conversation" since early morning. It was maddening.

At last Millard nodded minimally. "So I understand. But your facilities out there at Uranus are rather limited, aren't they?"

Before Abbott could frame a reply, Millard went on, "Pity."

Pursing his lips momentarily, he went on, "I suppose I should take a jaunt out to where you are and look things over for myself."

"You'd come all the way out here?" Abbott blurted.

And then waited.

At last Millard replied, "I believe I have to. See the evidence, talk with this Gomez fellow and the engineer. They've stirred the pot rather vigorously, haven't they?"

Abbott nodded wordlessly.

"Very well, then," Millard said, with just the hint of a grin touching his lips. "It'll do me good to get away from the office for a while. I should be able to reach Uranus within a week."

Within a week, Abbott echoed in his mind. When the IC's executive director wants to go someplace, he has one of the commission's private ships at his beck and call.

I'll have to tell Reverend Umber about this right away, Abbott thought. And Waxman. We've got to—

Millard interrupted his thoughts. "My people will fill you in on my schedule, Gordon. See you in a week or so."

The wall screen went blank.

Well, Abbott said to himself, he's not one to waste words.

Kyle Umber was sitting up on his hospital bed. The bandage that had covered his left cheek was gone, replaced by a translucent covering that clearly showed the scar running from his temple to his jaw.

"Harvey Millard is coming here?" he asked.

Standing at the reverend's bedside, Gordon Abbott nodded vigorously. "He's already on his way."

"Because of this discovery that Gomez and Zworkyn made?"

"Yes."

"Is he bringing many people with him?" Umber asked. "Will we have enough space to house them all?"

Abbott replied, "Knowing Millard, he's probably coming alone, or with one or two aides, at most."

"We can accommodate them on *Haven II* then."

"I should think so."

"Good."

"He's scheduled to arrive the day after tomorrow."

"I'll have to get up from this bed to greet him."

Abbott held himself back from shaking his head. "Millard isn't a great one for formalities."

"Still . . . he's the Interplanetary Council's executive director."

"True enough." Abbott took a step back from the bedside and turned to leave.

But Umber stopped him with, "This discovery that Gomez has made, what does it mean, Gordon?"

Abbott paused and turned back to face the minister. "It might mean that our solar system was visited by an intelligent alien race some two million years ago."

"An intelligent alien race," Umber repeated.

"And they sterilized Uranus. Completely sterilized the entire planet."

"My God."

"That's what Gomez thinks."

"Do you believe it?"

Abbott shrugged wearily. "It's an outlandish hypothesis, on the face of it. But it accounts for the facts that we've uncovered."

"My God," Umber repeated.

The trip to Uranus should have seemed like a vacation to Harvey Millard. He was away from his office; underlings were handling the niggling details of the day-to-day affairs of the Interplanetary Council. But he realized that he was heading into a new problem, a question that might well involve the future of the entire human race.

As he stood in the otherwise empty observation blister of the spaceship *Icarus* racing out to Uranus, he stared at the universe of stars emblazoned across the black infinity while the enormity of the situation weighed on his slim shoulders.

All life on Uranus was wiped out, extinguished some two million years ago. How? By alien invaders? The idea was preposterous on the face of it.

But is it right? He remembered a bit of wisdom from his university days: Just because an idea sounds crazy doesn't mean it's wrong.

But is it right?

Millard shuddered in the chilly emptiness of the observation blister. Could there be an alien race out there that sterilized Uranus? How? More important: Why?

Will they return? Will they want to drive us into extinction?

He stared out at the stars. And found no answer.

*   *   *

Evan Waxman sat in his office, unconsciously counting the minutes he had left to live.

I can't stay here on *Haven*, he told himself for the thousandth time. Umber will force me to leave. To go where? Back to Earth? Dacco and his bosses will want me dead. Returning to Earth will be a death sentence. Even Mars or the research stations orbiting Jupiter and Saturn won't be safe for me.

Maybe I should just kill myself and get it over with.

But he didn't move, couldn't move, could not force his hands to open the desk drawer and pull out the vial of Rust he had cached in it.

It won't be a bad way to go, he thought. Drug overdose. You'll be floating on a cloud when the end comes.

Still, he could not force his hands to open the desk drawer.

Raven opened her eyes slowly. Tómas was already up and dressed, she saw: a steel-gray tunic over darker slacks. He looked handsome, she thought. His face so serious, so intense.

As he stood before the mirror, smoothing down the tunic he had just put on, he noticed her stirring in the bed. And smiled.

"Good morning."

"You're up early," Raven said.

"You've slept late," he answered.

In a mock-accusative tone, Raven replied, "You kept me up half the night."

A wide grin flashed across Tómas's face. "I could say the same about you."

Raven tossed a pillow at him.

He stepped to the bed, bent over and kissed her.

"I've got to go," Tómas said, almost apologetically. "The IC's executive director will be arriving tomorrow, and we've got to be prepared to show him our findings."

Raven nodded. "I suppose I should open the boutique. It's been shut since the riot."

"You'll need help, won't you?"

"I'll find somebody."

"Sure. Good luck."

"Same to you, Tómas," said Raven.

He went to the bedroom door, turned and blew her a kiss, then departed. Raven sat on the rumpled bed, telling herself she should get up and start the day. Yet she didn't move.

The phone buzzed. "Phone answer," she called out.

Reverend Umber's round, slightly pinkish face appeared on the screen. Raven pulled the bedclothes up to her armpits. Then she noticed that the left side of the minister's face was covered by a translucent bandage.

"Raven . . ." He hesitated.

"Yes, Reverend," she said. "What can I do for you?"

Umber was silent for a moment, then he answered, "I need your help."

Raven showered and dressed quickly, then hurried to Umber's office. The minister was alone amidst the ornate furniture and decorations, sitting at his desk, looking somewhere between worried and expectant. A livid scar ran down one side of his face. Raven tried to keep from staring at it.

As soon as she took one of the chairs in front of his desk, Umber said, "I need an assistant."

"An assistant?"

"The executive director of the Interplanetary Council will arrive here tomorrow, and I need someone to help me with the arrangements . . . and the agenda for our meeting."

"Isn't that what Mr. Waxman does for you?" she asked.

"Evan has resigned," Umber said. Then he amended, "Actually, I expect him to resign. I'm sure he's going to."

"But I'm not trained to do his job," Raven protested. "I don't know a fraction of what he knows about how to run your office."

"You can learn," said Umber, his face dead serious. "And you have one important trait that I find indispensable."

"Indispensable?"

"I can trust you."

arrival

Harvey Millard sat in the bridge of the *Icarus*, the interplanetary council ship that had carried him from Earth orbit to the twin habitats orbiting Uranus. He watched as the ship's six-person crew went through the final moments of countdown to the berthing at the orbiting station.

In the bridge's sweeping display screens, Millard could see the rim of the bluish-gray planet and the two circular man-made habitats hanging side by side in orbit around it.

Millard felt tense as the ship approached the docking port. *Haven II* was obviously unfinished, bare skeletal metal ribbing making up half its circular structure. He saw flashes of what must have been welding torches here and there along the structure.

Then they passed *Haven II* and aimed at the original station, *Haven*.

From his command chair at the focal point of the bridge's control stations, the ship's captain announced, "Rendezvous in six minutes. Confirmed."

The six-person crew sat at their stations, relaxed, at ease, as the ship's master computer guided it into the docking berth of *Haven*.

Seated behind the crew members, Millard nodded, even

though none of the crew had turned to look at him. His palms felt sweaty, his fingers gripped his thighs rigidly. Although he enjoyed traveling, even over interplanetary distances, this business of docking a spaceship with a rotating habitat was something he had never been able to feel comfortable about.

The time stretched interminably, then Millard felt a barely noticeable tremor and finally a slight thump.

"Docking confirmed," announced the master computer.

The captain turned in his seat and smiled at Millard. "That's it, sir. We're docked."

The crew all got to their feet, grinning at one another. Each was dressed in a ceremonial uniform, black with silver trim. The captain's shoulders were heavy with braid. Millard, in a civilian's undecorated jacket, turtleneck shirt and slacks, pushed himself to his feet, happy that he hadn't wet himself during the approach.

Reverend Umber was determined to stand when he met Millard. Sitting in a hospital-provided wheelchair, with a fresh-faced doctor and an even younger nurse behind him, Umber tensed as the reception area's hatch swung open.

Gordon Abbott stood at one side of the minister's chair, wearing a crisp hip-length sky-blue tunic and sharply creased darker slacks. On Umber's other side stood Raven Marchesi, in a simple buttercup-yellow sleeveless mid-thigh dress.

The first man through the hatch was the ship's captain, smiling and looking splendid in his black-and-silver uniform. Right behind him was a civilian, modestly dressed, smiling gently.

Abbott stepped forward and put out a beefy hand. "Harvey," he said, loud enough to have his voice echo off the reception area's metal walls. "Good to see you again! Welcome to Uranus and *Haven*."

Millard allowed Abbott's hand to engulf his. "It's good to see you, Gordon."

Umber pushed himself to his feet as Abbott half turned and introduced the minister. "This is the Reverend Kyle Umber, founder and leader of the *Haven* habitat."

As he shook hands with Umber, Millard said, "Please sit down, sir. There's no need for formalities."

Umber smiled at the smaller man. "I prefer to stand, actually. I've been sitting far too much."

Millard dipped his chin in acknowledgement. "As you wish."

"You're alone?" Umber asked. "No staff?"

Millard grinned, almost maliciously. "'He travels fastest who travels alone,'" he quoted. Then he added, "I can reach my staff when I need to."

The ship's captain and crew were led toward a shuttle that would take them to *Haven II* as Umber introduced Raven. Scarcely taller than Raven, Millard took her hand in his and smiled radiantly at her. Raven muttered a greeting.

Turning back to Umber, Millard glanced at the scar running down his cheek and said, "I heard you had some unpleasantness here a fortnight ago."

Umber nodded as he pointed toward the moving stairs that led down into *Haven*'s living quarters. "My attempt at a nonviolent demonstration turned bloody," he said, his voice going low, guilty. "Thirty-eight persons were killed."

"Something about narcotics?" Millard asked.

His face grim, Umber said tightly, "Yes," as he slowly, haltingly led Millard and the others to the moving stairs.

Millard listened in silence as Umber—clearly embarrassed—explained Waxman's drug manufacturing and sales.

By the time they reached Umber's offices, the minister was saying, "Unfortunately, we never outlawed narcotics here in *Haven*. It never crossed my mind. I thought that the refugees we took from Earth would want to be free of drugs here in *Haven*. And most of them did! The only real trouble we've had has come from the top, not from the refugees but from my own staff!"

Millard nodded sympathetically. "That's often the way. The rich don't really believe that the law applies to them."

dispositions

++
++

once the little group reached umber's office, the reverand sank gratefully onto his desk chair while millard ensconced himself on one of the comfortable armchairs in front of the minister's desk.

"Now where is this man Gomez? I want to hear what he has to say."

As if answering a cue, Tómas and Zworkyn entered Umber's office. Umber introduced them and they sat down.

Without preamble, Millard asked, "You believe you have evidence that several of Uranus's moons were torn from their orbits around the planet some two million years ago?"

"Conclusive evidence," said Gomez.

Millard raised an eyebrow. But he smiled as he said, "Show me."

Nearly two hours later, Millard was nodding agreeably as he said, "I've got to admit, you seem to have it nailed down quite conclusively."

"Thank you," said Zworkyn.

"Of course, I'm not an astronomer. We're going to have the real stargazers look over your evidence."

"I am an astronomer," said Gordon Abbott, sitting at Millard's side. "They've convinced me."

"Uranus's moons were disturbed just two million years ago," Millard mused.

"Give or take a few millennia," said Zworkyn, with a wily grin.

Dead serious, Millard went on, "By alien invaders."

"That's one possibility," Zworkyn said.

"The most likely one," Gomez added.

"Fantastic."

Abbott said, "This has enormous consequences. If it was an alien invader . . ." His voice faded away.

"But why Uranus?" Millard asked. "Why didn't they strike any of the other planets?"

"Maybe they did," Gomez said, in a low, anxious voice.

Millard fixed him with a hard stare. "What do you mean?"

"The last ice age on Earth started about two million years ago."

"Ice age?"

From behind his desk, Umber disagreed, "Surely you're not suggesting—"

"That the ice age was caused to wipe out the ape-like creatures that had arisen on Earth," Gomez said, in a near whisper. "That's exactly what I'm saying. The aliens tried to prevent the human race from being born."

Kyle Umber's elaborate office went dead silent.

Meanwhile, in his own office a few paces down the passageway from Umber's, Evan Waxman was contemplating his future.

The safest place for me is right here, in *Haven*. Even if Kyle gets the Interplanetary Council to accept this space habitat as a member nation, I'll be protected here. I'm an important man here, respected. There's no reason for me to run away.

Unless Kyle Umber banishes me, he realized. I've got to prevent that. I've got to convince Kyle that I can still work for him. That I'll follow his rules.

Then it struck him. I'll become a penitent! I'll beg him for my life. I'll swear to be a good, upstanding, rules-following citizen.

I'll throw my life at his feet. He won't be able to cast me into the outer darkness. That would be the same as killing me. He's too softhearted for that.

I hope, Waxman said to himself. And he noticed that perspiration was beading his forehead.

Raven sat silently in Reverend Umber's office as Tómas, Zworkyn, Abbott and the newcomer from Earth discussed the consequences of Tómas's discovery.

In her mind she understood what the men were saying. But it didn't seem real to her. Alien invaders sterilized Uranus two million years ago? They caused the ice age on Earth to prevent the birth of the human race?

It was too fantastic, too outlandish to be believed. Where are these murderous aliens now? she wanted to ask. Do you have any shred of evidence that they really exist?

But she kept silent. She noticed that Reverend Umber had also lapsed into silence as the scientists tossed ideas and discoveries at one another.

It's too crazy to be believed, a voice in her mind insisted. Destructive aliens swooping through the solar system two million years ago, killing and destroying?

Then she looked again at Tómas's face. He believes this with all his heart, she realized. He's positive that he is right, that he's discovered an enormous threat to the human race. A threat to all the life on all the worlds in the solar system.

What if he's right?

decisions

Kyle umber felt weary. millard and the others had left his office hours earlier, still debating gomez's idea that the solar system had been invaded some two million years ago. Now Umber sat alone at his ornate desk, pondering, worrying.

Gomez's discovery is just too big to be believable, he told himself. Alien invaders sterilizing the planet Uranus. Causing an ice age on Earth to prevent the birth of the human race. Fantastic! Unbelievable!

Yet, deep within him, he feared that Gomez might be right. Abbott believes it and he's an astronomer. Millard seems to believe, although he says he wants to see more evidence.

If it is right, it means that somewhere out there among the vast clouds of stars there is an alien race that is our implacable enemy.

A superhuman force of evil. The devil incarnate. All the superstitious terrors of the human race made real, living, waiting to strike us again. Maybe they're already on their way here, coming to smash us again!

Despite himself, he shuddered. All the ancient fears of the human race come alive. It was too much to be believed. Too much *not* to believe.

His desk phone buzzed. Almost happy to have his morbid train of thought interrupted, Umber glanced at the screen.

Evan Waxman was calling.

". . . and he wants me to be his assistant," Raven was saying, smiling with excitement, "to work with him and learn how to help him run the whole community."

Tómas Gomez grinned at her. "You're coming up in the world."

The two of them were sitting across from one another at the tiny fold-out table in Raven's kitchen. They had hardly touched the dinner plates set before them. They were both too excited to eat.

Her happy grin fading just a little, Raven continued, "I don't know if I can do it, though. It's an awful lot to learn and—"

"You can do it," Tómas assured her. "You're a smart woman, Raven. You can do anything you set your mind to."

She glowed. "Do you really think so?"

"I'm positive."

"I'll have to find somebody to run the boutique," she mused. "It's doing too well to shut it down now."

Tómas nodded and leaned across the table toward her. "You're going to be an important person, Raven. Reverend Umber's personal assistant."

"And you, Tómas," she said. "You'll probably have to go back to Earth, at least for a while."

"No," he said firmly. "I'll stay here. If anybody on Earth wants to talk to me, he'll do it by video conferencing. Or they can come out here."

"But suppose—"

Reaching out to clasp her hand, Tómas whispered, "It's taken me all my life to find you. I'm not going to be separated from you. Ever. Not by anyone or anything."

Raven put her free hand atop his.

Then Tómas straightened and said, "We should talk to Reverend Umber about marrying us."

Raven gulped with surprise, but agreed, "I suppose we should."

This is going to be uncomfortable, Reverend Umber said to himself. But it's got to be done.

He was sitting alone amid the greenery and fancy furniture of his ornate office, frowning at the lavish ostentatiousness of it all. It's too much, he told himself. You're a man of God, not some oriental potentate.

His desktop phone buzzed.

Startled out of his self-incrimination, Umber said, "Phone answer."

The phone's screen lit up and announced, "Evan Waxman is here, Reverend."

Umber drew in a deep reluctant breath, but answered, "Send him in, please."

His office door slid open and Waxman stepped in, slowly, almost hesitantly. His eyes cast downward, he walked to Umber's desk and stopped in front of it, hands folded in front of him, still staring at the floor.

Umber got to his feet, yet Waxman did not look up at him.

"Have a seat, Evan," Umber said softly, gently, as he sat down again in his capacious desk chair.

Waxman sat, still avoiding Umber's eyes.

"I suppose this isn't going to be easy for either one of us," Umber said.

"No," Waxman replied, in a near whisper. "I suppose it's not."

Waxman and Umber

sitting tensely in his desk chair, umber said, "The chemlab building is a total wreck."

Waxman nodded mutely.

"I've decided to let it stay that way, at least for the time being," Umber went on. "To serve as a reminder for all of us."

"But there was nothing illegal about its operation," Waxman protested, in a soft, almost whining voice.

"Legalities aside, it was immoral."

"I suppose so," Waxman admitted.

A cold silence descended upon the two men.

At last Umber stated, "Tomorrow I'm going to ask the Interplanetary Council's executive director to admit *Haven* as a Council member."

Waxman nodded.

"Once we are admitted we'll have to obey the laws that all the other member worlds obey. Including the law prohibiting the manufacture and sale of narcotics."

Waxman's expression shifted slightly. "Kyle, you know that I decided to manufacture and sell narcotics as a means of supporting this habitat."

"It was an unacceptable means."

"But you took no steps to stop it."

Pointing to the scar running down his cheek, Umber said, "Until last week."

"Yes. Until last week. At the cost of thirty-eight lives."

Umber's sudden intake of breath told Waxman he had hit home.

"No one blames you for that," Waxman quickly added, meaning just the opposite.

"I feel the guilt," the minister said, his voice low, miserable.

"So do I," said Waxman, in an equally low voice.

Reverend Umber studied Waxman's downcast face. It was a picture of defeat, humiliation.

"I'm sorry it's come to this," Umber said.

Waxman nodded silently.

"Are you returning to Earth?"

"I suppose I'll have to."

"Will it be safe for you?"

Waxman smiled slightly and shook his head. "No. It will be the death of me."

"You really believe that they'll try to kill you?"

Locking his eyes with the minister's, Waxman replied, "They will try, Kyle. And they'll succeed. It's people like Dacco and his ilk that led you to build this habitat, to get away from them and their evil."

For a long moment Umber did not reply. At last he murmured, "Yes, I suppose that's true."

Suddenly Waxman burst, "Give me another chance, Kyle! Please, please, I beg of you! Don't send me off to my death. They'll kill me! At least here on *Haven* I have a chance to survive. Your colonizers are screened, scanned. You reject the violent ones, the dangerous ones."

Umber nodded slowly. "I've tried to make this habitat a true haven for the downtrodden people of Earth. I dreamed of bringing millions of them here, to this new world, where they could live in decency, where they could build new lives for themselves, a new world."

"And you can still do that, Kyle! Your dream isn't dead. You can go ahead with it. Build more habitats. Take in Earth's weary, poor, downcast people."

"Yes, I can still do that," Umber replied. "But what about you? What am I to do with you, Evan?"

"Let me help you! Let me continue as your strong right hand. Let me live!"

Umber leaned back in his chair, as if driven by the force of Waxman's plea.

"You told me that *Haven* will be bankrupt within a year," he said.

"We can survive! We can adopt an internal economic system, like the early colonies in the New World on Earth. We can grow our own food, manufacture all that we need—"

"Would that be possible?"

"I'll make it possible! You'll see, Kyle. We may drop down to a subsistence economy, but we can survive. And as newcomers arrive, our economy will grow! Just as the Americans and Australians and other colonists on Earth survived and prospered."

"Could we create a self-sustaining economy here?" the minister wondered. "Without importing goods from Earth?"

"But if you're accepted into the Interplanetary Council you could establish trade links with Earth and the other worlds. *Haven* could prosper, eventually."

"You could make that happen?"

"I'll work night and day to make it happen!"

Umber nodded. "That would be a magnificent undertaking."

"We'll make it happen, Kyle," Waxman said. "You and I, working together."

"Working together," Umber repeated. He nodded again. But then his fleshy face settled into a hard frown.

Waxman saw the change in the minister's expression.

"What is it, Kyle?"

"Quincy O'Donnell," said Umber.

"Quincy . . . ?"

"He was murdered."

"By a robot," Waxman claimed.

With a reluctant sigh, Umber replied, "By a robot that was programmed to tear off his space suit's helmet."

"Programmed?"

"Robots do not spontaneously attack people, Evan. We both know that."

"But—"

"But that particular robot attacked O'Donnell and killed him. Who programmed the robot to do that?"

"Nobody! The damned machine went wild. That's why we destroyed it."

"You destroyed it so that no evidence of your programming remained for anyone to find."

"Kyle, that incident is over and done with. I—"

"That *incident* was cold-blooded murder, Evan. You murdered O'Donnell."

Waxman sat frozen in his chair, his face white with shock, his lips parted, as if trying desperately to breathe.

"I . . . but . . ."

"The Interplanetary Council's penalty for murder is cryonic freezing," said Umber, his voice low but implacably unyielding. "You'll be frozen until medical science learns how to eliminate the violence in your brain."

"No . . . please, Kyle. Forgive me."

"Only God can truly forgive you. I'm merely His representative here on *Haven*."

Waxman slid off his chair, crumpled to his knees. "Please, Kyle. Please!"

Umber had to get to his feet to lean over his desk to see Waxman's kneeling form. "Evan, you're going to have to stand trial for murder. I will recommend leniency to the judges. If they grant it, you can resume your duties as executive director—but with Raven Marchesi as your assistant. She will work side by side with you every moment of the day."

Clawing his way clumsily back into his chair, Waxman said, "Yes, yes, that would work out. I could live with that."

As he resumed his chair, Umber repressed an urge to smile at Waxman's unintended pun.

"The mark of Cain is upon you, Evan. I don't know if it can ever be expunged."

"God is merciful! I've heard you say that a thousand times."

"Let us hope so."

the bargain

"He murdered Quincy?" Raven gasped.

Kyle Umber nodded solemnly from behind his desk. "He programmed the robot that killed the man."

"And you're recommending leniency?"

"Yes."

Sitting in front of Umber's desk, Raven stared at the minister's stony features for several silent moments.

Then, "I can't work with him."

"You must, Raven. We must all help to redeem Evan's soul."

"Redeem his soul? I'd rather send him to hell!"

Umber shook his head sadly. "No, Raven. We're not here to condemn or to punish. Waxman's soul should be saved, if we have the strength and the grace to save it."

Raven felt hot anger simmering within her. The bastard murdered Quincy, and the reverend expects me to work with him, to forgive him, to help him?

As if he could read her thoughts, Umber said, "I know it won't be easy for you. Vengeance is a very deep emotion. But forgiveness is better, Raven, far better."

"I don't know if I can forgive him."

With the slightest hint of a smile, Reverend Umber replied, "This will be a test for you, then. A test for all of us."

A test, Raven thought. We're all being tested: Waxman, myself, even the reverend.

"Will you try to work with him? Please?"

Raven heard herself say, in a barely audible voice, "If that's what you want."

Umber responded, "I believe with all my heart that it's what God wants."

Raven suppressed an urge to shake her head in denial. Instead she said, "God doesn't make it easy for us, does He?"

Glad to have the Waxman business behind him, Reverend Umber watched Raven leave his office, her face clouded with suspicion and doubt. He settled himself back in his desk chair and saw that his next visitor was to be Harvey Millard, from the Interplanetary Council.

Millard arrived precisely on time. Umber rose from his chair once again, as Millard—slim, elegant, wearing an ordinary suit of light brown jacket and darker slacks—entered his office and went straight to one of the chairs in front of the reverend's desk.

Before the IC's executive director could say anything, Umber asked, "What do you think of Gomez's theory? Truly."

Millard's light brown eyes widened with surprise. "I'm not an astronomer—"

"Neither am I," Umber interrupted. "But I would appreciate your honest opinion of the idea."

"That Uranus was sterilized by an alien invader some two million years ago? It sounds fantastic to me."

"But is it right?"

Shrugging his frail shoulders, Millard answered, "We don't know. It could be. It fits the available evidence. But . . ."

"But?"

"It's too big to be swallowed in one gulp. We need more evidence, more *facts*, before we can definitely decide if it's right or wrong."

Umber nodded unhappily. Scientists, he thought. They always want more evidence. Then he remembered that Millard was a civil servant, not a scientist.

"More facts," the reverend muttered.

"Which is why I asked to speak with you, actually," said Millard.

"Oh?"

"I want to discuss the possibility of having the Interplanetary Council rent your *Haven II* habitat."

"Rent it? The entire habitat?"

With a single nod, Millard explained, "I've discussed this with my colleagues back on Earth. They agree that we should set up a research station here at Uranus. Your habitat, *Haven II*, is a godsend for us."

"The entire habitat?" Umber asked again.

"Yes, all of it," said Millard. "It will be the base from which we direct the dredging of the buried Uranian civilization. We will also establish an astronomical station here to study the stars for possible evidence of an extraterrestrial civilization."

"Really?"

"Really. Your *Haven II* is going to become a first-rate research center, my friend."

Umber blinked with confusion. "But *Haven II* is being built to house refugees, Earth's poorest peoples."

"You can build other habitats," said Millard. "Our rental fees will help finance them. We can even bring construction teams out here to teach your people how to build them. You'll be able to expand much more quickly than the pace you've reached so far."

"Do you mean that the Interplanetary Council will join us in our effort to create new abodes for Earth's downtrodden people?"

Millard hesitated only a moment before answering, "Yes. I believe we can get the IC to help finance your noble work."

"That . . . that would be . . . wonderful."

A big smile broke out on Millard's thin face as he extended his hand across Umber's desk. "We can accomplish a lot together."

"Together," Umber agreed, clasping Millard's hand warmly.

cerebrations

Hardly a dozen people sat in the church. The décor was nondenominational, the walls bare, the altar equally lacking any paintings or statues.

The tiny group of people waiting for the wedding ceremony to begin sat in hushed silence as simulated sunshine poured through the arched windows of the nave.

Harvey Millard felt well satisfied as he sat staring at the undecorated altar. We've got the foundation of a research station, he told himself. *Haven II* has to be renamed, something more appropriate to a scientific facility, but it's there for our taking. Reverend Umber seems more than pleased with the rental fee we'll be paying for the habitat. It's a win-win situation.

Looking into the future, Millard saw a thriving research establishment orbiting Uranus, probing the remains of the planet's destroyed civilization, searching the stars for evidence of an intelligent race of extraterrestrials.

A shiver of apprehension gnawed at his self-satisfied mood. Can it be true? he asked himself. Did an alien race sterilize Uranus and cause the ice age on Earth? Might they return someday? Is the human race in danger?

We'll have to handle the information we release to the general public very carefully. Very carefully. We don't want to start a panic.

Lord, he thought, if we're not careful we could have the old UFO scare on our hands again.

Sitting several persons away from Millard, Evan Waxman was going through the motions of praying. Kyle will be watching me, he reasoned. Not right at this moment, most likely, but he'll have videos of this entire ceremony at his desk tomorrow morning. I've got to show him that I'm penitent, that I'm going to be well behaved.

Briefly he thought of Raven Marchesi. The little tramp has come a long way in a short time. From a whore to the assistant to the habitat's executive director. Umber's snoop, planted in my office to make sure I stay on the straight and narrow.

Well, Waxman said to himself, when handed a lemon, make lemonade. I'll stay on the straight and narrow. I'll help Umber to make his retreat for the poor into a huge success. We'll fill up *Haven* with Earth's castoffs and build more habitats for more of them.

I'll become Kyle's shining star. His right-hand man. Hell, I might even enjoy it.

Suddenly organ music filled the church. In the tiny vestibule to one side of the altar, the Reverend Kyle Umber turned to Tómas Gomez with a soft smile and said, "It's time."

Gomez nodded and fell in step behind the minister, with Vincente Zworkyn behind him.

As they walked out to the altar, Tómas thought, This is a big step. Marriage. A big commitment. Will I be a good husband to Raven? Can I make her happy?

And what of my work? Am I right? Did a race of aliens actually sterilize Uranus, totally extinguish its civilization? Did they cause the ice age on Earth? Try to prevent the human race from coming into being?

Then he saw Raven stepping down the aisle in a measured pace, with Cathy Fremont—the woman she had picked to run the boutique—behind her. Raven was wearing a white sleeveless mid-calf dress and clutched a bouquet of flowers in both hands. She looked solemn, unsmiling.

Raven marched slowly up the aisle, trying to keep in time with the organ music. The meager audience rose from their pews as she approached them.

As Raven strode along the aisle, she wondered, Can I really take on the responsibility that Reverend Umber has placed on my shoulders? Do I have the strength, the intelligence to do it?

Then she looked up and saw Tómas standing there, waiting for her, smiling at her. And she knew she would do anything in the world for him.

As Reverend Umber stood at the altar with Tómas and his best man to one side of him, he tried to clear his mind of the thoughts swirling through his consciousness.

Waxman is devilishly clever, he told himself. Throwing himself on my mercy like that. Depending on my being too soft-hearted to throw him to the wolves. I'll have to be careful with him, watch him every step of the way. I hope I haven't pushed Raven into a job that's beyond her capabilities. Evan is very clever, he might run rings around her.

Standing there at the altar, he suppressed an urge to shake his head. This will be a test for Raven. She's intelligent, sharp. But will she be able to keep Evan in line?

With an inner sigh, Umber said to himself, We'll see. With the Lord's help, perhaps she'll prevail.

And these murdering aliens that Gomez believes swept through our solar system two million years ago. Is he right? Are they real? Abbott seems to think so.

Raven stepped up to the altar and Tómas took his place beside her.

Reverend Umber tried to push all other thoughts out of his mind as he smiled at them. This is what's important, he told himself. The union of a man and woman. The procreation of the human race.

Despite everything else, Umber told himself, the human race will persevere, will expand out to the stars, will face our ancient enemies if we must. With God's help, we will not only survive: we will grow and learn and prosper.

With a benign smile on his fleshy face, Reverend Kyle Umber raised his hand and intoned:

"Dearly beloved, we are gathered here this day to join this man and this woman in holy matrimony."

The habitat *Haven* continued in its circling orbit around the planet Uranus. The stars shone across the spangled sky as they had for billions of years.

Life went on.